left
in
the
care
of

# left in the care of

A Novel Of Suspense

## Dinah Küng

Carroll & Graf Publishers, Inc.
New York

First Carroll & Graf edition 1997

Carroll & Graf Publishers, Inc.
19 West 21st Street
New York, NY 10010-6805

**Library of Congress Cataloging-in-Publication Data**
Küng, Dinah.
    Left in the care of / Dinah Küng. — 1st Carroll & Graf
    ed.
      p.      cm.
    ISBN 0-7867-0494-2
    I. Title.
    PS3561.U449L44    1997
    813'.54—dc21                                      97-28180
                                                       CIP

Manufactured in the United States of America

To my husband, Peter

left
in
the
care
of

# chapter one

"There are witches in this room." Father Fresnay paused and looked down from his makeshift altar. Claire saw his eyes scan the hundreds of solemn, upturned Filipina faces. The soft chatter that always accompanied a Sunday Mass for *amahs*, domestic servants in Hong Kong, died away. The room was almost still. Slowly, the choir of ten white-robed women standing along one wall behind a portable electric piano stopped jingling their tambourines.

Fresnay's voice rumbled and his usually soft Scottish accent gave each word a threatening ferocity. "You know who they are. Some of you have told the nuns of strange rituals involving the Host, the Body of Our Savior. We've also heard of someone taking money in exchange for casting secret spells, not for good, but for evil. None of this is approved by the Church!"

Claire had never seen her friend Fresnay look so severe, but then, she'd never attended one of his Masses at the Catholic Centre before. During the week, his ponytail of unruly black curls sprang away from his head in Hong Kong's humidity. Now it was tightly tied back. Instead of his weekday garb of pullover, baggy khaki shorts, and worn Chinese leather sandals, he was wearing livid purple and red vestments. Claire knew him Monday through Friday as a fellow China-watcher—a gentle, humorous 43-year-old Jesuit scholar in a tradition of Church sinologists stretching back to the sixteenth century.

Even when he offered Mass on Friday nights out at his country house in Tailong in the New Territories for friends and wandering hikers, he threw on a faded cotton chasuble over his T-shirt and well-worn running shoes. She was startled this morning to see the traditional pastor in him, the guardian of faith and doctrine, so unexpectedly roused.

She tried not to turn her head to look at Xavier, or the Filipinas on all sides of her, but surely the others were just as surprised at Fresnay's outburst. Claire, her Swiss companion, and their newborn son were the only people there besides the priest who weren't from the Philippines, four white faces in a sea of light brown and yellow faces. The crush of women filled not just this floor, but four other stories of this aging harbor-side office building donated to the Church. Xavier and Fresnay were the only males in this room of more than two hundred souls, unless you counted tiny Caspar in her arms. She bounced her little bundle rhythmically, waiting for her friend's tirade to end, but the newborn slept soundly anyway, his tiny mouth making sucking movements as he smelled the milk in her breasts.

"Any of you who participates in these unholy practices puts your soul at risk. This is not religion," Fresnay scoffed. "It is something evil. It twists the teachings of Christ into the work of the Devil. Anyone tempted to play God is not welcome in this parish, and I hope those of you who know about this will confide in me or the other priests. Now," Fresnay's expression softened a little, "we come to the Words of today's Gospel."

Finally, Claire stole a glance at her lover, but all she got was a view of Xavier's sharp profile, softening around the jawline with middle age. His narrow eyes, "the legacy of some Magyar who stopped at our house a few hundred years ago," were firmly focused on the altar. Xavier must have felt her gaze, for he crossed his right hand over to find her smaller hands clasped underneath Caspar's warm midriff. His grip was brief, but firm and reassuring. She had never said to him how important a man's hands were to her, but he seemed to know instinctively that his strong-muscled touch could calm or arouse her faster than any declarations.

He was a man of so few words, so unlike the American men she had known. Was it due to the vast language gap between his careful Swiss-German reflections and her American journalistic habit of thinking in snappy one-liners? Or would she find in the years to come that in any language he was less given than she to the obvious reactions and verbal navel-gazing of some of her reporter buddies? In the years to come . . . Again she caught herself assuming too much, but with Caspar in her arms and the soft wool of Xavier's jacket rubbing her sleeve, she felt enveloped, almost overwhelmed with the comfort of love, so recently acquired.

As for the Jesuit right now leading his congregation in Tagalog songs projected onto a white sheet in the corner of the room, Claire knew Fresnay well because she was a foreign correspondent covering China and Hong Kong for the American weekly *Business World*, and he was one of the two or three best sinologists in Hong Kong—foreign or Chinese. The lanky priest, holed up in his musty den with a team of monkish locals, shared his daily analysis of mainland papers and radio broadcasts with her as well as with a handful of other journalists and diplomats who met with him regularly. Claire and Robert shared a warm, but entirely professional relationship.

Her romance with Xavier had nothing to do with China. They had met in Hong Kong and dated whenever their paths crossed over the span of slightly more than a year—sometimes in Hong Kong, but just as often in Beijing or Canton or Taiwan. The

formality that such a schedule required had given their romance
a courtliness that Claire still savored. There was an inbred ele-
gance to his attentiveness when he was with her that gave her
confidence in his affection during the weeks they were out of
contact. But affection was not passion. Xavier had certainly enjoyed her company, but he didn't seem to have children on his
48-year-old mind.

Things had turned out a little differently, Claire mused to herself, no longer listening to Fresnay's thoughts on the three Magi.
She had tried to guess at the deeper longings beneath Xavier's
cool Swiss exterior and understood they weren't to be discussed. A man his age didn't remain a bachelor through careless
exhibition of his vulnerabilities. And now, Caspar? Well, here
he was, the reddish fuzz on his fragile scalp smelling of spit and
Claire's perfume, a bit of rash on one cheek and a blister on his
upper lip from sucking too hard.

She certainly hadn't planned on Caspar. Her only recent experience with children was admiring her neighbor Vicky's little
boy, Petey, over weekend coffees by the communal pool for a
few minutes at a time. Claire had to admit to herself, if not to
Vicky, that as a single working woman, she hadn't really felt
much interest in other people's offspring. She hated the way
kids interrupted conversations, nagged for snacks, and constantly needed wiping and feeding. She noticed that Vicky could
not sustain an intelligent exchange for more than a few minutes
without trying to listen with one ear while opening and closing
little Tupperware containers of dry Cheerios and animal crackers at the same time.

Petey, always dragging his careworn, threadbare, blue Ses-
ame Street Grover stuffed doll around the pool, was a clever
and quiet child, wonderful in his way. But now Claire realized
that the distance from Petey she had felt all along wasn't so
unusual—that no child was as special as your own, and only
then all children became more special by association with
yours. Because of Caspar, her relationship with other women

was now irrevocably changed. She had joined a vast sisterhood of tired, overextended, bloat-bellied females, office-bound or not, who answered first and last to tiny, sticky tyrants of love and need.

Since Caspar's arrival, Claire and Xavier had arrived at a tentative happiness, although they weren't an official family yet, despite Fresnay's promise to preside over their vows, whenever. Robert Fresnay, half-Scot, half-French, restricted his moral judgements to weekly duty in the confines of the confessional. Like many Jesuits over centuries of overseas missions, he liked to work virtually alone, wearing what he liked and socializing with whomever he found interesting. Fresnay knew that neither Claire nor Xavier was a particularly devout Catholic and that they had come to the Centre this Sunday ahead of Mass to post an advertisement for an *amah*. Fresnay had hinted that he understood Claire didn't want Xavier to marry her for the sake of propriety, or for Caspar. And Xavier considered one proposal in his life just about one proposal too many.

"Well, what did you think of my sermon?" Fresnay grinned at both of them wickedly as they later struggled through the flow of Filipinas along the narrow corridors and down by a creaky elevator to the sidewalk.

"Witches! Claire promised me a sermon about three wise men searching for a baby, not a Halloween show," Xavier exclaimed back over a din of Tagalog. Nearly a thousand Filipinas were pressing on all sides of them as they made their way out of the Centre up the road to Statue Square, the very heart of Hong Kong's downtown district. It was one week before Christmas, a brilliant sunny morning. The main business area of Victoria Island was deserted by the colony's weekday commuters, but the feel of the hustle for money lingered in the air, glistening all around them from the gold and silver high-rises. Garish Chinese holiday decorations in red, orange, gold, and green dangled twenty stories high in the breeze.

"And they all go to Mass on Sunday!" sighed Fresnay, his

towering frame protruding like a tent pole from the crush of
women no higher than his elbow. It was a weird sight if you
didn't realize that there were 128,000 Philippine nationals in
Hong Kong, most of them domestics in kitchens and nurseries
all over the territory. They were almost all Catholics of some
variety, from the most sophisticated college graduates who
earned more cleaning bathrooms in Hong Kong than teaching
math at home, to illiterate girls from the far reaches of the Philippines' archipelago. From Luzon to the central Visayan Islands
down to the southern island of Mindanao, long ravaged by the
effects of civil war between the government and Muslim rebels,
these women were their country's most lucrative, docile, and
exploited export.

A block away, the trio entered a hotel coffee shop crowded
with foreign tourists lingering over long breakfasts and local Chinese from the advertising and film circles who liked the stylish
anonymity of Hong Kong's many four-star hotels. Fresnay was
still in a jocular mood as they ordered coffee for three and for
the priest, a big breakfast of sausages, tomatoes, and omelette.
He had offered three Masses back to back and he was hungry.

Through the plate glass windows looking onto Des Voeux
Road, they could see thousands of Filipinas camped out for the
day—reading, eating, dancing to bootlegged pop cassettes from
Manila, doing manicures, and selling jeans and makeup to each
other. Every Sunday, the government cordoned off two blocks
just to accommodate the crush of maids who had few other
places on the island to relax en masse.

"But witchcraft?" pressed Claire. "Aren't you exaggerating the
problem a little? I don't see any broomsticks out there."

Fresnay nodded. "We wondered too, at first. Sister Iglesia
heard some stories at the clinic about *amahs* laying out Chinese-
style offerings of fruit and flowers at little home altars, muddling
up Buddhist prayers to the Goddess of Mercy, Kwan Yin, with
the Hail Mary. Or they would tell each other to say prayers a

certain number of times for guaranteed returns." He smiled as he stretched the "r" in guaranteed with his Scottish tongue. "We were a little concerned when we caught some of the women putting the Host into their handbags instead of their mouths. Apparently, they took our sermon that the Host was the Body of Christ quite literally and thought they would take Him home for a date!"

Fresnay's expression darkened. "Then we learned that someone in our parish here in Central District had set herself up as a sort of priestess. We're trying to find out who she is, because she's very clever and she must have frightened the women who could identity her into a fearful silence. We suspect she's something of a spiritual vulture, feeding off their loneliness. That certainly wouldn't be difficult to do, especially these days, when no one can say whether their lives will continue here as before after next June's Communist takeover."

"You think Beijing would change the labor policy? Force the Filipinas out?" Xavier asked.

"Not right away. But mainland China isn't exactly short of cheap labor, is it? As Hong Kong and China merge, would it make sense to continue seeing jobs and remittances drained away from China by the Philippines? And there's another, less political threat. You must have noticed that the Indonesian girls coming into Hong Kong are undercutting the Filipinas, as if those girls outside were making a decent living," Fresnay said.

Caspar woke up, his blue eyes staring solemnly as if he had just again entered the world for the first time. Xavier sniffed at his backside playfully and then took him from Claire. "I'll change him before he empties the restaurant."

"That big nose of yours is actually useful." Claire gratefully handed him over. As Xavier headed for the men's room, she laughed to Fresnay, "This is the man who said, when I told him I was pregnant, that he was very happy to be a father, but he would never, ever touch a diaper."

Fresnay stared thoughtfully at Claire, certainly long enough for her to register an unusual look of amusement in his eyes. "You realize that man loves you?"

Claire shifted in her chair, a bit uncomfortable. "Well, what I think is that he might not be sure about me as the partner of his dreams—things have moved so quickly—but he can be sure that that is his first-born son. He's transferring all of his doubts about me into twice as much love for Caspar. He's gone from bachelor to devoted father overnight. I think it's natural. Things are good the way they are, at least so far, so don't worry. We're just digesting it all, bit by bit, day by day."

Fresnay tamped down his pipe. "Any woman in your situation would grab the first offer that came from the father of her newborn child, especially if he were as good-looking and intelligent as Xavier."

"You know I'm too proud to settle for a mercy proposal. I've got a job, a housing allowance, and enough for a full-time, live-in babysitter." Claire thankfully stretched her arms out wide, freed of Caspar for a few minutes.

"That's not it. I think you're afraid he might be unhappy tied to you and you think you're putting his happiness before your own. That is real, generous love, but it's totally misguided in your case. But if you can't see it now," he shook his head slightly, "I wonder . . ."

Claire interrupted, "Anyway, you say these Filipinas like to mix up other religions with Catholicism?"

Fresnay loved to display his scholarly talent for esoteric research into Asian politics and history. "In the old days, I mean old, when the Franciscan Juan de Plasencia got to the Philippines in 1577, he found the locals were animists, with a whole army of witches as part of their practices. The earth and sky were filled with spirits that had to be worshipped and placated. To make their gods happy, for example, the Filipinos killed slaves to accompany the master of the house to the world beyond—"

"Like Egyptians burying slaves with the mummies? Or Indians burning widows on the funeral pyre?"

"Exactly. Plasencia wrote that the Tagalogs of the hill country bound slaves to the corpse and buried them together. He wasn't the only eyewitness. A Spanish explorer, Diego de Artieda wrote to Philip II that he saw a Filipino captain buried at sea in his vessel with all his oarsmen still alive on board!"

Fresnay paused to fiddle some more with his pipe and enjoy Claire's grimace. In over fifteen years in Asia, working her way up from stringer to staff correspondent and finally bureau chief, she had covered a deadly flood in Bangladesh, a train crash outside Shanghai, and a horrific fire in a Thai toy factory that maimed dozens of young women. She'd seen dismembered limbs, interviewed lepers, escorted refugees suffering gunshot wounds off sinking vessels in the China Sea. Still, she was capable of cringing at cold-blooded murder in the name of religion.

Fresnay had warmed to his subject with his Jesuit's precision. "More to the point for us now, the pre-Christian Filipinos used all kinds of sorcerers and quacks. The *mangagaway* healed the sick, or pretended to. The *manyisalat* bewitched lovers with potions. The *hokloban* killed people by magic, just by raising his hand. The *silagan* tore out the entrails of their victims—" Fresnay was happily ticking off voodoo men on his elegant fingers.

"You're kidding!"

"There's more. The *magtatangal* showed himself at night headless. The *asuang*—not among the Tagalogs, but among the Visayans—he flew around and ate people. The *pangatohojan* was a fortune teller, the *bayokin* was a man with a woman's nature, well, perhaps these days we would call him gay, and the *mangagayoma* bewitched people with herbs, something like the *manyisalat*."

"My God, Robert, you're ready for another PhD, this time on Filipino magic!" Claire exclaimed as Xavier returned bearing

Caspar. "Xavier, you've just missed an encyclopedia of Asian ghouls!"

"I'm sorry I did, because I've always found the Filipinos' image today a bit too—what's the word, Claire?—saccharine. You know, Robert, I spend so much time staying in hotels for my job, and no matter where I go in Asia, I hear these Filipino bands crooning sweetly in cocktail lounges, as if the whole of Filipino manhood was signed up for a five-year tour with a major hotel chain. Every time I go out to dinner at someone's house, there's another sweet-faced Filipina in a little white apron taking our coats and serving the dinner. It makes you wonder how the whole country was emasculated—"

Xavier was interrupted by the banging of drums and a crackling loudspeaker outside the windows. It was hard to see what was happening on Des Voeux Road. Groups of Filipinas who had settled along the sidewalk in Statue Square around the corner and in the street right outside their window were hurriedly gathering up their picnic baskets, boom boxes, and hawkers' stands. Squeals of excitement and argument filled the air. Scurrying off the street and onto the curb, female bodies of all ages and shapes were starting to press up against the coffee shop's plate glass windows. The megaphone was blaring the voice of a Filipina woman speaking Tagalog.

Claire felt the atmosphere all round them change. There had been more and more demonstrations in the last year, most of them by Chinese students and Democratic Party activists demanding more political dialogue and less threat of political retrenchment from the incoming masters in Beijing.

This time, it wasn't immediately obvious what the demonstration was about. Even though Fresnay was a sinologist, he had had to master some Tagalog like all the other priests in Hong Kong serving the Filipina community. He strained to make out the speaker's words over the racket of the coffee shop. "It's a labor protest. They want to raise their minimum wage to $3,500 Hong Kong a month. But I bet most of them are too scared to do anything but watch from the sidelines."

That was less than $500 in American dollars, thought Claire. Not much for six- or even seven-day weeks of twelve to sixteen hours a day. And most of it had to be sent home to the islands to support the old and very young, who couldn't work. Suddenly, she heard screams as the bodies, even the faces, of women were visibly squashed against the café's large window.

Claire looked with alarm at her two companions, gesturing at the window pane to Xavier over the racket of women's hysteria. Now the screams competed with the sound of police sirens and whistles. "I think the window could break!" she shouted. The three of them darted out of their chairs to move to the back of the dining room. Caspar started squalling.

"Let's go now," yelled Xavier, leaving cash with a waiter. They bid a hasty farewell to Fresnay who signalled that he felt needed out on the street among his parishioners. They headed out the back of the hotel for the high-rise carpark at Beaconsfield House. They were driving the same old rusty Honda Claire had owned long before she first met Xavier. They buckled the whimpering Caspar into his baby seat and headed up the steep incline of Cotton Tree Drive toward the island's Midlevels district.

Claire sighed, as much with regret as with relief. "In the old days I would've been out there interviewing, taking pictures, running around with everybody else. God, Caspar's changed everything for me. All I thought about was getting him out of there."

"A lot has happened very quickly for us, Claire." Xavier stared ahead at the road and, glancing at his expression, Claire saw his mood had changed.

"What's on your mind all of a sudden? Not the Filipinas' protest? Don't worry, I'll find someone reliable to look after Caspar. I've got a list of recommendations from Vicky Sandford next door. You know, the mother of that little boy at the pool the other day?"

"You mean the one who dropped his blue animal toy in the water, and Mr. Li fished it out with a basket?"

They both laughed at the memory of Petey's little Grover, a soggy sight dangling from the long end of the pool-keeper's sweeper. Petey had cried, "Is he dead?" until Grover had completely dried out in the sun. Xavier had been attentive to Petey's distress, his three-year-old face crumbling with tears as he waited for Grover's restoration. Claire had watched Xavier comfort Petey and knew from that moment on he was going to be an excellent father. It was Xavier as husband she couldn't envisage. All the girlfriends tucked away in Geneva, and outposts of Xavier's past in the Middle East and Africa. What about them?

The *amah* question hung in the air. They had borrowed a part-time *amah*, Consuela Barang, from friends of the Sandfords over the Christmas holidays, but would have to give her up and hire someone full-time soon after the New Year. Claire's maternity leave was up in two weeks, and she had postponed the arduous chore of interviewing applicants while she recovered. She wasn't looking forward to any of it. In fact, she still missed living alone.

Xavier's mind turned out to be on something else. He hesitated. "Please don't get upset at what I'm going to say."

Claire looked at him, startled, and then laughed. "Thanks. Now I'm upset." She wasn't really, not yet, but Caspar started to whine.

"Please, just listen first. Can you get him to be quiet? Give him a cracker or something."

"Xavier, he doesn't have any teeth. He can't eat crackers yet."

"What about one of those plastic sucker things? A *nuggi?*"

"Xavier, nookie means something quite different in English from Swiss-German. You mean a pacifier. Anyway, it's bad for his teeth."

"I thought he didn't have any."

"Teeth formation. Xavier . . ."

"All right. Anyway, I got a phone call from Fabienne."

Claire was unprepared for his news. "The Fabienne. The one you dated for a century or more?"

"Fabienne Jaccard. She's forty. Only two years older than you. The photographer from Geneva. She has a project in Cambodia starting after Christmas and she thought she'd spend Christmas in Hong Kong."

"With us."

"Not exactly." Xavier's eyes never left the road.

"With herself?" Claire deadpanned.

"No. Claire, I haven't had time to inform all my girlfriends, I mean my ex-girlfriends, that I met you, and we had Caspar so fast. I mean, some of them had been going out with me for five or six years whenever we were working in Geneva at the same time, or our paths crossed in the field. I didn't keep up a constant correspondence. It wasn't necessary. It was just nice whenever we met."

"I see." Claire saw precisely because it was the kind of relationship she had had with him herself. She hated this feeling, this heat of insecurity burning her throat. Now in addition to red hair, she had a red face. Say nothing, say nothing. She must love him, she hurt so much, so suddenly, and without any warning.

"So I told her to stay at the Furama or the Conrad, or someplace else on the island, and that we'd show her around. At least we shouldn't let her be alone on Christmas Day."

"Great. Our first family Christmas. Let's start our own special traditions now."

They drove on in a cloud of tension. Xavier turned off May Road to Tregunter Path and hit the brakes. A police inspector, a tall Westerner, was smack in the middle of the road.

"Please show me some kind of identification, sir," he said. "Where are you going?"

"We live at number three, Branksome Towers," said Xavier.

The officer talked into a walkie-talkie. "*Sam ho, Honda lai-a.*" Claire forgot Fabienne and studied the policeman intently. He looked a bit like an old-fashioned movie idol of the forties, dark-haired, with expressive eyes, polished somehow. Not a typical English look. He was relaying their destination and car type to another officer ahead in Cantonese, but after all those years in Hong Kong, Claire knew his Cantonese was freshly acquired from language training. He waved them on, but they had to drive slowly to navigate past three police vans partly blocking the curve of the narrow two-lane path. For another hundred or so feet, they were waved ahead by young Chinese officers, silver numbers shining from their epaulets, walkie-talkie bursts squawking at their hips.

"Slow down, Xavier. I see John Slaughter. He can tell us what's going on."

The Chief Inspector saw their car approaching and was about to usher them peremptorily into their building's parking lot when he recognized Claire and nodded. His weather-beaten skin and heavily freckled hands would have given away his long years in colonial Asia even before you were close enough to catch his fluent Cantonese bark. Claire knew his past anyway, having worked with him over the years on stories involving fraud, triads, kidnappings, even crimes across the border in China.

"Hello, Claire, my dear. Good morning, sir. I'm afraid there's been an accident. Very sad business indeed. We've found a body in the *nullah* near your building. We're examining the scene now and want to keep the traffic to a minimum."

"I see," Xavier answered. He was not so much younger than Slaughter, who was in his early fifties, and not the sort of person to rubberneck into another man's official responsibilities. Claire was more curious by nature than Xavier, and fifteen years of reporting in Asia had made her feel proprietary about excitement in her own backyard, but for Xavier's sake, she said nothing.

In a moment, her curiosity was painfully, awfully answered. She strained to see more of the ambulance in the curve of the road just before Xavier turned into the lot. She could make out two Chinese ambulance workers and a Chinese policeman gently easing a stretcher into the back of the van.

"Oh, God, it's Petey. It's Petey," she cried out, and Xavier braked hard to a full stop. "It's Petey!" Claire cried again, looking desperately at Xavier, as if he could magically fly from the car to change the terrible scene laid out before them. The small, limp, blond, doll-like form of Vicky's only child Peter Sandford lay still in the middle of the long canvas. He made no protest as a rough blanket was pulled up over his face.

"Sorry, sir! You have to move on." A Chinese constable, polite but firm, was leaning gently into Xavier's window.

# chapter
## two

The police cars were gone. There wasn't much of a breeze and the sun had already burnt off the morning mists on the Peak above Tregunter Path. Still, it was jacket weather, a treat in a semi-tropical city. Excellent morning for golf out at Fanling's eighteen holes near the border, if you could get away from the office for a few hours. A pleasure to open the windows of the 9:07 residents' shuttle bus and feel the fresh air brushing your cheeks as you thundered away with the other commuters from Midlevels to Central's office towers seven minutes down Garden Road.

Claire walked across Branksome's parking lot and dodged the shuttle bus as it started off without her. In thirteen days, and she was counting, she would be back on it, headed down to the bureau, Caspar entrusted to someone else's care for the day. She craved a return to her normal life, and in the same instant, wondered how she would manage to leave her son for more than a few hours.

She headed up the Path's fifty feet to the next apartment block. A phone call yesterday had been enough to learn that no one could see Vicky until this morning. Claire imagined her own face was still puffy from tears of shock and sympathy, but she was resolved to be as strong as she could for her friend's sake.

From the outside, the Sandfords' building, Tavistock, was once again just another number on Tregunter Path, another stark high-rise residence lining one of Hong Kong's better neighborhoods. The swimming pool lay glistening blue, but unused, next to the building. The slapping and thumping from squash courts beneath the asphalt hinted at a regular Monday morning game for two resident housewives.

Claire was so immersed in her own worries about how to comfort Vicky that she almost missed a note pasted on the floor-length mirror inside the elevator. It was in Chinese and Tagalog, addressed to the maids working in the building. "Please do not disturb us anymore. Take the service lift where you belong. If you don't like it, go back to the Philippines. Don't forget that you are employed here as servants! Don't ruin the reputation of your own kind who disagree with your attitudes and actions. This applies to the use of the shuttle buses also."

No English version, thought Claire, who had studied Chinese and music with equal fervor some twenty years before at U.C. Berkeley. So this was intended to be a nasty secret penned by Chinese tenants, who were relatively new to this neighborhood. The *Economist* had tagged such Hong Kongers as "the new yellow sahibs." In their heyday, the British might have felt the same about servants using the front "lift," but handled it differently. No, ten years ago, the maids would have stuck to the servants' entrance without question, Claire reminded herself. Lines weren't drawn so clearly now as they were even in the late seventies when she first arrived in the British colony.

Tensions were rising and with the takeover by Beijing in less than a year, where was Hong Kong heading? Of course, everyone loved a colony, as long as they were top dog, or, as Connie was already calling Xavier, "Master." And the families that had been *nouveau riche* Chinese industrialists in the seventies—the Foks, the Paos, the Kwoks—why they were more elite these days than any faded colonial bureaucrat.

Who was running the show during these final days of the countdown? The incoming mainland Communist Party officials, or the billionaires with their Cantonese forebears and Canadian passports? The elected legislature, now almost a lame duck body, and the newly created "provisional legislature" of Beijing-appointed toadies? The American Chamber of Commerce, controlling eight billion American dollars of investment in the territory, or some Cantonese front man acting as Beijing's "chief executive"? Certainly it was no longer the British.

Claire hesitated in front of the Sandfords' apartment. She felt yesterday afternoon's hole of horror open up inside her stomach all over again. The front door looked as if no tragedy had occurred. The buzzer burred the usual way. The Angel of Death had painted no Biblical sign on the door. Fate could land on your doorstep, Claire thought, and look as mundane as the daily paper waiting on the mat.

When the front door opened, and Claire was admitted into the apartment by an exhausted-looking Filipina maid, she saw Victoria Sandford sitting like a collapsed marionette, legs apart, arms between her knees. Claire couldn't see her face from the doorway but already she knew that the chirpy, precise, athletic, young Englishwoman had vanished.

"Who is it, Manny?"

"It's Claire, Vicky. Are you alone?" Vicky nodded wearily and Claire walked straight over to the young woman's side and sat down. Vicky's short brown hair was unbrushed, her delicate features swollen with crying, her sweater and woollen skirt obviously slept in. It was clear that at nine in the morning, the bereaved and shocked mother was very alone indeed.

"Ian's flight arrives back from Sydney this afternoon. They found another pilot to take over his routes. I spoke to my father last night. He and Mother will arrive tomorrow from Wyverstone. The doctor gave me a sedative. I'm still feeling rather numb. I'm sorry. Would you like something, some tea or . . . ?"

"Some tea would be nice," Claire said directly to the *amah* Manny standing mutely at the edge of the large living room in her blue and white striped uniform.

Claire could not think of any words of comfort that would not sound like bad television dialogue, especially since she had only just come to know maternal passion. In those early weeks of new motherhood, it was not unusual for Claire to wake suddenly, apparently for no reason. While Xavier slept, some animal instinct would lift and carry her into Caspar's little room.

She would see the pale face, the heavy awkward head, the red wisps sticking to his skull, damp with hot sleep. She would check his breathing, and then, like some lioness alone with her cub in a dark cave, lick his cheek, move close to his soft mouth and smell the milky sweetness. Did every mother feel this sensual tie to flesh that had so recently been her own, and yet was never hers from the moment of life? Was losing a child like losing your arm? Would Vicky feel Petey's loss every single day for the rest of her life, like the twinges of a phantom limb?

"John Slaughter stayed with me until I felt ready to rest last night. I didn't want to see Manny—I was quite hysterical, I believe. But I have to believe it wasn't her fault, it all happened so suddenly," Vicky said softly.

Then she forced herself to carry on. "Did you know John and Daddy fought in Malaya together? They were both very young then, it was practically the first posting for both of them. Now there's Daddy sitting back in the pub near the Old Rectory House and here's Uncle John holding my hand, telling me Petey is dead."

"At least it was someone who knew your family."

Vicky sighed almost cynically and sat up straighter, tugging her skirt back down to her knees and fiddling with a gilt button on her cardigan. "Yes. Not likely next summer, hmmm? At least it wasn't some PAP or PLA soldier barking at me through some foul interpreter. But it's not much comfort, is it? You and I have talked about it so many times. We've known he had epilepsy since he was about nine months old. Before this, there was always some warning that he was going to have an attack. He'd say, 'Mummy, I don't feel good. The singing is in my head again.'" Vicky paused. "Last night all I could imagine was how he must have suffered in those few minutes before Manny got to him, wanting someone to come and help him, and I wasn't there."

She looks wretched, thought Claire. Imagine, there were moments when I got pregnant that I didn't even want Caspar. Wasn't sure.

Vicky turned her tortured face toward Claire. "Did you see him, Claire? John said Xavier and you drove past on the road. John identified the body for the family and they've still got him. I just don't think I'm up to seeing him today."

"Yes, I saw him just as he was put into the ambulance. I felt just . . ." Claire caught herself verging on tears, the last thing Vicky needed to keep herself going. She started over. "You know, they say sometimes, 'He looked just like he was asleep,' but Petey looked more peaceful than that. I can't believe he suffered long."

"Ian's going to want to fly the body back to England." Vicky was staring away from Claire, out toward the harbor, so it wasn't obvious how she felt about this. Ian Sandford was a pilot working for Cathay Pacific, a decent man in his late thirties, but inclined to dominate his efficient and dutiful young wife.

"And what do you want, Vicky?"

Vicky turned, almost incredulous, her eyes welling up with pain. "Want? I want my baby back, I want to hold him. God, Petey, why—" Claire took the young woman in her arms and held her sobbing young friend for endless minutes. Tears coursed down her own face. Manny brought in the tea tray stiffly. When no instruction came, she placed it, gleaming, on top of starched embroidered linen on the table at their knees, and then disappeared back into the kitchen.

Finally, as Vicky collected herself, Claire poured the tea. For a while, the two women sat in silence. Claire took in the utter Englishness of the room. If you forgot the bright sunlight reflecting off the white ferries in the harbor at the foot of the steep slope and just scanned the chintz-covered easy chair, the silver-framed photos on the side tables, the clumsy watercolor seascape by Vicky's mother, and the ceramic dog lying near the front door, you'd think you were in Putney or Hampstead.

Then you might notice that the seascape was of a beach in Penang, the fishermen wearing sarongs as they gathered their nets at dusk. The chintz on the large reading chair in the corner pictured orchids and parrots, not roses or sparrows. The throw cushions were covered in contrasting Indonesian batik, not needlepoint. The ceramic dog faced a cheap foot-high porcelain elephant from Thailand. Claire could never forget an old New Zealand news hack nicknaming these ubiquitous doorstoppers, "Buffies." "Tripped over the buffie again," he would exclaim drunkenly at parties. Finally, Claire demanded to know why "buffie," and he had shouted, "B-U-F-E, Bloody Useless Fucking Elephants!" at the top of his lungs while his hostess blushed.

Vicky's side tables were dwarfed by a large Korean chest in the dining room. The dining table was of rosewood, with ten highly polished matching chairs, each chair carved on its back with *ming*, the Chinese character for brightness. And the tea set was not silver but pewter from Selangor. The whole picture was painfully neat and unoriginal. A blandly tasteful, timeless room of the former British empire readied for the constant flow of adults, not children. Vicky had trained Manny well, with a colonial rigor learnt at her mother's knee, thought Claire.

Vicky seemed to read Claire's mind. "Mother's already saying she wants me to come home for good. But England's not my home. Never was. Even during school days, I wanted to be here." Vicky wiped her eyes carefully. "Got to pull myself together. That policeman, you know, the sergeant with John, Anthony Crowley? He's coming back at ten to ask me some questions to file his report."

"He'll be here soon, then." Claire gave her another hug. "I'll come back tomorrow."

But Vicky didn't let her go. "No, please stay. You know, hold my hand a bit." Vicky seemed almost embarrassed by her own human need for support. "I'm sure he's going to be terribly nice, but I just need someone here. Please stay. I mean it."

It was the same inspector Claire had seen on the street yesterday. Crowley was on time, ready with a notebook and a comforting expression on his face. He reminded Claire of a young undertaker she had once met, professionally pleasant, pleasing to look at during difficult times, and a better actor than anyone in the party of genuine mourners when it came to expressing grief. It made Claire strangely uncomfortable and glad she could stay for Vicky's sake.

"Hello, sir." Manny's voice was hardly even a whisper as she opened the door to him. Claire glimpsed a strange expression— was it distrust or fear of his authority?—on Manny's wide, almost Chinese face.

"Hello, Manuela, good morning, Mrs. Sandford." Crowley paused, looking at Claire expectantly.

"How do you do, Inspector Crowley. We met on the street yesterday. I was in the Honda. I'm Claire Raymond, a neighbor." Claire stepped forward to shake his hand while explaining, "Mrs. Sandford asked me to stay a bit longer. I hope that's all right?"

"Well, I have to ask some questions as part of the official record. I'm not sure you—"

"I'd like her to stay very much." Vicky's face looked stricken, but her voice was firm. She didn't say "Please." Claire thought again of Vicky's upbringing. If her father had retired from the

Colonial Services at the high end of the ranks, Crowley was a nobody to a daughter whose life was still lived in the fading shadows of the old era. Crowley nodded as if to say he had no further objections.

"Mrs. Sandford, we know, of course, that your son died of a sudden epileptic attack while playing on the other side of the Path near the *nullah*. Your servant Manuela said yesterday he liked to play in a favorite spot of his in the woods there, very close to where she and a group of friends were picnicking. Was this routine, that your *amah* would watch the boy on Sundays?"

His tone betrayed something. Do you make your help work even on Sundays?

Vicky had heard it, too. "Well, officially it's her one day off," she admitted. "But when Ian is flying, she takes him along with her friends for an hour or so to give me a rest. I'm expecting another child. I'm in my ninth week."

Claire took her friend's hand. "Oh, Vicky, I didn't know."

Vicky managed a wan smile and murmured to Claire, "We haven't even told my parents, Claire. We were going to keep it quiet for a few months until we knew everything was, you know, well on its way. Now I almost hate this life inside me. I can't explain it. How dare this new baby be so safe and healthy inside me, as if nothing had happened to Petey. I don't want another child if this is what it leads to, all the love and the happiness just ends, like some, some," Vicky was determined not to crumble into sobs again, "some massive great thing landing on top of you, and you can't breathe, you can't believe you'll survive one more minute knowing what has happened."

Claire held Vicky's shoulder tightly, until she felt her calm down.

"Excuse me, Inspector, but is this really the right time to interview Mrs. Sandford? Couldn't we wait for her husband to return home?" Claire found Crowley a strange combination— good-looking, but somehow too eager and a little pompous all at the same time.

"I'll only need another few minutes. Then I'll confirm the report of the *amah*, and we'll be finished. Mrs. Sandford, how serious was his illness? I recall you telling me a bit about it a few months ago, when I bumped into you at the bus stop while I was on duty. You were on your way to the doctor, weren't you? Didn't you tell me his illness was under control? Did he have these attacks often?"

"Just a few at first. And as soon as we got him on the medication, the seizures were much less frequent. But lately, say, over the last year or so, they started getting worse. The threshold, as Dr. Trythall at Matilda Hospital calls it, that threshold was lowering. We all found it strange, including the doctor, because we caught it early enough and we thought the outlook was quite good. Usually the threshold gets higher the older a child gets, and as long as they get lots of sleep and not too much excitement, and you keep the anticonvulsants like Dilantrin on hand, you worry less and less. There are the side effects to watch out for, of course, sometimes nausea, anemia, and other things, but we didn't have any problems with those. You can talk to Dr. Trythall . . ."

"Yes, I suppose we should have a word with him. I, um . . . it must have been very hard for you and Mr. Sandford to watch him suffer, I'm sure. I once read about these *grand mal* seizures."

He was unctuous, Claire thought. Vicky was on the defensive. "They don't use that terminology anymore, Inspector Crowley. Petey had partial seizures; he stayed conscious, but they were 'complex' partial seizures. Something inside his brain, his temporal lobe, would misfire. He might start to talk nonsense or not quite nonsense, but not quite sense, if you see what I mean. Sometimes, as he was so little anyway, it was hard to tell. As the seizure spread, he would hear songs, or voices, recall previous places or people. He'd say, 'Mummy, I feel funny and' . . ."

Vicky stopped and sighed. Then she drew herself up again

and seemed determined to finish. Crowley was taking notes and nodding sympathetically. "We tried to remove Petey from anything that we noticed might trigger an attack. It could be certain songs, loud sounds, a lot of stress. It wasn't easy in a city like this with all the construction work, the traffic, just constant noise. I tried to keep the house as restful as possible."

But never really relaxed, thought Claire, remembering Ian's demanding personality and the airline's constantly expanding schedules, the stewardess strikes, the safety rows with the Chinese staff, the budget worries, the localization policies. No, Ian never rested. It was unlikely Vicky relaxed.

"Did you consider removing Petey from Hong Kong?"

"He was still too young to go away to school. I take him to England, of course, to visit my mother every summer," she stopped, realizing she had forgotten that Petey was dead.

"I am so sorry, Mrs. Sandford. Please convey my condolences to your husband as well. You know, I walk the Path as part of my rounds some mornings with Constable Yueng. I used to see Petey regularly with Manuela buying vegetables at the truck that stops along the road. He was an absolutely delightful child." There he goes again, thought Claire. Vicky was looking at him almost resentfully.

He returned to business. "Well, yes. Um, we'll get back later if we have any further questions. In the meantime, I'd like to interview your *amah* just to complete the routine." He slapped his notebook shut and Claire noticed his smooth, well-manicured hands. He was such a strange combination of smooth manners, offset by an unfashionable northern accent, the working class vowels muffled by effort and probably some years in London.

"Thank you." Vicky sat upright as if she were holding her breath until he left. "Claire, would you show him back to Manny's room? Thanks so much for stopping by. It was good of you, really."

Claire kissed her friend gently on the cheek. "Then I'll slip out the servant's door. Get some rest. Only a few more hours until Ian gets here. Try and hold on."

She led Inspector Crowley through the heavy door connecting the dining room to the long, pristine, tiled kitchen and pushed open the equally heavy door leading to the servant's corridor. Manuela opened the door of her own room just two inches, enough to see who was knocking. She was crying now and her face was flushed to a deep magenta. She looked shocked when she saw Crowley waiting outside her door. Still shuddering, she took in Claire's presence, too.

She gestured sobbing to the Inspector to sit on a folding metal chair next to the bed, but he declined, so she remained standing in front of her two visitors. "Please stay with me, ma'am," she pleaded. Claire turned for consent to Crowley, who nodded an okay. Relieved a bit, Manuela wiped her brows and eyes with a large white handkerchief.

Claire had lived in Hong Kong since her early twenties. Looking around the small space barely large enough for three adults to stand in, she could see Manny was relatively lucky. She'd seen the inside of enough Hong Kong homes to know how many Filipinas slept under the dinner table every night, or shared the bed of the youngest child in the family. Some slept in kitchen pantries or closets converted into bedrooms, their clothes hanging directly over their heads in a long suffocating row, the television set attached somewhere near the ceiling, if they were lucky enough to get one. The unlucky ones were expected to sleep on mattresses next to the washing machine in the laundry room.

Most old Hong Kong apartments didn't have Western toilets for the servants, only Chinese-style holes in the floor for squatting over. Many servants' rooms didn't have baths or even proper showers. Landlords installed garden hoses or shower heads on pipes over the toilet. Most ate their meals from a rice cooker next to their beds. The kitchen was for the master's family.

Manny lived in privacy in a whitewashed room with its own separate bathroom with a shower, sink, and toilet. Her single bed had fitted sheets. She had a plywood standing closet and a small television. On her bedside table was a statue of the Virgin Mary strung with tiny necklaces of plastic flowers. Leaning against the statue was a snapshot of a small boy sitting on the back of a jitney in Manila, one of the ubiquitous jeeps bedecked in garlands and neon paint and wild slogans that served as the city's fastest form of public transportation.

Crowley waited for Manuela to stop her sobbing, but the woman showed no signs of calming down, so he plowed on, a bit too loudly.

"Please tell us, Manuela, everything that happened yesterday up to the time you came running up to me on the sidewalk and took me to see Petey's body."

Manuela gasped for breath, wiped her eyes, and her shaking slowed down enough to talk. Claire tried hard to suppress the thought that came into her mind—the typical colonial daughter keeping a stiff upper lip in the living room matched by a Filipina's Hispanic sense of melodrama. Yes, these were clichés come to life, perhaps. But damned if she hadn't seen in her years of reporting the same things again and again. Maybe she'd been in Hong Kong too long.

Manuela was talking between taking deep breaths. "Yes, sir. In the morning I went to Mass at St. Joseph's with some of the other Filipinas who work in this building. We took the shuttle bus from the parking lot and came back by the Peak tram to the May Road station. It was after eleven. When I came home I made lunch—egg mayonnaise salad—for Mrs. Sandford. I got Petey and took him downstairs to meet my friends for a picnic. Mrs. Sandford was going to have a rest."

"How did Petey seem to you? Did he appear to be sick? Were there any warning signs of an attack?"

"Nothing, sir." Manny's shoulders were heaving up and down.

"Where did you have your picnic? Who was with you?"

"There were three of us. Usually there are more, but this time it was only Narcisa and Aurora. We usually have our meetings—"

"Meetings? Or picnic?"

"Well, both, sir. First we have the meeting of the Charismatic Society and we pray at the clearing above the Path just past the footbridge."

"Where Tregunter Path meets May Road on the other side of the bridge?"

"Yes, sir. The building construction workers eat lunch there during the week. That is where they pile up their working materials for the building next door they are working on. We usually meet there about one o'clock."

"And where was Petey?"

"He went up the Path to a little place where he likes to play."

"By the *nullah*?"

"Yes," Manuela seemed suddenly eager to make a point. "But this time of year, there is no rain, sir. There is no water. It is not dangerous. And sometimes he goes to play with the gardener on the slope next to the clearing, where they grow the plants. But the gardener knows where we are."

Crowley nodded sympathetically to Manuela as he took notes. There was no backyard or park for kids to play in along the Path, except for an old mini-tennis court that had fallen into disuse and stayed locked up much of the year. But a footpath led up from the road, cutting gently across the slope through the brush and trees. Sunday walkers used the footpath to descend from the top of Victoria Peak all the time. It was reasonable of Manny to let Petey potter around nearby; safer, in fact, than trying to play closer to the road where speeding cars were a problem.

"There, there," said Crowley awkwardly. "Nobody is blaming you. Did Petey go over to the nursery to see the gardener yesterday?"

Was Manny hesitating? She answered quietly, "No, sir. He did not go near the nursery yesterday."

Claire leaned quietly in the doorway, watching Crowley ask the questions, just doing his job. As a journalist, she would have let Manuela do more talking.

Crowley probed again. "So what happened?"

"We had finished our prayers and we were dancing to some music, sir, and eating some *adobo*, singing and laughing, just having a good time. Every ten or fifteen minutes, I would check on Petey. I knew where he was because I could always see his red sweatshirt through the trees, and I was watching where he was sitting on the ground. Suddenly, I noticed he was very quiet. I told my friends I am going to look at Petey. When I got to the place where he was, he was lying on the ground, sir. He was very quiet, but his mouth was full of saliva and his face was blue."

Manuela's expression turned inward as she relived the fear all over again. "So I say to myself, Oh, my God, my God, and I call out to my friends to come help me. He didn't close his eyes or say anything, and I was shaking him and crying and shouting to him, but he didn't answer. I was very, very frightened, sir. I had been watching him all the time, when we were praying, through the trees."

Manny's head sunk and her shoulders heaved and a deep wailing came out of her chest. "My God, my God," she repeated, shaking her head in her hands. "I am so sorry, sir. I knew Petey could get sick very fast and needed his medicine. But this time I gave him his medicine and it did him no good. It always protected him before this. God has cursed him with this sickness."

"So that's when you came running down to the road below and saw me?"

Manny wiped her eyes carefully and recited slowly, reliving the order of events as accurately as she could. "First, I saw that neighbor lady, Mrs. Reynolds, Imelda's employer, driving past and I tried to stop her, but she ignored me, even though I was waving and shouting from the sidewalk. She does not like the Filipinas. Then I saw you. Yes, sir, I was very happy to see you."

"But by then, of course, it was too late. How long did you stay by the body before you came for help?"

"Only one or two minutes, sir. My friends, they were crying and crying and I had to make sure they wouldn't touch him if I left him even for a minute. They were hysterical and didn't go for help when I told them to. Just stood in one place, screaming and crying. It was very hard to think what should I do. I was afraid. My little boy Ramon died in Bontoc last year. This is Ramon's picture. He got sick and he died, too." Manuela took the photo of the little boy in the jitney in her hand. Claire realized Manuela might be on the verge of a long story. "He needed some medicine, but he didn't get it in time. I miss him every day."

"We're very sorry, Manuela, but I'm afraid we have to go now. There may be more questions later, and you're going to have to stay here with the Sandfords, even though it might be uncomfortable for you."

Manuela starting crying louder. "I have a big pain in my heart for my Ramon. If only I could talk to him once again, but I will never talk to him, never again, and he wonders where I am. I feel a very big, big pain in my heart now for Mrs. Sandford, too."

Crowley looked at Claire and muttered curtly, "You might recommend Mrs. Sandford pass on some of those sedatives to her *amah* here. I'm very sorry to hear that, thank you, Manuela. We'll go now. Please take good care of Mrs. Sandford. Do everything you can to help her, and try to be kind if she loses her temper or is short with you. She would have to be a saint not to hate anyone connected with this tragedy right now." Crowley put his notes away.

"Yes, sir, I will, sir. Thank you." Manny gathered herself shakily to show them out through the kitchen. But Crowley said,

"Thanks, that won't be necessary. We'll go out this way." He opened the back entrance's heavy door to lead Claire out to the steel and cement landing that faced the servants' elevator. It was a sharp contrast to the front entrance with its bevelled mirrors, tropical plants, and gold handrailings.

"We'll speak to the gardener and Mrs. Reynolds to confirm what Manny says, but it seems fairly straightforward. I hope I didn't seem brusque, but I've interviewed Filipinas before. They can be a terribly emotional lot."

"It worries me. Oh, not the crying, I mean, the whole thing of leaving your children with someone else, all day, every day," said Claire, half to herself. "I'm just about to hire an *amah* for my own newborn this week. This kind of thing makes you think twice about giving your children five days a week to anyone, no matter how well meaning they are. I wonder if there was anything that could have been done? Can anyone take care of your own child as well as you can? Was she really watching, I mean *really* watching?"

Crowley spoke coolly. "Am I right in thinking you're a journalist? Yes? The name rang a bell. No, I don't have much time to read, but I think I saw you on a talk show discussing the crisis between the Chinese army and the American navy last March in the Taiwan Straits."

"Yes, that was me."

"Well, in my short tour of duty here in Hong Kong, I've learned that there are some questions that are very dangerous to ask. All middle-class women hire working-class women to look after their children, who in turn give their own children to their mothers to raise. All this money earned goes in circles, and the children? From what I've seen, the Filipinas are as careful and kind as any sort of nanny you'll find anywhere in the world. If a mother has to work, well, she could do worse.

"But," he gestured dismissively back at the Sandford flat, "these women aren't working. If I had a child, I would want his own mother to be at his side, not someone with a third world primary school education and half-baked English. But then," Crowley smiled wryly, "I wasn't brought up in one of these colonial families with hot and cold running servants. My mother raised me by herself in Leicester, with no thanks or apologies to anyone. She cleaned other people's houses during the day and worked a second job on Friday and Saturday nights. Left me those nights with an auntie."

He was obviously quite proud of his mother, but stopped there, as if embarrassed by the direction their chat had followed. Claire wondered to herself what had brought him to Hong Kong, especially with the handover imminent. There was no future in the force, no possible promotion opportunities for a good-looking Englishman with ambition, and if he didn't have the education and push to make it in banking or commercial circles, it was a strange dead end. It was policy to make sure that the upper ranks—at one time almost all British—were increasingly filled with talented Chinese as the colonial administration came to a close. Crowley would certainly never see himself made Senior Superintendent in the service of the Special Administration Region of Hong Kong to come. The Hong Kong government had stopped actively recruiting in London many years ago. Even the Hong Kong Governor's deputies were Chinese, save one Australian-born press spokesman.

They said good-by politely at the gate of Claire's building. It was only ten-twenty in the morning. Claire's first interview with a candidate to be Caspar's *amah* would be arriving at ten-thirty. She felt momentarily like calling the whole thing off. She opened her front door heavily, filled with misgivings. Did she really have to work? For her sake? For whose sake? Until a year ago, work had been all she had besides her music. Studying the piano had been a way of life from the age of four. There had been a time when she had even considered making music her career. Instead the lure of travel, with journalism paying her way, had won out. She'd earned this job the hard way, by sticking out long years of freelancing in the field, rather than joining the corporate race for overseas postings back in the States.

Maybe it was hard for a man like Crowley to understand that her identity as Claire Raymond, the byline, was more than a persona, it was her source of financial, social, and emotional support. What was it her ex-lover Jim had said to her that amazing night when they both admitted their feelings? "I can't believe the famous Claire Raymond is with me tonight." Well, even if Jim was now gone, or disappeared rather, in a strangely abrupt departure on U.S. government business somewhere else, her identity as Hong Kong's longest serving resident American correspondent was immutable.

Now for Xavier she was just Claire. Bylines and ten-day assignments in Shanghai wouldn't impress little Caspar. Those two men, large and tiny, had opened up her hope of being other things, maybe simpler or better things? Was she giving those other choices a fair shot?

Claire felt depleted by the emotions of the morning. Letting herself into their apartment, she thought again of Petey's laughter, then tears, at the swimming pool the last time she had seen him alive.

Suddenly, strong cigarette smoke hit her nostrils as she entered her living room. Neither she nor Xavier smoked. A small figure lounging on the shaded balcony was silhouetted against the bright morning light beyond. The woman turned at the sound of the front door slamming behind Claire. She rose sinuously and came in from the balcony, a tentative smile framed by dark brunette hair cut into a perfect fringe. As she came into the room, hand outstretched to greet Claire, the other hand took away a cigarette from dark, full, red lips. "*Salut, Claire. Je suis Fabienne.* I'm so sorry, I hope you don't mind. Your girl let me in. I don't know which hotel Xavier booked for me. So I thought I should just come here until I will reach him."

Fabienne paused, taking in Claire with large eyes. One gamine hip was cocked upwards in well-cut jeans, barely topped by a soft oatmeal-colored sweater and finished with small suede boots. Still recovering from childbirth, Claire knew that her black trousers stretched obviously across her slack stomach and the white cotton shirt she had thought looked chic was already more than fashionably wrinkled.

Fabienne smiled again, almost too knowingly. "What a beautiful baby you have, but so unlike Xavier. I would never have guessed he is the father."

Claire fumbled a recovery and managed a perfunctory handshake. She decided to let the slur on Caspar's illegitimacy slide past her, and having regained composure sufficiently to ask if the flight to Hong Kong had been comfortable, she asked Connie to get the woman a cold drink and settled her guest on one of the sofas in the living room.

They chatted about the weather, life and liberty, sitting opposite each other, marking time while Claire waited for Xavier to return her quick alert by phone.

"I have my career and my personal life, and that is enough for me," said Fabienne.

Claire wasn't idiot enough to ask Fabienne to detail what or whom she reckoned her personal life included. "I have my career too, and then Caspar came along. He's changed a lot of my ideas just by being here," Claire admitted, "You never wanted children yourself?" She wondered if they could, after all, strike a sympathetic chord somewhere.

"I wasn't meant to play the cow," snapped Fabienne, lighting another cigarette.

Claire wondered what face Fabienne showed to Xavier, because it was hard to picture these two together. There was nothing left to do but wait for Fabienne's speedy departure for the hotel and moo good-by, Claire thought ruefully.

# chapter
## three

Fabienne could probably have repeated the day's weather report and managed to make it sound to Claire like a recital of intended barbs. It only needed a few more comments from the Genevan and the taxi might not have been necessary—Fabienne was welcome to take the quicker route over the wall of Claire's balcony, roll down the hillside, and plunge into the harbor's polluted waters. Worse, Fabienne exuded an air of satisfaction, even patronizing approval, at having gained entrance to the apartment, thanks to Connie, in order to inspect Xavier's offspring alone.

Her tiny hands cupped gracefully around a mug of mint tea, the Swiss-French woman had rattled off all the places she had seen, "except Hong Kong, of course, and Cambodia, this is the first time," but it didn't take Claire long to realize that she was actually listing, carefully, all the places she had visited with Xavier. Was it her imagination or was Fabienne watching for a sign of recognition from Claire of familiarity with Xavier's past?

For someone so spare and light, she was remarkably immovable. She sat for a full five minutes while Claire stood, she stood in the middle of the room chatting for another five while Claire waited patiently, hand on the doorknob. When Claire finally did open the front door to bundle Fabienne, her camera bags, and expensive black calf leather carry-all downstairs for a taxi bound for the Excelsior Hotel, there was Leo standing right in their path.

Leo Franklin was the three and a half year old Eurasian child who lived in the only other apartment on their floor. Since moving in next to the Franklins, Claire had not felt too much warmth from his parents, the Australian financier, Giles, or his well-groomed Chinese socialite wife, Lily. But Claire had loved Leo immediately, for his light laughter trailing from under the front door, for the infectious games he played with Petey Sandford in the swimming pool shared by three buildings along Tregunter Path, for his toys left strewn along the stairwell, and for his ribald "I-can-see-your-butt" humor.

Today Leo was wearing his latest Disney promotional T-shirt over tiny jockey briefs. But no matter what his current video passion, Claire had nicknamed him "Little Boo-Boo," after Yogi Bear's sidekick, the first time she met him months before. Not knowing the reference, it had immediately offended Lily, who was sensitive to any imagined interracial slur.

"You are so sweet! You are so cute! What is your name?" Fabienne had dropped to her knees. So Leo had dropped to his.

"Poo-poo," mugged Leo.

"That's Boo-Boo," corrected Claire. "He's a little cartoon bear I loved when I was his age. Actually, his name is Leo Franklin."

Fabienne was rubbing his cheeks and ruffling his hair ferociously.

"Where do you live, *mon cheri? Mon petit homme*!!" Fabienne was pouring verbal syrup on the boy's head so thick it would glue them both to the foyer marble for weeks, thought Claire.

"In the zoo," Leo's eyes were narrowing.

"Oh, you are an animal. What kind? What kind of animal?"

"A bumposaurus. They go like this." And Leo went down on all fours and hopped around, his thumbs and two fingers making raptor-like grasping gestures. To Claire's delight, he then sunk his teeth into the suede-covered ankle of her guest.

"Now you're dead," he said, shaking his head with sympathy.

Claire instructed the taxi driver to take Fabienne to The Excelsior with ill-disguised haste. The hotel was not offensively distant from their apartment, being on the same side of the harbor as Tregunter Path, nor was it smack under their noses in Central. How Swiss of Xavier, thought Claire sourly, to be so neutral and diplomatic.

The morning had already had its fill of emotions—grief, resentment, jealousy, indecision—and it was still so early. She sighed and leaned back against the dining room wall and surveyed her living room.

What had Fabienne seen? And what impression would it make on a Filipina applying to work for her? A room, not very different in proportion from the Sandfords', but certainly a world away in taste and history. The walls were lined with a hastily unpacked jumble of her own books—Chinese poetry, literary biographies, murder mysteries. In the corner, with the light pouring onto the unpolished surfaces, stood her Russian-built grand piano, dragged to Hong Kong from Shanghai by some emigré family and unloaded on a small Chinese music store in Wanchai to be discovered by Claire one Saturday afternoon. There were her piles of yellow Schirmer music scores and her cherished map of China drawn by sixteenth century Jesuits, bought under the appraising eye of Father Fresnay at an auction downtown. The rest of the room was a sorry collection of battered whitewashed rattan, its cushions covered in faded salmon linen.

Six months ago, it had all been unceremoniously thrown together with the help of a team of sweating Sichuanese moving men alongside Xavier's Corbusier chair, Balinese masks, and wall hangings, stereo, and CDs. The final chaotic decorator touch was the collection of hurriedly purchased baby gear: a stuffed lion from Tokyo, a hand-me-down babywalker from the *London Times* family in Beijing, a shiny British stroller from friends at the Hong Kong and Shanghai Bank, and a bouncer hanging in the kitchen doorway from Claire's friend in the State Department, Harris Hillward.

No wonder *Architectural Digest* hasn't called, she sighed. She slid the balcony doors as wide open as possible to air out the room. When she went to the nursery to check on Caspar, he wasn't there, and startled, she discovered him instead in a Moses basket in the center of the kitchen floor. Consuela was ironing a shapeless velour item about ten inches long.

"Connie, what are you doing?"

"Ironing the baby suits, ma'am."

"Connie, you don't have to press a baby's stretch suit. I appreciate your thoroughness, but I don't think it's going to make much difference. That's like ironing towels—it's just not necessary."

"I already ironed the towels, ma'am."

"I see. Thank you." Claire suppressed a smile. Connie's expression was a mix of pride and fear of a reprimand. Claire had no intention of going through such a scene every day. She would have to overcome her initial instinct to virtually hide from her domestic help in the hope they would know better than she how to run a family home. The whole idea of some poor girl working six days a week from breakfast until after dinner left her feeling a mixture of gratitude and embarrassment. This lifestyle was a given for working mothers in Hong Kong, but Claire came to it desperately in need of relief and yet uncomfortable.

No, there was no avoiding her responsibilities, even if she was backing into them so reluctantly. She saw she was going to have to establish priorities with the permanent *amah*. For years she had done her own laundry and shopping in between assignments in Taiwan, Bangkok, and Beijing. Saturdays had meant a quick swipe at the bathroom, a vacuum over the worn Chinese carpets, and a spray or two on the mirrors.

She had realized in the last few weeks that Xavier's job required a certain preparedness as agency people arrived with little warning from Geneva, Washington, New York, or the field, and expected drinks on short notice, if not dinner. Caspar, too, wasn't just a bit of housework she could catch up with between assignments. For a brief second, she stood motionless in the corridor of her own home and, realizing that every room of her home was shared with another presence, hated the new burdens of home and motherhood, the very burdens that drew the ill-contained resentment of the tired, virginal Filipinas all around her.

Connie had gone to answer the door to Ysidra Pangilanan. Ysidra looked about twenty and wore her hair down the back of her neck in a braid. She was dressed in a black skirt and red shirt and smiled tentatively at Claire. They sat in the living room, Ysidra perched on the edge of the long rattan sofa.

"Connie says you are a relative of hers?"

"Yes, ma'am."

Claire smiled warmly. "What kind of relative?"

The two Filipinas exchanged mumbled consultations.

"A cousin, ma'am."

"Can you tell me something about your work experience?"

"Yes, ma'am." Nothing followed. Claire looked at Ysidra, who smiled politely back, fiddling patiently with the end of her braid.

More Cebuyan urgent exchanges initiated by Consuela who was bobbing anxiously around the dining table behind them, pretending to polish it.

"Connie, does your cousin really speak English?"

Connie smiled helpfully, "She is very, very shy, ma'am. She works for a Chinese family now in Mongkok. That man is very bad man and he is always making trouble for my cousin be-

cause she is so pretty. He climbs into her bed when she is sleeping. She beat him away many times. Anyway, my cousin wants
to work for you very much, ma'am."

"So you said, and I appreciate her eagerness, but you said
she spoke good English."

"She learns very quickly, ma'am. And she loves children very
much."

"I see."

In the negative sense, Claire thought ruefully, this might be
easier than she thought. She could do nothing for Ysidra, and
having compared Ysidra's features with Connie's, suspected
they were more closely related by bus lines than bloodlines. For
the moment, there seemed to be nothing she could do but send
Ysidra back to the Mongkok bedhopper.

The next candidate, "Teddy" Agrava, was anxious for the job,
but wasn't available until her current employers emigrated to
Canada in three months' time. She had seen the advertisement
at the Catholic Centre's bulletin board asking for applicants with
experience with newborns. Actually, she had no experience
with children, although she was a trained nurse. Someday, she
would like to emigrate to the U.S., where her half-sister was a
nurse in Washington, D.C. Check.

The third candidate, Luisa Tarlac, had forgotten her references, then admitted she was breaking her contract because her
employers were "very picky about everything, changing sheets,
watering the plants. Always very tough on me. They show me
no consideration, and the employer's wife is not healthy in her
mind." Check.

The fourth candidate, Arellina Santos, didn't show up.

Claire retreated with a wad of tissues and emptied herself of
grief over Petey and frustration with the morning. A cold beer
and cheese sandwich now sat half-consumed on her desk. Guilt-
ily, she wished to be removed from all these intimacies. Life in
the bureau was so safe, she thought. You wrote about other
people's tragedies, bankruptcies, wars, and divorces with equa-

nimity. You polished off strangers' successes and failures with a white wine and soda at the Foreign Correspondents' Club.

She looked up to see Xavier standing in the doorway of her office, a particular look of amused and loving disgust in his eyes.

"I see you and my child have shared a San Miguel together for lunch."

Claire straightened up. "Oh, you should have called. You've missed lunch. He's sleeping soundly."

"I'm not surprised, although you keep telling me beer is good for the baby. Anyway," he sat down on the end of the chair, "I didn't come home to see him. I was a little worried about you. It's only ten minutes from town and I couldn't think of anything I wanted to eat and the secretaries ordered all these smelly take-out noodles in fish sauce." He sighed, "I just felt like clearing my head."

He sat down and leaned over her, stroking the long stray red curls that hung over her shoulder. While he played with her hair, she reciprocated by straightening the collar of his light-weight wool sportsjacket. He never had to dress too formally for his agency job. She loved the way he wore his clothes, thoughtlessly, perfectly, *décontracté*.

As she brushed off his shoulders, she thought to herself, This is how monkeys in love must groom each other. They don't make promises or take vows. They bark until the rival monkeys head off into the bushes and then they sit quietly in the shade of the midday, picking out lice. He wasn't even wearing a tie for work, just a turtleneck sweater. The back of his hair curled over the cashmere, so she played with his hair, too, and smiled.

Possibly it was a little too brave a smile, because he sat back and asked pointedly, "Did everything go all right with Fabienne?"

"Of course," Claire said, shrugging indifferently. "I've been airing the house out for the last couple of hours."

"Yes, well, she's always smoked. I used to smoke heavily too, remember."

"I wasn't referring to her cigarettes. She also implied the baby wasn't yours."

Xavier sighed. He kissed her softly and murmured, "I'm with you. You . . . remember? You have no reason to be nervous about her little comments."

Claire turned away slightly, embarrassed, and Xavier pulled back at her small rejection.

"Remember, you are a little shock for her, too. But she means well, so don't worry. Anyway, she called me from the hotel and suggested lunch, but I told her—"

"So that's why you're here in the middle of the day."

"Well, maybe I'm not ready to see her. It's strange, the idea of you both in the same city. She told me she has friends here in town besides me, as it turns out. I don't think it's going to be a problem for us, and Claire, it shouldn't become a problem. Okay?"

Was she being scolded or loved, or both?

"Did you spend some time with your friend next door?"

"Vicky, yes. Nobody realized Petey's epilepsy was so bad. There's nothing you can say in such a situation. I wish I could have checked back with her, but I've been interviewing *amahs* all morning."

"I hope you didn't hire someone without my meeting her," Xavier protested playfully. "I want someone beautiful, who calls me 'Master,' cooks me *rösti*, has a warm bath waiting when I come home every night, and folds the dinner napkins into little orchid shapes on the plate."

"I think you're joking, but the pathetic thing is, I can't be totally sure. Is that really what you expect in a servant?"

"No, I was talking about you, not the *amah*."

Claire laughed. "Right. You've spent so much of your life in hotels and tents, I'm not sure how you expect me to run your first real home."

"You should know me better."

"I say that to myself every morning now that I wake up with

a man in my bed and a baby next door yelling for my body."

"You'll get used to it. You haven't got a choice. You're stuck with two new men in your life."

Claire was about to say, "Is that a promise?" but Xavier reacted badly to Claire's insecurities. She could look at her cards every day and still not know if she was playing a weak hand or a winning streak. Why was that?

Dovie Ocampo came on time, but she just missed meeting Xavier. She was a woman in her fifties, wearing no makeup, her short hair tucked behind her ears. Claire was surprised to see she was wearing a woollen bouclé suit, the sort English-women of a certain type would wear to a tea.

"I learned about the job from Mrs. Sandford, ma'am. Only on Saturday."

"I've just seen her. She's holding up incredibly well. We're all shocked by what happened," Claire replied.

But Dovie knew what she was there for. "I have worked for Mr. and Mrs. Evans-Smith since 1973." She handed Claire her typed references in a business envelope. Claire immediately recognized the government letterhead.

"As you probably know, Mr. Evans-Smith is retiring from the post of Secretary for the New Territories. He'll join his wife in England in a month's time. Mrs. Evans-Smith had already made arrangements for me to work in Sha Tin, near my daughter and her family. But then my daughter decided to return to Manila next year and I thought I would like to work on Hong Kong-side again, closer to other friends who work for families in government."

Claire took in Dovie's introduction, privately absorbing the surprise of her introduction. So old Evans-Smith's time was up, she remarked to herself. Of course, all the old-timers, the men she had interviewed in her first heady days of local reporting in Hong Kong fifteen years before, they were *old* now. Those who had stuck it out were just making it to the handover for the big pensions. Even so, were they as sad as the younger men in their forties and fifties who were retiring early from the Hong Kong government to the shires, men who in another era would have had another good twenty years of colonial service ahead?

She was thrown momentarily back in time to her days starting out at the *South China Morning Post* as a local reporter. What confidence men like Evans-Smith had enjoyed then, shuttling between their offices in Government House, the Murray Building, and Beaconsfield House. At the end of the day, they would ease over to the Hilton Hotel's Dragonboat Bar for a few drinks, then mosey by diesel taxi back up to their government-paid flats with ceiling fans and large porticoed balconies overlooking the harbor. The weeks were punctuated by a share on Sundays in ownership of a little Chinese junk. Things seemed so much more straightforward then, well before 1984, when they signed away Hong Kong's future in a deal with Beijing.

And such men had been, for the most part, kind to her, the lanky red-headed and raw-boned American newcomer, brashly tackling the stodgy colonial hierarchy with her blunt questions and tart articles. Evans-Smith had been particularly courteous, she recalled, although she had seen much less of him in recent years. Her assignments for *Business World* were regional now, big-picture stuff for American readers.

With nostalgia, she recalled her own strangely carefree ways, if that was the right word for working eleven-hour days, ten days at a stretch, without a day off. Her wardrobe had consisted of denim mini-skirts and black cotton Chinese sandals, T-shirts, and for full effect, Chinese-produced "555" cigarettes. She had worked hard without union protection until late into the evening shift, then finished her evenings in the club for local journalists, Australians, and northern Englishmen as well as Chinese—the poor journo's version of the more glamorous Foreign Correspondents' Club, that haven for well-paid network cameramen and PR hacks.

When had she first seen Alistair Evans-Smith, with his wacky, unruly hair that sprang away from his foreheard like a rooster? He had been one of old Governor MacLehose's point men in pioneering relations with the powerful clan families living near the Chinese border back in the sixties and seventies . . .

Dovie's cough drew Claire back sharply.

"How is Mr. Evans-Smith?" she asked the older woman. "I haven't interviewed him in almost ten years, although we've brushed shoulders socially every few years since. You know how Hong Kong is."

"He's very well, ma'am, except, you know, a lot quieter since his daughter died five years ago. He never talked about how he missed her, but we all knew how sad they both felt. You know, he used to sing a lot around the house on the weekends—that was his Welsh side coming out—but after Viola's death, he never sang another note."

"I'm not surprised."

In fact, Claire had read about it one day, picking up an abandoned *South China Morning Post* while she waited for some faxes to come through to her in the business center of a Shanghai hotel. The *Post* was two days old, and five minutes after reading the item, Claire had pushed it to the back of her mind. In the seventies, she'd met the daughter once, but it was hardly a formal introduction. Viola had been a noisy young child romping on the balcony of a government flat through one of her parents' curry lunches for young members of the local press during Evans-Smith's stint with the Government Information Offices. She had totally forgotten. Totally. Single career-bound reporters on deadline weren't always the most sensitive people, she chastised herself.

"Well, the inquest was so quiet. I remember reading it had something to do with the swimming pool at the residence," Claire said.

"Yes, ma'am. She drowned."

Dovie fell silent. Nice to know she was discreet. The death of Viola Evans-Smith had never been explained publicly in great detail, and there were hints of something hidden, but who knew? Probably Dovie.

"Mrs. Evans-Smith has already gone back to the U.K. to prepare their home there. They asked me if I wanted to go with them, but I would like to stay nearer to my daughter. I'm really too old to emigrate."

"Actually, I'm wondering if the care of a newborn doesn't need a younger woman. Do you mind if I have a word with Mr. Evans-Smith?"

"No, of course not. That's why I brought my references. As far as pay is concerned, I am looking for the same level I was earning before this, and also, ma'am, I would like to continue to have my Sundays off, not Saturdays."

"You speak excellent English."

"I taught English as a young woman. But the pay in Hong Kong as a servant was much higher than as an English teacher in Manila. The Marcos days were very difficult for my family. My late husband was a newspaperman. We all left the country after martial law was imposed."

"Do you like working with children?"

"Yes, and I like to keep the house. I make fresh bread every morning, I can mend, cook Chinese and Western, and Mrs. Evans-Smith sent me on a Thai cooking course. I can do dinner parties, although I am not so good now at staying up past midnight to clean up. I feel it the next day."

"We all do," Claire joked, "and besides, we don't give many state dinners, Dovie. In fact, if I have any worries, it is that this household won't be anything like as grand to work in as the Evans-Smiths'."

Dovie looked clearly disappointed. "I thought your husband was a government official with the United Nations?"

"Yes, well, he's not my, I mean he is with a development agency connected to the U.N. but our style is not what you might think from your past experience. I mean, we don't have a lot of formal dinners or receptions. At least, not now."

Claire realized that she didn't even know what she was talking about. They had hardly shared a house before Caspar was with them. Nothing was normal yet.

"I see." This was a come-down for Dovie, who was putting her handbag back on her lap in readiness to go.

Claire was fearful of losing this candidate so soon. "On the other hand, you might find the location is good for you, since there are many government families along Tregunter Path, and of course, you'll have Sundays off to go to Mass, and we won't intrude on your private life at all. The hours will be as regular as a baby's schedule allows."

"I see," she said again. Clearly, she was not impressed. The telephone rang and Claire went into the television nook to answer it.

It was Fabienne. She didn't talk, she trilled. " 'ello, Claire, I spoke to Xavier this morning, just to tell him the room is absolutely perfect, with a view of the water, and so many boats, I really want to do some photographs of the harbor, during the night as well as during the day. This is just the way he described it. And I want so much to see the town, and thought perhaps we could all go out tomorrow night, for dinner, you know, nothing fancy, just the real Hong Kong. Would you like that?"

Caspar was crying in the kitchen. The ring of the extension had wakened him. Where was Connie? Probably sulking in the servant's quarters over her "cousin's" failed interview.

"Fabienne, I'm afraid I have to go see what's the matter with the baby."

"Oh, of course, I'm so sorry. Yes, I'll discuss the plans for tomorrow night with Xavier. He's so good at organizing things. Meanwhile, could I just ask you, do you know a good place to have my camera repaired? The little door that holds the battery at the bottom has come off. It's a Nikon, and I need it to be fixed very, very quickly, for my work, not just for my holiday here, and—"

"Fabienne, could we talk about it later?" Dovie was rising from the sofa to go.

"Well, it's something that I have to do right away, in case, you know, they don't have the tiny, tiny part I need—"

Dovie had headed to the kitchen without her handbag.

"—and I know that if I bring the camera in right away, that way they will be certain to have it repaired before I go to Cambodia. Otherwise . . ."

Dovie had returned with Caspar in her arms. The boy was pulling on Dovie's short hair, his face creased from sleeping on a toy left in his basket. Dovie was swinging and bouncing him almost violently from side to side, but despite Claire's alarm, Caspar was starting to close his eyes, whether from relief or motion sickness, Claire couldn't tell.

"Fabienne, I'll see you later." Claire slammed down the phone and took in the scene before her with a sigh.

Dovie was still swaying, more gently now, and she smiled at Claire over the baby's shoulder. He was cooing slowly, his sobs subsiding with huge heaves, his little hands holding tightly onto her collar. Dovie's smile was no longer polite, but truly warm, now directed totally at Caspar rather than Claire. Claire felt her shoulders, gripped by nervous tension, drop about two inches with relief. Caspar was making little "uh-uh," sounds of contentment and his mouth was moving into little kisses full of hope for milk.

Dovie handed him over to Claire without ceremony, saying, "I'm sure he'd like a little meal. He's not used to the smell of me, but he'll be more comfortable in a few days. Perhaps you would like to talk to Mr. Evans-Smith about my references?"

"Yes, I would. Thank you, Dovie. Thank you."

# chapter
## four

Claire decided she would drive Dovie all the way home to the New Territories. The forty-five minute trip gave them a better chance to know each other. Dovie had her opinions, there was no question about that, and she was anxious to explain how developments in the New Territories had come to obscure what had been, not so long ago, low-brushed countryside, perfect for hiking on a Sunday with friends.

Well, now, first Claire should know that those new towns were full of teenage gangs these days, Dovie told her, mainland kids who lived an unruly existence straddling Hong Kong's border with China. They harassed the Filipinas travelling in and out of town on the mass transit railway, making lewd remarks at the young women and showing no respect for the older ones.

"When I was young, it was the Chinese who worked in our homes as servants, not the other way around," she said plainly.

In the end, Dovie had had a good life, although she had always wished she could have stayed in the Philippines and used her university degree and continued teaching. Now that she was older, Dovie didn't feel so comfortable working alone in a large old house, all but one of the staff—old Ah Lok—let go with the death of Miss Evans-Smith, then the departure of Freddy, and now the move of Mrs. Evans-Smith to England.

Dovie was very proud of Freddy. She had taught Freddy to read, in fact. Mrs. Evans-Smith was always very busy with charity work, so Dovie had coached him from the age of six, and of course, he had done his A-levels with flying colors and gone on to university. Dovie showed Claire a picture of the gawky Evans-Smith junior on an English lawn in front of what looked impressively like the Oxford common.

Claire realized after some twenty minutes of this that she was getting qualms about Dovie's motherly affection for Freddy. Claire hadn't planned Caspar, that was true, but now that she had him, she wanted to enjoy her motherhood, not hand him over to a substitute bosom who would claim him as her own.

That prompted another fear on the heels of the first. As Claire listened to Dovie's affectionate description of Freddy's rowing prowess, Claire wondered if Dovie would see Caspar as some kind of leftover, an also-ran to Freddy, after her long tenure with the Evans-Smith family?

It would not be the last time Claire would find herself reciting an unspoken Working Mother's Prayer: Love my son, but not too much. Teach him to love you, but not too much. Help me in every possible way, but don't take over. Be more perfect than I could ever be, more patient, more wise, but never let him see your superiority over me, because I am his mother, the Queendom and the Glory, forever and ever, Amen.

The driveway up to the old Secretarial residence was a shock to Claire who hadn't seen it in a decade or more. On that long ago summer day, visiting one of Evans-Smith's predecessors, she recalled, the curb had been lined with bougainvillea, a long promenade of fuschia and green, the rest of the grounds protected from beating sun by a lush carpet of elephantine ivy leaves.

The ivy was still there, but had overgrown the flowers and spread across the gravel drive in greedy patches. The white house looked almost the same, but as Claire parked her car in front of the porch, she could see that the paint had broken off the bases of the columns near the steps, and that the window trim was broken off in places.

The Hong Kong government had never been poor, in fact, it was sixty billion U.S. dollars rich these days, but recently the allocations were going in different directions. There were two legislatures, the outgoing one broadly elected under the last British governor and Beijing's puppet appointees waiting for their turn after the handover. It was hard to know where the public works money was going to go, should go, or would go, once the Communists took over. The Brits had only shown the Communists the colony's accounts for the first time this year. Even an optimist had to expect a comedy—or a tragedy—of mismanagement, at least for a while.

The government had once held up the Secretary for the New Territories as the man on the front line, juggling the delicate relationship between the colonial government—safe and snug back on the island south of the harbor—with the clans that ran the rural areas to the north, bordering China. Many of the villages still ran according to the inheritance and property laws of the Ch'ing dynasty. Visiting Father Fresnay's weekend house in Tailong village near Hamtin beach on Sai Kung Penisula was to return to the final decade of the nineteenth century. But not far away, expressways plowed through the New Territories past walled villages, clan shrines, and traditional cemeteries like laser lines of the future cutting through time.

The border the Brits had so vigorously patrolled all those years was now fast becoming a historical artifact, as thousands of trucks, ferries, buses, and trains surged up and down the land

and sea corridors that connected Hong Kong's commuters and
traders to the industrial boomtowns of Guangdong province.
That border was dissolving, and now the man, who as a talented
young deputy Secretary had more than once singlehandedly
cowed the clannish *Heung I Kuk* elders in fluent Chiu Chow
dialect, sun-bleached cox's comb bobbing with political determination, that man was now sitting in his garden looking out
across the bluff toward the distant seacoast, patiently waiting
for his tea tray.

"Lovely winter weather for a bite outside," he said as a welcome, with hand outstretched, rising out of his garden chair.
Claire noticed one of his knees seemed a little undependable
so they both sat down rather quickly. Dovie had slipped discreetly into the house by the servants' entrance off the garage.

Even in the sunshine it was chilly, and Claire kept her green
wool coat belted around her. Evans-Smith wore an old tweed
sporting jacket over one of those handknitted sweaters mainland Chinese had always worn before they started getting Hong
Kong fashion shows by satellite dish.

Now Dovie reappeared, half-supporting an old Chinese servant in white shirt and black pants, a woman so bald only three
or four strands of hair crossed her scalp before winding into a
tiny bun at the nape of her neck. Claire recognized her as one
of the dying breed of famous "black and white *amahs*," a highly
regarded sisterhood of Guangdong women who took vows of
chastity and served families from young womanhood until
death.

"A mother now," Evans-Smith said looking over Claire ap-
provingly. "Finally!"

"Hmmm, rather late, but what the hell, why not?" Claire answered cheerfully.

"Got your hair? Yes? Well, let's hope he has your spunk."

"He's got his father's bellow, that's for certain," Claire said,
helping Evans-Smith arrange the tea things.

"Haven't met the father, have I? Well, you're the mother, at any rate, and I bet he's a devil, your little fellow. Well, they all are, and then, just when you've humanized them, got them to stop bunging their food all over the Tibetan, they're off, like Freddy. Ta, ta, and that's it!"

They laughed together for a moment and then fell quiet. Claire sighed. The view stretching beyond the garden and across the hills had once been an uninterrupted, magnificent stretch of Chinese farmland. Now to one side, there was an expressway heading northward, thundering with huge trucks headed for Shenzhen and Guangzhou.

"This is a great lookout point for seeing how the New Towns are now the *old* New Towns," commented Claire, pointing to the older estates crumbling in a welter of hanging laundry and peeling painted numbers on the water-washed concrete walls.

"Yes, and over there are the new New Towns," he rose and gestured to a couple of steely towers catching the late afternoon sun some miles away, "and," his finger moved again to a slope overrun with Mediterranean-style villas, "there are the newest of the new, at a million-plus for what we used to call a two-up-two-down back in England. I thought it was a speculator's folly when it first went up, but I guess the world isn't going to run out of upwardly-mobile, middle-class Chinese any day soon." He chuckled, more to himself, than to Claire. They sat down again to enjoy their tea.

"Tell me a little about Dovie," asked Claire.

"Well, I'll say it straight out." He thrust both hands into his jacket pockets. "She may not be right for you. She's used to the government lifestyle, you know, and she hasn't handled an infant in more years than she'll admit. I'm not sure you could expect her to do the night feeding on a regular basis, not the way Althea handed Freddy and Viola over during those first couple of months."

"Well, given I'm going back to work soon, that's the one feed

I'm sure to be around for. It's the others that are a problem."

"I'm always careful with women in your generation, but I must ask anyway. Do you have to go back to work?"

"Well, you know better than others, it's been my life for more than a decade. I love this city, and things are really getting interesting now up in Beijing with the changes in government. By this year next time, I'll bet you Deng has died and we're watching a real power struggle behind the scenes—"

"Oh, they'll never change up there, whatever they call themselves down here. It's the corruption you have to watch, not the Fifteen Party Congress or who they finally make a scapegoat for Tiananmen once the old man goes. Their imperial tendencies go back centuries, but—" His brow had furrowed up and he drew himself upright, "we're talking about childcare, not the Communists, my dear! No, I only asked whether you had to return to work because the time with your children is very short, however you look at it. Very precious years, indeed."

He glanced across the lawn almost despite himself. His gaze lingered in the middle distance, where the empty swimming pool, a rudimentary, old-fashioned cement hole lay accusingly, full of cracks and brown strands of vine leaves. Claire imagined the ghost of Viola walking across the grass, and glanced back at Evans-Smith, who was suddenly complacently sipping his tea.

Had she imagined such a disconcerting moment? No, the lines on his face were deep and no humor could erase his profound pain. Claire realized with a jolt that when they had first met, his most outstanding feature apart from his hair, had been his freckled, sunburnt complexion. The deep crevices were mottled with dark brown and stark white patches now, as if the skin had given up trying to make sense of its melanin over the many years in Hong Kong's blistering sun.

She spoke as soon as she had regained her composure. "I'd like to give Dovie a try, but I feel so responsible taking her. I gather the usual thing is to do a one month tryout to see if it works, but you'll be gone by then, and I couldn't just let someone with her experience wander the job market like a newcomer."

"That's not likely to happen. It's true I'm supposed to join Althea in a month, but I've got a lot to clear away. My departure may have to be delayed. Between the two of us, I expect we could make sure Dovie is happy one way or another. Have a go."

"All right, I will. Now I'll ask you a separate question."

"Well," he laughed, "it'll hardly be the first time you've put me on the spot!"

"Do you really want to leave Hong Kong?"

The white flip of hair flew up with a thrust of his chin. "No. No! It's been my life! First the languages at Cambridge, then the people here, and now the handover. They need us, God damn it! If only these arrogant little yuppie businessmen realized it, with their venture capital in Shenzhen, golf courses in Changan, housing developments in Zhuhai. And their loyalites! Marched 'em straight from Whitehall to Jongnanhai without so much as a nod to the interests of the average man on the street." He laughed unconvincingly but even an alert glance from Claire didn't deter him.

"Do they think they're so much cleverer than Shanghai's bankers in 1949? And suppose it all works? Suppose they do manage to turn southern China into one huge Hong Kong? Who ran Hong Kong so successfully for them all those decades they were making millions on plastic flowers in Hunghom? We did, our hundreds of nice boring bureaucrats in their summer knee-socks and white shorts! But no, now the British administration has to go, and God knows what's taking its place."

"Well, since last week we've known our fearless leader is going to be C. H. Tung."

"Of course, it was always going to be C. H. Ever since the Communists bailed his shipping operations out of the red in '85—"

"$120 million U.S., is more than bailing him out, they bought him outright!"

He nodded. "Well, let's just say we've suspected they've had their eyes on him for a plum job ever since. Six months ago, an old friend of mine saw him dining up in Beijing, but his hosts weren't northerners. They were his father's age, old friends of C. Y.'s from Shanghai, no doubt telling junior how loyal dad cleverly used his fleet to play both sides of the fence during the war. Yes, they can count on C. H., even though he's made such an obvious show of slanting toward Taiwanese interests. All part of the theatrics . . . well-planned, I must say," Evans-Smith sniffed and bit emphatically into a piece of cake.

Claire smiled at him. "We need men like you to stick around and pass on those tidbits of news we can use, the lore that makes it all make sense."

He scoffed. "No one wants us around, not even you journalists. Always looking for a new angle, not an old one. Well, that's what they always said about Hong Kong—borrowed place, borrowed time, and us, I guess that means we led borrowed lives? I hope they'll be happy with the mob that takes our place—a bunch of rubber stampers prattling on about understanding Asian values? Do Asian values make you feel better when you get tossed in prison for complaining about corruption or calling Li Peng the butcher he is? They haven't a clue of what's coming as soon as CNN and ITN leave town."

A fresh breeze ruffled his hair and he drew his jacket more closely around him. Claire was snug in her coat, but her tea had turned cold. She served herself another piece of lemon poppy seed cake and asked him, "But what about barristers like Max Pereira, or Rebe Wing? Won't they, or people like them, continue the traditions of judicial independence, accountability? After all, it's the rule of law that counts." These were two of Claire's friends, both popular advocates of constitutional law in local legal circles.

Evans-Smith shrugged. "Pereira's half-Chinese, half-Portuguese. He's a marvelous barrister, first rate. But he owns a house in England and has an English wife. You watch and see how the Party marginalizes him with racial inuendo. And Rebe? Well, maybe there's some hope there. Her uncle's an important intellectual up at Fudan University, and that'll hold water with the Shanghainese working down here. After all, Jiang Zeming will probably be in charge, and he's the core of the Shanghai mafia running the country. But look at it the other way. It's one more bit of leverage Beijing has over people like her. Call it sour grapes, my dear, but the signs aren't healthy. God, things looked a bit different in '84."

"But your friends in the Foreign Office got angry when we questioned you so hard about the agreement."

"We said then it was the best we could do. I'll tell you a secret, my dear. I wish we'd tried a whole lot bloody harder. It's too late now. Too bloody late."

By the time Claire reached Midlevels an hour later, the sun had long ago set in the gray waters to the west, and the lights of the city stretched below. A slow-motion camera could have traced the ferry routes into bright yellow strings linking the two sides of the harbor, the neon signs of garish blues and yellows and reds blinking off the water, and on toward the hills of Kowloon. It seemed a lonely night to be driving, and Claire indulged herself with the still-novel pleasure of anticipating warm bodies at home to welcome her.

Connie answered the door and to Claire's surprise, Xavier was not yet home. He had left a message on her answering machine saying that he was stopping to have a quick drink with Fabienne before coming home, "Just to get her schedule for her visit settled."

If his purpose was to settle one woman, it had only unsettled another. It had never occurred to Claire that in making it clear Fabienne wasn't welcome as a houseguest, she was encouraging Xavier to see Fabienne separately as an alternative.

She waited for him for almost an hour, and getting famished, accepted an omelette from Connie before excusing her for bed. Dovie had already retired after a long day of unpacking in the second half of the servants' room, conveniently partitionable by design.

Claire lay in bed, waiting for the sound of a car below. The "drink" must have started at the end of his working day, if not earlier, and it was now nearly half past nine. She put her head underneath the pillow to suffocate her anxiety. It was impossible to sleep, as tired as she was. Finally, just as she was dozing off, she heard the little "eh-uh, eh-uh," that signalled Caspar's hunger for the last feed of the night. She went to his crib and sitting on the daybed underneath a moonlit window, guided his mouth to the breast. It was calming and she ran through her mind again for any reason to doubt Xavier. She could find none. The telephone rang and she leapt up, answering as reasonably as she could.

"Oh, good, you're still up. I was afraid you'd gone to sleep. I'm sorry. This drink has dragged on and on. She really needs to talk, and the best thing is to just listen."

"I was worried about you," Claire lied.

"I wish I were home. I'll be back soon," Xavier said. Was he lying as well? "Do I hear the little sausage?"

"That's him, but he'll be asleep again by the time you get here." Claire couldn't help it. She felt the warmth of their child in her arms and the love in Xavier's voice. She curled up with a dozing infant in her arms on their bed, pulling a mohair throw over her shoulders, and fell asleep within a few minutes.

She awoke to screaming, a woman's voice, a shrill alarm coming from the foyer outside the front door. Claire rolled away from Caspar, who stirred, and put him safely in his crib. He didn't wake. She grabbed her bathrobe. She ran through the darkened living room, the bars of the bamboo playpen shining in the cool blue moonlight near the balcony door. She threw aside the bolts of the front door, as she saw Dovie and Connie emerging in nightgowns from the kitchen.

The three women stared into the landing outside the front door. Leo Franklins' *amah*, Narcisa, from the other apartment immediately opposite Claire's, was pulling at her hair and pounding on the elevator button, hysterically screeching, "The Devil took him. The Devil! Help me, please."

Seeing Connie and Dovie, the frenzied young Filipina started shrieking in Tagalog and both Connie and Dovie firmly seized her shoulders and head to calm her down through her sobs. Claire stood helplessly with them, towering over all three women. Nothing would stop the screeching.

"Dovie! What has happened?" Claire yelled over the hysteria.

"Ms. Raymond, Leo is gone!" Dovie was struggling to contain Narcisa's flailing limbs.

"Leo, LEEEOO!" Narcisa shrieked, her face a mask of fear. The three women half-carried her back into the Franklins' apartment. Claire quickly ran through the rooms, double-checking to see if Leo had wandered. His little bed was mussed, but there was no trace of him. She dashed back through the dining room and into the kitchen in her bare feet and opened the heavy door leading to the servants' rooms, a short corridor just like the one in her own apartment, with a bedroom door, a bathroom door, and a heavy steel-braced door leading to the servants' landing and facing the exit used by Dovie and Connie.

To Claire's surprise, the back door opened easily and Claire realized that Narcisa had first gone out to that landing for help and then decided to rouse the tenants at the front instead.

She returned to find Narcisa jabbering hysterically in Tagalog at the kitchen table.

"Has she reported anything to the police?" Claire demanded breathlessly, her heart pounding.

The answer came quickly from Narcisa herself, "No, ma'am."

"All right. I'll take care of it. Where are the Franklins?" Claire asked.

This time Dovie answered. "They're still out to dinner, ma'am."

"Get her something, some milk, tea, anything, Dovie."

Narcisa had thrust out a number written on a Post-it and stuck to the kitchen wall. Claire didn't recognize the host's name, but that wasn't surprising. Giles Franklin was an Australian stockbroker who worked all hours, as far as Claire could judge from their short acquaintance. On the weekends, he left early for the Aberdeen Boat Club leaving Lily to look after Leo. Lily spent a lot of time watching Leo play with Petey at the pool, but didn't mingle very much with other wives, Chinese or Western. While most of the women got a bit of a tan, Lily was careful to protect her skin. The Franklins moved in financial, not government circles, and in recent years, there had been a big influx of new talent in banking and brokering.

Claire wavered, wondering whom to call first. She called the police. They would know how to handle breaking the bad news to the Franklins. She asked for the officer on duty, and using John Slaughter's name as a reference, reported a missing boy.

Within the hour, what had seemed to Claire like an evening of private terrors had become a nightmarish carnival of public fear. Xavier found his front door standing open and his own child sleeping peacefully untended, while Claire called to him from the Franklins' living room where she was holding vigil with Connie and Dovie over Narcisa. After twenty minutes of Narcisa's uncontrollable hysteria, the Franklins had arrived in the carpark in their Lexus, escorted by a police car.

With barely a nod to Claire, they locked themselves in the master bedroom with a Chinese inspector. Claire could hear Lily crying and Giles' excited, angry baritone. More junior officers came and went from the bedroom while the inspector on duty, named Quek, heard but unseen, issued orders in terse Cantonese barks.

"What exactly happened?" Claire pressed Connie, who knew Narcisa, a delicate and beautiful brown nymph, better than Dovie could after only a day on the job. She was worried that

Narcisa had been assaulted by an intruder, but that turned out to be wrong.

"Narcisa came to check on Leo before she went to bed, and he was gone," said Connie.

"But how? How could anybody get past her bedroom through the servant's corridor without her realizing it?"

"She was watching television, and she says she didn't hear anything."

"But why? It isn't possible," Claire said, aghast at the simple idea that someone could enter a flat and take a child without discovery.

"It's happened," said Xavier somberly. "Wasn't there a case in America where a girl was taken during a slumber party, when other people in the house were awake?"

"Yes, of course. But how, here, with Mr. Liu on duty at the gatehouse, and all the *amahs* knowing each other?"

"Actually, it was probably criminally easy," Xavier said uncomfortably. He glanced back at their own apartment, and Dovie, reading his thoughts, said, "I'm going, sir. Come on, Connie." They muttered a few more words in Tagalog as they left to cross the carpeted foyer back to their rooms. Dovie looked exhausted by the drama of the evening, and suddenly Claire wondered again if she hadn't hired someone who was too old to take on the responsibility of Caspar.

Xavier was still standing by the sofa, wearing his raincoat. There was an awkward pause between them now that they were alone. The discomfort was tangible, but for a moment, Claire couldn't remember why she was annoyed with him. She had completely forgotten Fabienne. Xavier turned his back to look out the balcony doors at the harbor. Perhaps he feared a private interrogation of their own, but Claire had no energy to consider his long absence with the other woman.

The sounds of Lily Franklin weeping as Inspector Quek and Giles Franklin emerged in conference at the end of the corridor broke the tension between the two lovers.

"The police asked me to wait here and give them a statement about the time I arrived and what I found," Claire explained. "Why don't you go ahead?"

Xavier nodded, clearly tired and relieved, kissed her on the cheek.

While Claire waited for Quek to take her statement, she went to the Franklins' dining room window and looked at the blackness of the hill reaching up from the back of the Branksome building. There were no more buildings above them until you came to the Peak Tram station shining brightly at the pinnacle of the small mountain. There was no road behind them either, no streetlights, just low trees and undergrowth and one narrow walking path that meandered up the hill to the Peak café, the same little trail where Manny and her friends had picnicked.

Through the darkness, she saw flashlights playing among the trees, then disappearing, like sinister fireflies, and she heard Cantonese shouts echoing against the back of the building. The police were searching the wild jungle growth.

She murmured to herself, so as not to frighten Narcisa, who was sobbing more quietly now on the sofa alone. "Strange . . . first Petey, but that was an illness and this is different."

Suddenly, she turned to Narcisa. "Tell me something. Why was the back door unlocked?"

Narcisa looked at her in shock, enough shock to stop her tears. Claire went to a side table where a box of tissues stood and handed one to the maid.

"The police are going to ask that first. Why didn't you lock the back door when you retired for the night?"

Narcisa's face looked panicked, but then she realized she had the strength to answer. "I hadn't gone to bed yet, ma'am. I told you, I was watching television. I usually lock the door when I go to brush my teeth just before I turn out the lights."

"Yes, of course. I'm sorry." Claire knew she had sounded as though she were accusing Narcisa of negligence.

"I am sorry," she repeated.

Her thoughts turned back to Xavier and Caspar waiting for her in their beds. The sight of him standing there had been such a relief after the long, jarring evening. She felt a wonderful strength coming from him, this near-stranger she had flung her future at. But she was too old to tuck her fears under the pillow of a strong man, even one ten years her senior. Not even he could claim to guess what evil thread of coincidence had brought not one, but two dramas to Tregunter Path in the space of two days.

She glanced at a framed photo of Leo with his father on the deck of a pleasure boat, at laughing "Little Boo-Boo," and she felt maternal panic clutch at her throat.

# chapter
## five

A few weeks before, Claire had stumbled across some Christmas recordings in the discount bin of a music store. Feeling a mix of childlike enthusiasm and self-consciousness, she had scooped up "Jingle Bells" and other standards by Frank Sinatra, Elvis Presley, Leontyne Price, and Luciano Pavarotti, and she had handed over her credit card too late for sense to check her sentimental impulses. For years she had virtually ignored Christmas, apart from dispatching presents to her elderly parents in California on December first. There had been the obligatory phone call back to the States on the day itself, and then on to the next news assignment.

She wasn't sure now what Xavier expected of their first Christmas together, especially with a newborn suddenly in their midst as if tailor-made for their high-rise manger. Passing by a factory outlet in Wanchai specializing in tinselly exports, she had selected their first family ornaments. However, buying reindeer, music, and a new red felt stocking to hold Caspar's gifts couldn't disguise their lack of a shared history together.

The imported fir had been delivered this morning, a forgotten apparition of hope and good cheer that startled them all after the previous night's horror. It stood expectantly, reproachfully bare, in the morning sun. Claire spread out the yuletide junk, hoping Consuela and Dovie, who was spending her day getting to know the layout, weren't watching this virgin effort through the small window of the kitchen door.

There weren't nearly enough shiny balls, she could see that now. Other families grew naturally, and their trees accumulated a history with them, layer by layer, drummer by nutcracker. A family and its Christmas tree needed time. She was still so shy of Xavier's possible European coolness for her corny American yearnings that she hadn't suggested they trim the tree together. She would surprise him.

Instead, he had certainly surprised her. Fabienne was far worse than anything her jealous imagination could have conjured up—kittenish, intelligent, and chic. She and Xavier had spent many such holidays together in the years past. A few vacations at a spa in Saturnia, Italy, a motorbike sojourn along the southern coast of France, one Christmas on a Greek island. No mistletoe, no Elvis singing "Jinglebell Rock," or Harry Connick Jr. boogying up "Winter Wonderland."

Images of Xavier and Fabienne together, lurid sexual snapshots, flipped through Claire's vulnerable imagination. She fought them off valiantly, but was flung back again and again by her own appetite for confronting and surmounting the worst. Supposing they had done *that* together, and *that*, and *that*. Supposing he had wanted Fabienne more hungrily each time, that he had written love letters he had never penned for Claire, lingered over possible gifts for her, compared her favorably with every other woman he met. He had gone back to Fabienne many times, and with each reconciliation, his partner grew stronger, more independent, more equal to him in every way.

Claire would have liked more of a courtship, she realized now. After all, what little time they had spent dating before her pregnancy had been wonderful. She remembered that first night they met, an evening almost two years ago, she had rushed pell-mell—long, dark, red hair in the wind—to a hotel reception, but had gone to the wrong function room. The host was Xavier's U.N. development agency, not the Shanghai Stock Exchange authorities she was looking for.

It was typical of Claire's hectic days as bureau chief that it took her a few minutes to realize she was in the wrong room. By then it was too late. Xavier had seen her across the crowd, mentally met her, bedded her, and consigned her to his long list of global conquests. So he later confessed.

When, during all those early, carefully orchestrated months had Claire realized he was looking at her more intently than before? Not after their first night together, nor the first time they went out as a couple for a rather stilted junk outing with reporter friends of Claire's. Through all their sporadic lunches and dinners, coordinated painstakingly according to their deadlines and travels, emotional discretion was clearly Xavier's watchword.

It must have been that moment in Bali, she now realized. They had stolen a springtime week together in Indonesia, and Xavier was driving their rented jeep along the dirt road into the brilliant green hills around Tenganan. Heavy rains had come and gone before they ventured out after lunch into the refreshingly cool jungle. Just before they reached the picturesque village, their jeep had to cross under a waterfall that had sprung out of the terraced fields checkerboarding the slopes that rose above the one-lane road.

Xavier tried to maneuver the jeep left to the edge of the other side of the precipitous path, but even then, Claire was drenched by the spray as the jeep jounced past the torrential stream. Xavier braked and looked at her anxiously and tried not to laugh, she was so suddenly bedraggled. She glanced in the side mirror and saw a soddy red mop. She had tried hard on this holiday to straighten out her hair into a more sophisticated look, but now it hung wavy and matted on her shoulders. She burst into laughter, and tenderly he touched the thin, wet cotton of her dress and cupped her breast, kissing her deeply. Since then, she hadn't bothered to try any new hairstyles, perhaps because the expression on his face told her they weren't needed.

Claire could not have felt uglier this morning if she had grown claws and warts overnight. She tried to talk herself out of this evil funk, imagining the Christmas tree as a hostile witness to her distress. Claire's hair would be combed, her bathrobe clean, and her son bathed for Christmas morning. But the tree would stand in the middle of the room, every branch screaming, "Jealous, mean-minded, obsessive bitch! Right there, the one with the red hair!" Like those talking trees in Oz pelting Dorothy with apples.

There were so many serious, sad things going on around her, what a waste of energy to be scrutinizing the navel of Xavier's old sex life. She hadn't felt this kind of cancerous jealousy since high school. It had to be hormones, she concluded.

She wondered if it was too soon to look in on Vicky again, and then remembered that Vicky's parents had arrived by now and wouldn't want a near-stranger around. From reading the morning papers, Claire knew that the disappearance of Leo Franklin had cast a new coloration over Petey's death. Claire felt immediately outraged by the implication, and wondered what new suffering it was going to cause Vicky unnecessarily. What had been treated routinely as a tragic accident had to be reexamined, the articles claimed, from every angle. So on top of houseguests, the police would be back at Tavistock to interview everyone once again.

Maybe she could be of some help, by getting herself out of the apartment and putting her journalist's investigative skills to good use. She was feeling rather underoccupied, an unusual sensation for a woman who had spent her whole life studying and working nonstop and doing her own chores. Maternity leave was dragging on her and the murmurs of Connie showing Dovie around the kitchen hinted she would be *de trop* there, too. Claire's habitual fallback during idle moments was to lose herself at the piano, but she realized that there, too, lay a new irony in her life. Her freest time was when Caspar was napping and because he was asleep, the last thing she could do was ripple up a few noisy Bach fugues.

So, to get out and clear her brain, but what? She wondered if perhaps she could find out more from the gardener on the hill above Tregunter Path, Mr. Ip. Maybe Crowley's Chinese was too poor to earn the older man's confidence. The presence of a translating constable might have only created more distance. Years before, Claire's work at the *Post* had put her into daily partnership with the Cantonese-speaking staff photographers and her Mandarin dialect training had been the base to which she added some working Cantonese. The mix of dialects made those same photographers groan at her accent, but it was worth a try.

She told the two *amahs* she was going out for a stroll. She caught the glance of mutual relief on their faces. On her way to the front door, she wondered if she should remind them to lock up, then hesitated at the thought of overreacting, then thought again. Two children were gone. That was a fact, even if it was a tragic coincidence. One missing was one too many. She went back into the kitchen and instructed them to check the back door entrance as they came and went. She made sure they double-locked the front door as she departed. Of course, they would. They didn't need to tell her they were shaken up themselves by Narcisa's fate.

She paused outside the front door for a moment, remembering the scene of last night, and stood again on the very spot where they had tried to calm Narcisa down. Instinctively, she reached down and gently tested her own doorknob. It didn't turn. She was tempted to ring her bell just to make sure the *amahs* didn't open the door, but this was laughable paranoia, she told herself.

She recalled one of her deepest experiences of irrational fear from her childhood. Visiting her grandparents one Thanksgiving in Detroit, the five-year-old Claire had listened from under the dining room table in the dark to the adults gathered in the soft light of the living room just through the arch between the two rooms. She heard them talking about cyclones that had swept away parts of houses and whole cars in Michigan. As she listened, she had wondered if a cyclone might come up right as they were complacently winding down a pleasant evening and snatch that part of the house that was dark, where she squatted under the heavy oak table, leaving the brightly lit room intact and the grown-ups safe.

To the little girl, filled with her first conscious sense of separateness from her parents' embrace, it had seemed imperative that she reach the light of the living room in the few remaining seconds before a storm could strike. Just a few feet and she would no longer be alone and vulnerable, but surrounded by their comforting arms. Just a few inches to go. . . .

That was fear, and it returned suddenly with the old irrational power. It made no sense now, with Caspar under the care of two loving women. She braced herself and went downstairs. Just feeling the bright sun hit her cheeks made the morning better. She crossed the parking lot, wondering how she would approach Ip, when something caught her eye. In front of the gatehouse, three Filipina maids in their crisp cotton blue and white striped uniforms stood under the community bulletin board. Claire realized they weren't gossiping or waiting for the shuttle bus. They seemed to be chanting or praying, their heads bowed underneath the handwritten notices on the board. The girl in the center was sobbing as she mumbled her prayers.

Claire moved more slowly, trying to make out their words. She glanced up at Mr. Ho, the morning watchman. He shrugged indifferently to the scene beneath his glass window and kept on smoking his cigarette and chatting with a Chinese policeman on duty.

The weeping girl turned out to be Narcisa.

"Narcisa?" Claire ventured. Narcisa turned her tear-streaked brown eyes to Claire and nodded hello. Claire had forgotten how pretty she was, even without any makeup and in a boxy shirtwaist. "Narcisa, is there anything I can do?"

Narcisa hesitated, but walked slowly toward Claire, composing herself. "Hello, ma'am. You know, I am going to lose my job. I am advertising for a new one."

"No one talked to me this morning. I'm sorry to hear that. In fact, I'm just trying out a new *amah*. But if she doesn't work out, perhaps we can talk. Is it because of Leo, of course? Has there been any news?"

"Not yet, ma'am."

"Will you come and sit down and talk to me?" Claire's first instinct was to comfort the girl, who couldn't have been more than eighteen years old. But her second thought, as she helped the distraught Narcisa to a cement bench to one side of the squash court entrance, was to keep her wits and ask questions that might help bring Leo back. Could it be the police knew some reason to connect Leo's disappearance and Petey's unexpectedly fatal attack?

Narcisa clearly needed someone to hear her side of the story. "It's my fault, all my fault, but I never thought it would hurt Leo."

"Why is it your fault? What happened?"

"Now I will get no references from Mrs. Franklin and the law is that I have to leave Hong Kong within two weeks of the end of my contract. I will have to go back to Banaue. My family there is going to suffer so much hardship because they won't have the money I send them."

"Narcisa, start at the beginning."

"I can't tell anything, ma'am. I still need a reference from my employer."

"You mean the Franklins don't know the whole story?"

Narcisa sobbed and hid her face in her hands. Claire put her arm around Narcisa's small shoulders, a physical kindness so overwhelming that Narcisa burst into heaving wails that nearly choked her. Claire sat her down on the bench and Narcisa poured out her heart.

"Please don't tell the Franklins, ma'am. I lied to you last night."

"About what?"

"About the back door, ma'am. The truth is, a few weeks ago, I met a nice man, a Filipino gardener up on Lugard Road, on the Peak, and he wanted to see me at night. He has to work as a houseboy on Sunday because his employer entertains every Sunday at lunchtime, and I can only go out during the day on Sunday because I work on all the other days, and I have to be back by the evening to prepare the Monday breakfast." She looked up at Claire for sympathy.

"So this man, he asked me many times if he could come and see me in the evenings, but of course, I said to him the Franklins don't let me go out in the evenings."

"Did you ever ask Mr. Franklin for an evening off?"

Narcisa looked at Claire with her beautiful, wide eyes. "You know, ma'am, none of the *amahs* can go out at night, except Saturday night, but I work Saturday nights, too. Mrs. Franklin wants me to serve at her dinner parties."

Claire knew, of course, that whenever she visited friends in Hong Kong, their Filipina was on duty. She had never really asked herself how the Filipinas managed a private life of their own. They were, in fact, unacknowledged slaves, paid the minimum to do the maximum. She was impressed that Narcisa had even discovered there was an available Filipino man in the colony. The competition to catch his eye must have been Olympian, even for a beauty like Narcisa.

"So he pressed me many times to let him come to my room, but not tell the Franklins. Of course I knew it was very wrong, but I was tempted very hard, even though I know such a thing is a mortal sin. After the first time, I went to confession and after the second time, I went to confession again, but now I don't feel it is so wrong because this man is very kind to me. He says someday we can get married. And then . . . ."

"You left the back door unlocked for him, is that what happened?"

"Yes, ma'am, but how did anybody know? Who would do such a thing? The Franklins were out for the evening and I was taking a shower. I was not watching television. But now I am telling you the truth. It's true that even if I were watching the television, I would have seen someone coming past the door, but I was in the shower. That is the truth."

"Yes, yes, I believe you."

"I thought Jun might come while I was in the shower. I didn't hear anything."

"Jun?"

"Junior—my friend. But he didn't come. And I haven't heard from him today. There's no way I can make a phone call in private. Right now, Mrs. Franklin thinks I'm buying vegetables at the truck down the road. I didn't tell her I had to put up the notice today, and we were planning to say prayers for blessing."

Claire squeezed her shoulder. "Then what really happened last night, after the shower?"

"Well, I decided to go to sleep. It was about eight o'clock. I get up at five-thirty every morning, but I set up the coffeemaker the night before. About a quarter past ten, I woke up. I realized I had been thinking so much about Jun, about getting ready, and how he didn't come, and feeling so sad, that I had forgotten to set up the breakfast things. While I did that, I realized that I had forgotten to check on Leo and that's when I found his crib was empty. He was gone. I was so frightened."

"And that's when you came screaming out into the foyer?"

"Yes, ma'am, and I lied to the police, but I think they knew I was lying because they asked me what television program I was watching and I think I lied about the wrong one. I tried to check the program listing this morning, but the newspapers of yesterday were thrown out already. And then, Mr. Franklin, he told me after the police went away last night to start looking for another job."

"Did you tell him about Junior? Does he blame you for Leo's being missing?"

"I don't know about that, ma'am, but I think he has a bad conscience, because I had already had some trouble with him, so he knows that I wanted to go a long time ago. But until now, Mrs. Franklin was very good to me, better than my previous Chinese employers."

"Mr. Franklin also seems all right to me. What kind of trouble?"

Narcisa took a deep breath and whispered to Claire, "Twice he came into my room at night and said if I'm not nice to him, he will fire me without references. And my brother's family has many children to feed. But after the first time, I told him I would never let him come into my room again, or I would tell Mrs. Franklin and get her to write my reference for a new job. I don't belong to him, I don't have to do his dirty things." Narcisa was crying again, harder than before.

"Narcisa, that's a very serious charge to make about your employer."

"Now he leaves me alone, but he watches me all the time. Maybe he knows I got a boyfriend. One day he said I looked 'too pretty,' and 'who was I flirting with these days' right in front of Mrs. Franklin. So I feel really bad for her, and I don't want to leave her alone. I want to help her, help her until the police find our Leo. He is such a good little boy, ma'am." Narcisa was shaking and looked up at Claire with a wild look in her eyes, a mix of desperation and shame. Claire could see how the teenager's guilt was tormenting her.

She waited a few moments for Narcisa to calm down again.

"So the police really don't have any idea? Lots of people might get the television program mixed up when they've been through such a shock."

"Yes, ma'am. I told them I forgot to lock the door on time, only that."

"Did you tell anyone before last night you were leaving the back door unlocked for Jun?"

"I don't trust all the other *amahs*, only some. They get jealous over little things. I told Regina that Jun was visiting me, and maybe Aurora. I didn't tell Manny or Imelda because they are much older, already over thirty, and Manny's husband is a no-good back in the Philippines, living with another woman and having other children with her, and Imelda never got married. So they try to boss the younger girls around because they are jealous."

"But perhaps Regina or Aurora gossiped?"

"It is possible." Narcisa turned thoughtful. "So anybody could know."

"Last night I thought I heard you say, 'The Devil took him'?"

Narcisa looked at Claire with alarm. "You heard me?"

"Of course. That's what you were screaming at first. Before we came out of the front door, I think, or maybe just after we opened the door."

"Yes, ma'am. I was very upset. You must forget that."

"Did you really mean the Devil? Or did you suspect someone, a real human being?"

"No, ma'am." Narcisa fell silent for a moment. "I don't know who would want to take my Leo. Only the Devil would do such an evil thing."

"You believe in the Devil?"

"Yes, ma'am, all Catholics do. I am a Catholic."

Claire, who had been raised Catholic, hadn't imagined the Devil per se roaming the earth since her First Communion. Even at seven years old, she had suspected he would leave his pitch-fork and red suit at home when he visited suburban California, but she didn't contradict Narcisa.

"Do you think the Devil could take a human form?"

"Yes, ma'am, in fact, I know it is true." To imply otherwise seemed to offend Narcisa's sense of faith and the world. Her two friends were waiting for her. Claire said she would tell Narcisa if she heard of any jobs, and left them taking out their rosaries for a hail of Hail Mary's.

Narcisa's story had been more sordid than Claire had imagined. As sympathetic as she might feel toward Narcisa as a human being, she would never knowingly employ a girl who entertained men by the back door. Nor would anyone else in Hong Kong.

Narcisa's story about Giles Franklin was much more disturbing. Once before she had heard through friends that an acquaintance of theirs, a British reporter in the midst of a divorce, had been propositioning his *amah*. No doubt these things happened. Monday morning's account of the Mongkok Romeo sprang to mind.

Still, Narcisa's story was open to a wide variety of interpretations; it was possible that Franklin had actually raped her, or that Narcisa had coldbloodedly seduced him before she befriended Jun. Anyway one looked at it, it was a mess.

Claire started off for Ip's potted terraces overlooking Vicky's building next door. Another woman was marching toward her along the sidewalk, strangling a handbag under one arm, her head looking back over her shoulder in hope of a possible taxi. It was the wife of the Deputy Secretary of the Public Works Department, Fiona Reynolds. Claire had met her only a few times before her move with Xavier to Tregunter Path and only to rub shoulders at cocktail parties.

"Mrs. Reynolds? I'm Claire Raymond, we met at the National Day reception for Macau?"

Mrs. Reynolds turned straight to face Claire, her eyes invisible behind large black sunglasses with a little gold fish perched on each corner. She was dressed expensively in a fuschia linen suit, her golden hair sprayed off her forehead, which glinted in the sunlight with sweat and powder.

Fiona squinted at Claire. "Yes, I remember, you were chatting with Sunny Kwok? Reporter, aren't you?"

"On maternity leave. I'm taking a walk to get fit again."

"I never walk." She spat out the words.

"Don't you have a car? Someone said yesterday that you were driving past on Sunday near where they found little Petey Sandford?"

"Car's been stolen. Right out of the carpark last night. With all this terrible news about the little boys, nobody has time to chase another missing car. That's the third this month from Tavistock, smack out from under the nose of our watchman. I told Barrie last night, the managment along Tregunter Path has just gone downhill since they sold the building to that new company—"

"Pacific Profits."

"Yes, that's the one. I believe our watchman must be part of some racket. I mean, how can these triads just drive our cars out of the gate without being seen? Two Benzes and a Daimler that belonged to the Hong Kong Bank man, what's his name . . ."

"Patrick White?"

"Yes. Listen, I absolutely must get a taxi. I'm late for the Club."

Claire had the distinct impression that Mrs. Reynolds had already warmed up her morning with a breakfast sherry. A taxi whizzed past them, a red blur already carrying passengers. He came worryingly close to Mrs. Reynolds who was teetering on her white pumps a few feet into the Path, her free arm wagging vaguely in the breeze.

"Bloody man, he could have struck us!"

Claire waited for Mrs. Reynolds to join her back on the sidewalk. "There'll be another one soon. Did the police ask you if you saw anything on Sunday when you were driving past the *nullah*?"

"God, yes, that Office Crowley. Dreadful person, a sort of wideboy in uniform. Have you seen the types turning up at Kaitak these days? Barrie tells me that the other day he went into the loo off the Mandarin Grill and he couldn't believe his eyes. The attendant was a boy from Watford. From *Watford*, would you believe, standing there in one of those little Chinese outfits with a little black cap and red tassel on top—the exact same outfit they put their Chinese boys in."

"Anyway, this detective Crowley—kept insinuating things, as though I should have stopped, as though I would have even noticed one of the *amahs* waving at me. I was in a frightful hurry that day to pick up Barrie at the Aberdeen Boat Club. Driver was off. Between you and me and the gatepost, I can't remember seeing any girl on the road."

As Fiona Reynolds sputtered out her excuses, Claire realized that she had less than a decade on Claire, but certainly it felt as though they were separated by a generation. Claire thought of Vicky and reflected, here were two different versions of colonial females, Vicky so direct and clearheaded even under the greatest duress, and Fiona in a humorless fluster because she had to take a taxi.

"Anyway, it's an appalling story, this disappearance of the little boy right on the heels of the Sandford child. Something terribly amiss around here. I blame the police in the end. They should keep a better eye on things. The whole place is going to go to the dogs anyway once we leave. Barrie's got to stay for the handover ceremony, of course, but we've already booted out our lodgers back home in Sussex. Thank God our son is in public school back in England. As far as we were concerned, there was no question of his staying on here after he turned seven. The Island School, the International School, even the Swiss-German school, well, some of those kids are using drugs. This Ecstasy rubbish. Read about it in the *Post* the other day."

"You must miss him a lot, though," Claire sympathized.

"Terribly. But it's really better for him, you know. We see him during the summer. I'm used to it. Here's another one."

And like a hunter in hot pink bagging a diesel tiger, Fiona pounced on an empty taxi and tumbled in, shouting, "*Hoi joong wan*," to Central.

As the driver shifted into gear, she leaned out the window. "Better to have them in a proper school back home, especially as there's no real future for them out here anyway. By the time they reach ten, they're bored."

Claire hadn't taken the time yet to reflect on the life she was offering Caspar. Would Xavier want to send his son to the monastery school in Switzerland that had educated him forty years before? The thought clutched at her. They'd never talked about where they would live after Hong Kong, provided there was an "after Hong Kong" for them as a couple. If she didn't marry Xavier, would he leave this posting for another without her and Caspar? She realized that in the rush of work at the bureau, the strain of pregnancy, and the move, there were profound uncertainties she hadn't broached with him.

A hundred feet above where she stood, Ip emerged from his shed on the slope and started hoeing along a bed of small flowered plants. From behind, with a cloth around his head protecting him from the sun, he looked almost like an old woman. At the sound of Claire's footfall, he turned and watched her, almost indifferently curious, leaning on his hoe. She realized he was waiting for her to finish her ascent. He stood patiently as she pulled herself up off the road onto the hill, then skirted irrigation ditches and rows of knee-high snake plants, then passed a few rows of strange, low herbaceous borders, to reach a footpath cluttered with hoses and fertilizer bags.

She greeted him in Cantonese, "*Jo sann.*" He grunted and waited, expressionless. Of course he had no idea who she was,

unless he had noticed her new habit of taking daily walks with
Caspar in a baby harness.

She started again in Cantonese, "My name is *Lei Mun Ch'ing*."
Claire's Chinese name was a mix of sounds and meaning. "Raymond" become "*Lei Mun*," and the meaning of Claire, clarity,
became the Chinese word for clear, "*Ch'ing*." She continued, "I
heard you were here on the day Petey Sandford, that little boy,
died."

He nodded and went back to repotting a fern, answering in
strangely slow Cantonese, the eight tones of the dialect riding
high and low as if in spoken opera, "*Pei-tei*. A good little boy.
He liked to visit my garden. He was sick."

"I'm a friend of his mother. She's suffering so much." Claire
used the phrase in Chinese, so resonant, "eating bitterness."

Ip nodded and looked up at her from where he was squatting.
His face was deeply tanned and furrowed, and his hair cut short,
like a stiff brush. But oddly for a Chinese who worked all day
with the earth, he wore new gloves.

He stood up and stared at her, "Have you come to ask me
questions? I told the police, I didn't see *Pei-tei*. He didn't come
play here."

"Did you see the *amahs* eating over there?" Claire gestured
in the direction of the picnic site about fifty feet across the slope.
A clearing beyond was nestled at the foot of a grove of trees
that shaded Tregunter Path.

"I *heard* them." Ip nodded. "When they discovered trouble,
they made loud noises."

"You didn't help?"

"I didn't know it was the boy. Then I saw the police and
ambulance. Every week, they dance, they shout, they cry. I
don't listen every week. It's their religious custom. *Meng cha-
cha, chi hsin-a*."

Claire could well imagine that the sight of a Charismatics
prayer meeting, especially with *amahs* speaking in tongues,
would strike any Cantonese as "crossed wires crazy."

Ip was ending his account. "I've finished. *Tso-ah*." Claire realized he was now shooing her off with a dismissive flick of his hand. Certainly he had the right, but she had done nothing to offend him. She stood her ground.

Her stillness angered him. He shouted, "*Ma Faan ah*." Hassle. "*Tsuo-ah*." Get going, this time in the accent of northern China. Perhaps he had switched to Mandarin because he noticed her Cantonese betrayed traces of Mandarin training.

"But—"

Then Ip exploded into a string of curses Claire could only partially understand. His inexplicable temper shook her. "*Deng-ah*," Wait, wait, she pleaded, but she was getting nowhere.

She stumbled a little, backing down the slope. He was still irritated, and kept rattling out phrases too fast for her simple Cantonese. He'd said what he had to say. Claire was humbled to think she had presumed she could do any better than Crowley with his constable. Ip might just be another irascible old man who wanted to be left to himself. But if Claire had detected a trace of affection for Petey underneath Ip's gruff exterior, it also crossed her mind that Ip's interest in Petey might not be as innocent as he played. And there was no doubt in her mind that, despite what he claimed, from where Ip lived and worked seven days a week, he had enjoyed a clear view of almost everything that had happened the day Petey died.

# chapter six

The police were streaming all over Branksome, floor by floor, door by door, their walkie-talkies screeching up and down the lifts, as they interrograted every single one of Claire's neighbors about Leo Franklin.

They carried copies of Leo's picture for the residents who weren't familiar with his curly hair and elfin face. They stopped everyone, asking them whether they had seen him, here in the parking lot, or there, by the swimming pool last summer. Excuse me. Who had been seen talking to him in the last week? Did you ever see any stranger initiating play or conversation with the boy by the poolside? In the carpark? Who knew the Franklins had gone out for the evening? Who saw them drive out of the carpark?

The officers were polite, but there was a new tone in their interrogation, a tone that had nothing to do with the case. Old-timers noticed a new assertiveness, less deference than in the old days. No doubt about it, the handover had happened already behind the scenes, in the locker rooms, somewhere back-stage when the *guay-los* weren't watching.

Moreover, the standard of their English was noticeably low. In the old days, good English had been a prerequisite of pro-motion. Now it was Mandarin that kept the ambitious in night school. This morning, the questions were clearly stated, the an-swers cooperatively given, but the comprehension of some of the policemen was less than perfect. The investigation was lum-bered down with misunderstandings.

The questions were straightforward nonetheless. What time that evening did you go out, sir? When did you return, miss? Did you see anyone in the corridor? In the lift? In the servants' stairwell? In the lobby? Behind the building? In fluent Canton-ese, uncertain English, broken Tagalog. All morning, all after-noon. It seemed like the whole of the Hong Kong police force was on Tregunter Path, putting all its public strength, its visible support, behind apprehension of the culprit.

So why did Claire feel no comfort? Why did she feel like escaping the inevitable failure she was witnessing in slow mo-tion? She knew that superb police work had just located a vio-lent criminal who had carried out three bank robberies in less than a year. They had found his arsenal of bomb equipment, remote control devices, and AK 47s, all hinting at expert training as a soldier in the People's Liberation Army. That was the kind of crime they could solve by paying off informers, tracing weap-ons, and twisting arms attached to the underbelly of the territory.

Tregunter Path was not their territory. The nastiness here was somewhere hidden, not in closets nor in the trunks of cars but in the recesses of someone's mind.

She had retreated to her bedroom to try on clothes. Nothing fit. On her bed lay the discarded reminders of her pre-baby figure: the lithe silk flowered dress cut on the bias, the natty black linen cigarette pants with the matching sleeveless vest, the rose chemise in light-weight wool crepe with the halter neck. Either her hips strained the seams of the skirt, or her milk-laden bosom, once so girlish, pressed against her bodice like that of a middle-aged matron.

She sighed, realizing there were horrifying hints of her mother's figure reflected in the mirror. Even some of the red seemed to have faded from her hair. How she had anticipated her first real evening out again with Xavier. She had imagined wearing something casual, but seductive. He would be wearing the same black cords and cashmere turtleneck she had admired on a date shortly after they met.

In her fantasy, they would stop first for a drink at the Foreign Correspondents' Club, long enough to show friends that she'd come back to life from the strange and unfamiliar world of maternity to the old gang. Ah, but unlike many of them, she wasn't stuck at the bar for the night with the lost and lonely; she was going to move on in every sense of the word.

Maybe they would head then to the Café de Paris, where Maurice would hang over their table for a minute or two recommending the walnut, roquefort, and endive salad. Xavier would pull out a picture of Caspar, all purply-skinned, puffy-eyed, and beautiful, and Maurice would exclaim in professional admiration, "But who would guess that Madame just had a baby!"

She had to continue this courtship for her own satisfaction, to know not only how she felt about Xavier as a partner for life, but also to reassure herself that Claire Raymond still prevailed over that tiny dominus called, to lull an unsuspecting world, "baby."

In fact, she was in a rotten mood, angry with herself and the innocent red-headed peanut in the Mickey pajamas for her dilemma. She didn't really have a clear idea of what she wanted more: to drag herself back as much as possible to her safe routines of China reading, watching, analyzing, with Caspar and Xavier in the margins, or to let that life take a backseat to her relationship with Xavier, make it work, go the whole bristle-bearing hog.

She wasn't used to feeling unkindly toward her child. How
could this quotidian anger have survived the sadness and terrors
of the past three days? She blamed Fabienne and the ugly fears
her arrival provoked. Claire didn't have all the time in the world
to make up her mind about Xavier. Because Nature, in the form
of unmarried other women, abhors a bachelor.

Fabienne even had prior claim. What did Fabienne want? In
fact, why was she here, *really?* Claire didn't give much weight
to Fabienne's assignment in wherever, whenever, Cambodia,
sure, that led to this stopover in Hong Kong.

Now, on top of everything, Fabienne was the occasion of
their first evening out on the town. It wasn't even worth leaving
the baby for.

And that was hard enough without Xavier and Fabienne
standing at the front door of the apartment looking—was it
Claire's imagination?—as if *they* were the couple heading out
for a night of fun. She reviewed the evening drill with Connie
for the third time.

"You understand that the bottle of my milk in the freezer is
only in case I call you and can't get back in time for the eleven
o'clock feeding."

"Yes, ma'am." Connie smiled obligingly. Perhaps the other
*amahs* had warned her about the panic of the first real evening
out for a new mother.

"And I will get back in time. Don't let anyone in the apartment
for any reason. If you feel like laying down, leave all the doors
open so you can hear him crying."

"Yes, ma'am. I always do that." Connie's answer was unre-
proachably patient, but she was clearly counting the seconds
until they all left and she could watch a soap opera on the little
black and white TV in her room behind the kitchen.

"Come on, Claire, it's going to be all right," Xavier's tone was
at its most Teutonic, but he hadn't learned yet that it rubbed
Claire the wrong way.

"I'll try to call from the restaurant around nine-thirty."

Connie hesitated. "That might wake the baby, ma'am."

"She's right, Claire. Please, come, everything is going to be all right." Now she felt Xavier taking her by the shoulders and moving her gently but firmly out the door.

"The number of the doctor is above the telephone, with the telephone number of the police—"

"Claire! Half the police force is on duty inside this very building for the entire night!" Xavier seemed in a hurry to get the evening started.

Fabienne stood waiting behind him in the foyer in a short red knit mini shift with wide cowl neckline, a skinny, shiny, black patent belt and chic black slingbacks. It went well with her dark Louise Brooks sort of charm. Claire had settled on a straight black dress and covered up the bursting seams with an antique Japanese short kimono tied in front over her still-round tummy with a gold embroidered cord that matched the gold threads woven through the silk.

They paid off the taxi at the top of Lan Kwai Fong Street, the L-shaped alley-like lane that had become the epicenter of night-life on the Hong Kong side of the harbor in a wave of yuppie development in the late '80s. The short foot of the "L" was highest on the steep hill that backed the business district of Central. It was noisy, but dark; some kitchens and small cafés operated along this quieter stretch. Fabienne's heels clicked perkily on the street, and once or twice, when she tripped in the semi-darkness of the uneven asphalt, she instinctively reached for Xavier's arm for support.

They reached the turn of the "L," and paused before navigating the steep descent between two rows of blazing clubs and restaurants.

"There was a huge street fair here five years ago, and so many drunks carousing in beer foam—they started a landslide and a panic, and twenty-one people were crushed to death," Claire told Fabienne.

"How morbid! That explains the police, I suppose?"

Claire had noticed, too, the patrol striding purposefully uphill to pass them two abreast on one, and three on the other.

"You see the two men squatting down by that nightclub, 'California,' the two Chinese leaning against the wall?" Claire gestured farther down the street. "They're probably point men for drug suppliers to the kids around here . . ."

"It's not all that nasty," chided Xavier. "C'mon, Claire, you're just feeling bad because of Petey and Leo, I know. Everything looks a little dark to you tonight. Try and cheer up."

"No, Xavier, don't be so tough on her, she's right to be feeling so low. It's the hormones, right?"

Claire felt like some grandma being taken for a walk. Don't coddle me, chick, she thought, I'm postpartum, not senile.

"Here's the place I was thinking of," Xavier stopped triumphantly outside a small doorway under a sign, "The East is Red and the Blues is Here! Hong Kong's best spot for jazz!" He did a little shimmy and grabbed Claire's hand affectionately for a two-step on the curb.

"Jazz! I don't believe it, Xavier. You promised me something exotic! I can hear jazz in Zurich or Paris any night of the week!" Fabienne pouted, the shine of gloss on the lower lip reflecting neon colors hanging overhead.

Claire interrupted. "This is the place we always planned to check out, but never got a chance, Fabienne. Let's try it."

"Nooo, Xavier, you didn't used to be so square, so straight."

The small shoulders had completely turned away from Claire and the boat neck of Fabienne's top was slipping slightly off on one side. Xavier's strong hand moved protectively to cover the bare neck so vulnerable in the night air and Claire felt her gorge rise.

"I haven't changed that much, you may remember I always loved jazz. You should know, you're the one who stole my valuable collection of Coleman Hawkins."

"Borrowed. You never said you're weren't coming back. I've

also got your racing bike, your collection of Asterix and Obelix books, your espresso machine, and—"

"I consider we've got a fair trade," Claire interrupted, putting her arm around Xavier with the cutest and meanest smile she could muster.

"*Ça va, ça va*, girls, the jazz was just an idea. Claire and I will go there another time." He kissed Claire's temple, gently.

"He wasn't such a bore in the old days," Fabienne tried to joke with Claire. She wasn't giving up.

"What's she talking about?" Xavier joked apologetically to Claire.

"That's what I don't want to know," Claire said dolefully.

"Okay, Fabienne, what did you picture when I said something exotic?"

Fabienne smiled like a child who is unashamedly satisfied to see she can make trouble.

"Let's see!" She clacked away, maneuvering the steep, long steps sideways on her little heels and waved them to follow her. About fifty feet ahead was a turning off Lan Kwai Fong where newer clubs were sprouting up. Claire felt a certain rush of adventure, despite herself, as they started to follow the woman in this new direction. The street narrowed and took another sharp turn uphill past a Vietnamese noodle stall and many small hardware and tool-die shops, their roll-down metal frontages padlocked firmly against the night crowd. The raucous music that filled Lan Kwai Fong was quickly muffled by the narrow prewar buildings standing four or five stories high in this part of Central's backyard.

"*Voilà!*" Fabienne stretched out one arm dramatically, like the doorman of a four-star hotel and bowed, then winked knowingly at Xavier, "Maybe something a little kinky, *monsieur?*"

Claire had to admit Fabienne had good eyesight. There was little immediately visible from a distance, but next to a darkened doorway was a small glass cabinet showing a few photos. Over

the showcase were Chinese characters advertising a proctolo-
gist's specialty in hemorrhoids, but Claire decided to let this
information go unexplained to her companions who didn't
share her knowledge of the language. The photos themselves
were, at first glance, of famous Western film stars, although
there was so little light, it was hard to make out much more.
From the top of the narrow and twisted stairs leading to a simple
landing came an ominous *thump, thump, thump, bump da
bump bump, thump, thump, thump.*

"Not exactly Miles Davis," murmured Claire to Xavier.

"Sour face, sour milk," he joked back to her, and put his arm
around her encouragingly. "We never found this place before,
give the girl some credit, you never know."

Claire looked at him intently. "I give her more credit than you
could imagine. Oh, you bet, I reckon she's full of tricks."

Two Chinese men had emerged at the landing to collect a
cover charge which Fabienne had already produced from a fistful of cash in her pocket. For the first time, Claire saw Fabienne
the Photographer in action on the battlefield, in the remote village or under pressure of the studio lights.

Fabienne wasn't sexy simply because she wore cute clothes,
although they didn't hurt. She was an *allumeuse*, a magnet of
positive, unknown action. Claire felt more at home in one of
her silk dressing gowns, tucked into a corner with her volumes
of Chinese poetry, history, and biography through which she
escaped the claustrophobia of a dying colony through time and
place.

The club stank of male sweat and cigarettes. A tall girl in a
long red *cheongsam* and heels moved them toward a table near
a small stage by pushing customers out of their way with her
strong thighs. One male customer laughed and squeezed her
leg in appreciation and looking up for acknowledgement,
laughed again. He ignored Claire and Fabienne and looked
questioningly at Xavier. The waitress dismissed the little ha-
rassment with a deep chuckle.

The next act started and without further ado, Claire's ginger ale was left melting in its ice as she stared at the strange apparition that emerged from behind a curtain. A Eurasian girl with an almost Korean flatness of feature, but gingery-streaked hair, strode out on stage in a simple, short, black cardigan sweater, the sort that sold cheaply at the China Products Emporium a few blocks away, worn over a short mini-kilt.

The Scottish motif was sustained by a comically small tam on her head and a real set of bagpipes which she made clear were far too heavy. The stripper laboriously blew at the pipes, but wiping real sweat off her brow, smiled at the audience knowingly and began to slowly unbutton her sweater.

"More hot in Hong Kong than in Edinburgh!" she yelled hoarsely over the general hubbub and thumping disco background to her act. The Scottish theme was a kind of insider's joke in Hong Kong, since many of the founding fathers of Hong Kong's powerful colonial trading houses, or *hongs*, had been Scots. Early intermarriages between Chinese and foreign devils, or *guay-los*, were commonly alliances of equally clannish Cantonese and Scots.

Claire surveyed the audience. Many were slight Chinese boys sitting with foreign men. She glanced more quickly around for women and realized, now that her eyes had adjusted better to the dim lighting, that Fabienne and she were the only two women in the club, unless you counted the stripper on stage.

Which clearly you couldn't, because the stripper, having revealed two natural-looking, large, pale breasts, which made Claire surer of the girl's northern bloodlines, was now unwinding the kilt to reveal a small erection encased in white Jockey underwear.

"*Ho yeh! Ho yeh!*" shouted some of the Cantonese drinkers with approval. The whole act was one big visual pun on mixed race, mixed sex, and mixed culture. The Chinese, whose monosyllabic tonal language lent itself generously to punning, were clapping with the beat of the disco bass in a kind of intent and hungry way.

"Well, I have to hand it to you, Fabienne," Claire joked her uncomfortable way out of the first shock. "It's my first Asian hermaphrodite, and you found it."

The gingery brown pubic hair as well as the heavy, unsupported swing of the breasts made it clear that there was nothing artificial about this artiste.

"I could imagine we were in Bangkok, not Hong Kong," said Xavier. The music sped up a little as the erection grew larger under the stripper's guidance. Claire realized how far off the beaten track they were, by Hong Kong's standards, when the climax of the act lived up to its name. The audience yelled out some crude catchphrases as the "Scotsman," as the performer was billed, exited with a lot less dignity than "she" arrived.

Claire had been dragged to sex shows years before during her first assignments in Bangkok, for the most part. It was a sort of initiation rite for women forcing their unwelcome way into the ranks of foreign correspondents in Asia. At least she hadn't had bosses coming in from overseas who made such excursions a job requirement, but she knew of many such instances imposed on her colleagues with the implicit understanding that being a good sport included going along with the executive's off-the-record excursions and keeping quiet back at headquarters. Claire hoped that Fabienne's appetite for the kinkier side of the East was satiated.

"Exactly how long will you be staying in Hong Kong?" Claire asked her across the clinking of ice and insistent bass of the interval music.

Fabienne looked up in surprise at Claire's tactlessness. Such a full frontal assault was clearly not her style. She was more of the hide and seek type.

"You're afraid I might stay on forever?" Fabienne avoided Claire's direct gaze by lighting a cigarette.

"A lot of people do. In fact, you could say there are two kinds of people in Hong Kong at this point in time—the people who are staying on until they are due to leave, and the others who are just stuck."

Claire's mind darted to Evans-Smith. He was actually leaving the colony, but lodged forever in its colonial history, the only context in which he belonged. Her friend Father Fresnay was staying on until his job was done, whenever he and the Church and for that matter, the Chinese government, decided enough was enough. It was more than a physical fact, it was the subtext of every relationship in Hong Kong. Are you staying until your tour, your time, your travel is finished, or are you trapped by marriage or investment or time to a life in this uneasy future with the Communists?

"Oh," Fabienne smiled understandingly, "I'm only staying for a little bit, but what about yourself with the Communists taking over? Haven't you made China your whole career? Are you one of the people who is stuck?" The Genevan glanced minx-like in Xavier's direction, but he wasn't really listening. "Or did the arrival of Caspar change that for you? Now you have a Swiss baby to consider and the father? Maybe you're not as stuck as you were before?"

Claire laughed off the offense. "I already had a perfectly good passport when I met him."

She wants to know if Xavier and I are permanent, Claire thought. Is that why she suddenly has a photo assignment in "nearby" Cambodia? She's really here to stake her claim. It's worse than I let myself imagine. That's why he hasn't told me much about their meeting the other night. He's afraid to let me know her real intentions. Does he think I'll panic? They both underestimate me, in their different ways, because Europeans always confuse American transparency for stupidity. He thinks I might make a fool of myself, and him, and she actually believes she can seduce him away from me and his child with an old suitcase of memories.

As if reading Claire's mind, Fabienne raised her voice to get Xavier's attention, "Do you think I could take some photos?"

Xavier hated to draw attention to himself. It was a natural modesty and also arrogance, born of knowing precisely who he was in the context of six hundred years of his family living in the same Swiss village.

"Oh, I don't think—"

But Fabienne was already squeezing between the tables toward the back of the room with her large shoulder bag in tow, carrying her camera, Claire realized with dismay.

"Xavier, I'm kind of tired!" Claire protested as soon as Fabienne had left their table.

"Do you want another juice?"

"No, um, frankly, I've had enough."

Oh, God, she sounded like a martinet, kill-joy, *mom*. She had become somebody's mother and there it was. All these people in the room had mothers who didn't know what they were doing right now. What a filter through which to watch the world's turpitudes. Now her figure was ruined and her mind was warped. She seemed to have left her sense of humor back in the maternity ward.

"You're right," Xavier said unexpectedly. He kissed her lightly, "The Swiss-Hong Kong Tourist Association does not approve."

But Fabienne was already back, more victorious in her quest for kink than ever. "The manager said I could take a photo when they finish the next act, and he promises it'll be great! What, is something the matter?"

"Well, if he said yes, we'll stay, then maybe the jazz club, okay?" Xavier looked for compromise.

"It's my fault, Fabienne," said Claire. "There might not even be time for the jazz. I want to get back for Caspar's last feed."

Fabienne was miffed at this show of solidarity between Xavier and Claire. "Okay," she tossed her head, "I might even stay without you." Claire didn't quite believe her, but after more than fifteen years in Asia, she appreciated anyone trying to save face.

Over the tape system, a drum roll sounded abruptly and cheering started from some of the tables in front of the stage crowded with Hooray Harrys—British types who looked like they hadn't bothered to change clothes after a day trading stocks on the Hang Seng Index a few blocks away. Some incongruous, old-time honky-tonk music started up and without any introduction, a Chinese manager leaped on stage and led the audience in a familiar countdown, "*Yet, yi, sam!* One, two, three, who's there?"

"The Fairy Princess, who do ya think?" answered an astonishing vision sashaying across the boards to a wave of delighted applause in dripping pearls and sequins, feathers and platinum wig. It was a six-foot-plus "Mae West" with shaven shoulders, hips and bosom heaving with padding, and an enormous fan of feathers coquettishly wielded with all the subtlety of a jib sail on Hong Kong harbor.

"Mae" paused dramatically, and then came a bump of the hips and a drum roll and "Mae" soaked up the guffaws from the flushed fans at her feet. "Is that your real hair color, honey, or are ya burning up for someone?" "Mae" taunted a red-headed man sitting across the audience. Claire blushed out of solidarity for him. Thank God "Mae" hadn't directed such a joke at her.

"*Ley ho ma*, and hello, boys," "Mae" swaggered and swept. "Although my mother says *boys* should be in bed after nine o'clock at night." More laughter. "Little devils need their sleep for school, um-hmm, yeah."

"Hello, hello, pleased to meet'cha." "Mae" scanned the audience who had simmered down appreciably, and focused intently on one guy sitting right in front, "And *you're* not bad to meet either. Say, do you believe in love at first sight, anybody here? Oh, good, I see a lot of hands, c'mon get 'em out of your pockets, there, save it for later. You do? You believe in love at first sight, do ya? Well, I don't know if I do, but it sure saves a lot of time, don't it!" Hoots and hollers.

Claire looked at Xavier and shook her head, chuckling resignedly. "I have to admit, whoever he is, he's got the voice and delivery down perfectly." Xavier was laughing, too.

"It's just Life to see you guys, c'mon, crawl to me baby, crawl to me." Instead of a kiss, the audience got an extended pelvic grind, which drew yet more applause. Claire took in the unmistakable change in the audience. The few waiters on hand were delivering beers and gin and tonics to the Europeans, as all Westerners were tagged in Hong Kong, at twice the pace, while the Cantonese in the audience sipped more gently at their fancy cocktails.

The show was like a smorgasbord of titillation, with something for everyone. And why shouldn't Hong Kong enjoy a transvestite evening when the whole city was becoming a metropolis in political cross-dress? Was it a capitalist enclave officially disguised under Communist sovereignty now? Or a Communist entrepot masquerading at capitalism? What did Deng Xiaoping's "one country-two systems" mean, anyway? "A whole city in a sort of political drag, left in the care of some long-distance pimps who care nothing for the people here, but everything for how much money Hong Kong will rake in for the north," Claire murmured bitterly. She surprised herself. She hadn't realized how cynical she had become.

The soundtrack of some new music began, an authentic wind-up for a real vaudeville tune. It seemed like the performer had tried to do something with class and some real theatrical preparation. "Mae" launched into a song tailor-made for the race track addicts of Hong Kong. With one hand on an ivory walking stick and the other on her hip, she purred to the lilting, suggestively syncopated backup:

*"Oh, I wonder where my easy rider's gone,*
*I wonder where my easy rider's gone,*

*If he was here, he'd win the race,*
*If not first, he'd get a place,*
*I never saw that jockey trailing anyone before,"*

The impersonator never dropped from a pitch-perfect nasal impersonation of the Original Blonde. Claire thought it was such a good rendition, it gave her the impression she was indeed watching someone she had met before, and the more she laughed at the song, the more she got an eerie feeling that "Mae" *was* someone she'd seen before—not the actress, although the likeness was beautifully executed, but someone she'd met before somewhere, but where?

The act took on a new fascination as she peered closely at "Mae's" features for a glimpse of the man underneath. For Claire, this was by far the greatest tease of the show. She was drawn in completely, marvelling at the evocative swaying of the hips, the delightful pursing of the lips.

"This guy is amazing," she whispered to Xavier. "What the hell is he doing in Hong Kong? Who is he?"

*"I'm losing all my money—that's why I'm blue,*
*If that boy was here, he'd sure know what to do,*
*I'd put all my junk in pawn,*
*To bet on any horse that jockey's on,*
*Oh, I wonder where my easy rider's gone,"*

The music built up for a slow final chorus, and the brokers and barristers slopping their drinks at the front, joined in for the last carousing phrase, "Ohhhhhh, I wonder where my easy rider's gone."

*"Merveilleuse, incroyable,"* gushed Fabienne. "I'm going to get a picture of this guy. I don't believe it! No, better, you take a picture of us together!"

Despite the lift some genuine talent had brought to the evening, Claire was now truly exhausted. She glanced at Xavier who was oddly distant, as if he was watching the show with his eyes, but not his mind. She wondered where he was. Protectively, she closed the kimono closer over her chest.

Fabienne thrust the expensive camera into Claire's hands. "It's my back-up camera while the other one is being repaired. Take care, just push here," and without hesitation, she jumped onto the stage to embrace a startled "Mae" in the middle of her bows. Claire poised for a moment, surprised that Fabienne had left her with a telephoto that needed delicate focusing. But she would take a photo if it meant she was then entitled to call it quits for the evening.

Putting her eye to the camera, she brought their torsos into alignment. Rising smoothly to the occasion, "Mae" put one hand on her gorgeous blonde wig of hair piled high, and one arm around Fabienne, obligingly striking a pose. Claire took the shot, then let the lens linger for a moment on the performer's face.

The lens was like a telescope, bringing "Mae" up close. Claire gasped as all illusion fell away. The lips had been styled with pencil and gloss to look much fuller than they were. Underneath the powder, the evidence of a closely shaven chin betrayed a dark-haired male.

The eyelashes, however, had needed little touching up. Naturally long, they framed eyes Claire had seen only the day before. The brilliant impersonator, whose "mother wanted boys in bed after nine," was Inspector Anthony Crowley.

# chapter seven

"Aconi-what? Aconitum? What's that?" Claire frowned in surprise at Vicky over her steaming mug of coffee. She had promised to drop over by nine, but that was already too late to catch the Sandford seniors before they left for a day in Sai Kung, "to get their minds off things."

When she realized Miriam and Gordon Forsythe were gone from the apartment, Claire hid her relief from Vicky, but Vicky probably knew already that her parents required a fairly attentive audience at the best of times. On a normal morning, Miriam would have hooted her delight and approval over Caspar, even though she hardly knew Claire—such was her sense of loyalty to any new mother far away from "home." There would have been a lot of "Do you know the whomevers" with unsolicited updates on people Claire had hardly met. Gordon would have grilled Claire for her impressions of the political situation, ending with his vague, "Time will tell. Couldn't be avoided."

Petey's death killed off that kind of chat.

Claire was also relieved that the elders were out of the house because she wanted to tell Vicky about the apparition of Crowley at the nightclub, and it was easier without Miriam around, her over-plucked eyebrows shooting to the ceiling in disbelief that Hong Kong had sunk to the level of the girlie bars in the Patpong district of Bangkok.

Anyway, Vicky had just divulged some startling news of her own. "Yes, some kind of herbal solution mixed with some chemical called aconite in Petey's stomach. Apparently it's a classic poison, but not very commonly used."

"I never heard of it."

"Neither had I. Neither had the Hong Kong police, apparently, but it turned up in Peter's stomach contents. A very clever young man on their forensics team just back from Canada decided to go a bit beyond procedure because of some strange results, and that led to more tests, and anyway, it's the strangest thing and the forensics fellows don't know what to make of it. They asked me any number of questions about his diet, his medication, even the houseplants. Asked me about seeing Petey with any purple or purply-white flowers. I could never get Petey to stop chewing on rubbish from the ground—leaves and twigs. But I can't say I ever saw any such flowers around Tregunter Path. Well, at any rate, it proved me right and Ian wrong."

Vicky's eyes were shaded from Claire's scrutiny by sunglasses, so it was hard to tell, even in the slanting morning light of the Sandfords' balcony, whether her expression matched a very slight note of triumph in her voice.

"Ian wrong? Why? He expected something else?"

"Oh, he didn't want an autopsy at all! I disagreed, I mean, what's the harm? There might be something, just something, we don't know. My parents backed me up, especially Daddy, and when Ian saw that Petey's own grandparents weren't sentimental about his remains, he couldn't very well object any longer. And you know what else the police told us? There were a lot of bruises on his body, more than they noticed on Sunday. John

Slaughter said the lab man hadn't any theories, but insisted it just wasn't a simple case of fatal epilepsy."

"Aconite and bruises," Claire repeated carefully, "*as well as* the normal signs of an epileptic attack?"

"Absolutely. But do you know they were also looking for signs of sexual molestation? Well, of course, there weren't any that seemed obvious, but I must say, they were remarkably thorough."

Vicky expelled her satisfaction with a hugh sigh of relief. "The saliva tests, the vomiting, not to put too fine a point on it, were completely consistent with Manny's story, thank God. The police questioned her all over again, and of course the other girls corroborated her story completely. Petey was already close to death when they reached him. The police wanted to know if they saw anybody else pass them, or talk to or approach Petey while they were having their picnic. Manny insists she didn't notice anything unusual, but you never know. Maybe someone else was passing along the path, or watching them without them knowing."

"How is Manny?"

"She hasn't come out of her room, except to leave the meals and dust and vacuum while I'm in my room. As soon as we've finished dinner, she disappears into her room, of course, but she did that before this all happened. Sunday was a nightmare for her as well. I think she also wanted to leave Ian and me some time alone. No, there's no doubt Petey had an epileptic attack, but," she paused, and her voice faltered, "it shouldn't have been fatal."

Vicky fell silent. Claire hesitated, not sure how to help. She had no idea of what suffering her friend was containing through sheer force of will, only four days after losing her beloved child. The funeral was tomorrow morning, rescheduled because of the autopsy. Maybe then Vicky would let herself go, release all her pain, when it was over, her parents were gone and, Claire prayed, Leo was found.

A ferry horn sounded in the harbor below. After a while, Vicky poured herself some more coffee. Claire broke the quiet. "Do you know the Franklins? Or Leo?"

Vicky screwed up her mouth in admission, "Lily and I weren't as friendly as we could have been, considering our children swam together downstairs when they weren't out boating. But of course, you must know them better than we do, living on the same floor."

"Not really, as we haven't lived here very long."

"Well, once you've spent a full summer by the pool minding your child, you'll get to know people much better than you'd wish, not to put too fine a point on it. Leo was a very boisterous little boy, I've noticed—it seems a lot of Eurasian kids seem either terribly quiet or terribly noisy. Have you noticed that?"

"I can't say I have. Actually the parents seem noisier than the child. Lots of dinner parties. Leo is quite cute. He and I sort of have a running joke together, nicknames we call each other. But his parents are quite aloof, stick to their crowd. At least, there is certainly a lot of traffic on our landing on some evenings."

"Lily entertains *ferociously*, mostly couples like themselves— you know, Chinese wife with *guay-lo* husband, very upwardly mobile, hot house orchids on the table, custom-made Italian motorboats, charity dinners . . . They weren't much interested in us and our fuddy-duddy share in an old junk. Ian doesn't care for him—not because he's Australian, but because he's, well . . .." Vicky stopped.

"You heard some rumors?" Claire hinted.

"The maids talk a bit." Vicky dropped her eyes down and sipped at her coffee.

Just then, Manny slipped through the sliding glass doors of the balcony, but Claire knew the roar of the traffic down on the slope had muffled what they had said so far.

Manny's eyes seemed filled with worry, but her manner was as gentle as usual. "Shall I clear the coffee, ma'am?" Vicky shook her head and asked for more. Claire waited until Manny had left.

"She talked to me, I mean their *amah*, Narcisa," Claire was sure that for all of her preoccupying grief, Vicky was as quick-witted as ever.

Vicky's eyes widened with curiosity. "Is it true?"

"Twice, at least. You'd think when she asked for a night off to date a Filipino boy, Lily Franklin would have been more than happy to say yes. Narcisa admitted to me that she was expecting a clandestine visit from this new boyfriend, some gardener named 'Jun' who works up on Lugard Road, about the same hour that Leo was snatched."

"Lily might not have noticed anything. The marriage wasn't in great shape. I could tell. It happens all the time. European marries Chinese, thinking he's getting a docile little poppet. It lasts about two years, and then he looks up one day and she's decked out in a fortune of designer clothes from the Landmark, expensive jewelry, a mobile phone in her crocodile bag, and she's off to the races—quite literally, off to Sha Tin—with her girlfriends for the whole of every Saturday afternoon."

"They've already dismissed Narcisa. Given her the usual two weeks. That means she's got about ten more days to find another job or be deported back to the Philippines."

Vicky had a sudden thought. "Do you think this boyfriend took Leo, I mean, for money? There's no ransom note that I've heard of, unless John's keeping it a secret. They often do, I've heard, so as not to encourage more snatching, with all these Asian-type kidnappings in Taiwan and all over now."

"It also means that if Slaughter can't find enough evidence that Jun and Narcisa were involved in Leo's disappearance in little over a week, Narcisa will have to go home and that trail will go completely cold."

Vicky sighed. "Poor girl. I can't believe she deserves any of this. It's Giles Franklin's fault. It's not the first time somebody's husband went jungly with a local girl, but right in your own house, ugh," Vicky shook her head in disapproval, her tough, practical colonial streak showing itself again.

The moment of distraction for Vicky was gone and she turned silent, again, thinking obviously of Petey. Claire reached over to hold her friend's hand for a moment of comfort. After all, that's why she was here, and she was grateful that she was on maternity leave, and had all the time Vicky might need.

"You handled his illness so well. And now you're dealing with his death more bravely than anyone has a right to expect," said Claire. She wondered momentarily if Vicky were on tranquilizers, but she should have known better. Vicky shook her mood off. "Simply what one does, Mummy says. Manage through the next hour, then the next hour, then the next. She's very solid, Mummy, but you know I don't think that makes her cold, even though she seems a little unemotional at times. Did you know my mother was married before?"

"Miriam? As in Miriam and Gordon, your parents?"

Vicky laughed lightly. "Oh, it wasn't always 'Miriam and Gordon.' She was quite a flirt in the fishing fleet. In fact, the year she announced her engagement to my father, the old gang had a kind of catchphrase about my mother—'Miriam'll marry'em.' Daddy's her second husband, you know. Her first husband, Ralph, was quite a bit older than she was, a real hero in the Malaya days." Vicky pronounced the name, "Rafe."

"Daddy only came into the emergency at the tail end. Then one day, Ralph was gone. Dicky heart was the verdict. Broke her spirit for a while, you know, in a quiet sort of way."

Manny had come in quietly with fresh coffee and smiled politely in acknowledgement of Claire.

"Thank you," Vicky said properly, but she waited carefully until Manny had left the room to continue her story. "After the funeral, Mummy says she went on a long holiday to visit a rather racy aunt who kept her soaked in G-and-Ts for about a month. Then she came back and that was the end of it, or at least she would shrug it off. 'Good or bad, it'll come in handy for conversation during the rainy season,' my Great-Aunt Julia told her. 'No experience is wasted, if not repeated, so don't waste your time over it.'" Course Great-Aunt Julia was a WREN in the war."

Claire laughed despite herself. "I'm sorry, I shouldn't laugh, but your family is really something. And, after all, what are we doing right now? Talking about it."

Claire looked more seriously at Vicky. "Is it possible to look forward to the new baby?"

Vicky thought the question over. "Yes. And somehow this autopsy report makes me feel better. Leaves me something to latch onto, something more to find out. It doesn't bring Petey back, but it lets me gnaw away at it without feeling guilty."

Claire chuckled. "Sort of legitimatized gnawing."

"Precisely. You know, I'd like to hold Caspar a bit," Vicky said softly.

Claire reached across her chair to the small sofa of striped ticking and rattan against one side wall of the balcony. Caspar didn't wake, but as Vicky took him gently, his little mouth started to twist over to one side in hope of a meal.

"Oh, I'd forgotten how they do that when they're so little," Vicky managed a small smile, and then tears started to flow silently down her cheeks. She lifted her sunglasses away from her eyes. "Got a tissue?" she laughed bravely, crying and smiling and holding Caspar all at once. "We'll be all right in a bit, won't we, won't we?" she said, more to herself than to Claire.

Claire watched her friend and decided it was a poor time to talk about Anthony Crowley.

───────────────────────────

As Claire emerged from Tavistock, she saw it was too fine a morning to spend indoors. The police were still everywhere, their questions drifting along the hallways, their Chinese and British accents mingling with the sounds of the city below and the breakfast departures, front doors opening and closing, elevators rising and descending to the waiting shuttle bus. Claire didn't feel like going home after leaving Vicky's.

Instead, she decided to give Caspar his breakfast feed outdoors. Positioning him a little more comfortably in his harness, she crossed Tregunter Path and wandered past Ip's gardening shed, up the well-worn dirt footpath that left the paved road and rose in steep curves all the way through the thick, green trees to the top of Victoria Peak. The hammer of pile drivers from building sites across the city punctuated the crisp air, slamming against the Peak and reverberating off the wall of tightly packed high-rise buildings at the foot of the mountain.

Claire couldn't remember a time, political winds notwithstanding, when Hong Kong hadn't shaken with the deafening clanking and pounding of construction machinery. It was the musical backdrop to all the new Asian capitals—Kuala Lumpur, Taipei, Shanghai, Jakarta, Saigon, and anyday now, Hanoi.

Nothing was as comforting these days as the baby's warm weight lying on her body, almost as curled up inside her as he had been all those long uncertain months. She could bury all fears for him when he was this close. Like this, no harm could come to him. She hadn't minded letting Vicky hold him, but it had been strange to see Vicky nuzzling her grief-stricken face against Caspar's tiny breast without flinching a little at the stolen intimacy. Did every new mother resent sharing her newborn this intensely? Would she ever be able to protect him enough from the world? His vulnerable red-downed head collapsed against her breast with the lulling rhythm of her step.

Claire realized she was going to pass the picnic site where the *amahs* had eaten last Sunday. They were all back at work now, of course, and the little clearing looked forlornly trashy, full of food wrappers discarded by the construction workers and barred by a police sign in English and Chinese. The rubbish can at one end of the clearing was stuffed with Tagalog tabloids, movie mags, and hairdressers' monthlies. The Filipinas' Sunday was a day of mutual praying, manicuring, politicizing and hairdressing, gossiping, giggling and eating, singing, dancing, and shared loneliness.

Petey had died some fifty feet away near the dried up *nullah*. Claire guessed this when she saw the police ribbons still tagged around trees to mark off the site. She sat down gingerly, careful not to jolt and wake Caspar, on one of the impromptu plank benches resting on rocks. She glanced up the slope toward the *nullah* that ran from the Peak downhill toward Tregunter Path. Yes, she could make out the banks of the ditch. She swung Caspar and herself heavily back to her feet and wandered farther up the footpath, but nothing apart from the police markers distinguished the place where Petey died. If there had been any traces, Claire knew, the police had already examined them with Manny in tow to point out the way.

This part of the footpath was fairly wide, rising at a leisurely angle to the slope. Then it turned steeper and narrower as it navigated upwards to the Peak and the tram station at the top. Through the trees, Claire heard the rumble of the wooden tram cars as they ferried their passengers—mostly tourists at this hour—up and down rolling cables of wire through the overgrowth.

Claire started humming a little tune she had often played on the piano when she needed a lift, but was breathing hard when she reached a small bench covered by a wooden roof, a rest spot for joggers and lovers. This wasn't the kind of exercise that was going to trim her down to Fabienne's fawn-like figure, but it was a start.

A definite gloom was descending on her as she sat down to feed Caspar, the canopy of the semi-tropical forest shielding them from the sun. The tune died on her lips and she listened closely to the sounds all around here. There was the regular little sucking sound that was such a comfort to her. Still, she felt uneasy. Her breath slowed, as if the slightest movement would wake the stillness of the brush around her. She could not say why she felt the presence of something, or someone, around

her. Some bird or animal? There were snakes in the undergrowth, she knew, and sometimes wild dogs that roamed the
Peak descended closer to the residential buildings hunting
down scraps in the back of the carparks where the garbage
awaited pickup.

She waited. She held Caspar closely to her heart. There was
no sound. None at all. She twisted her torso to the right, back
down the path, and even directly behind her, where the forest
floor slid sharply down some thirty feet to Tregunter Path. She
saw nothing on the slope below her—no animal or bird. Perhaps it was something smaller, a gecko. She twisted to her left,
to peer through the trees to the back of the buildings lining
Tregunter Path.

She waited, holding her breath. She could not shake the sense
of being observed, and why not, she laughed to herself nervously. This footpath was a quick shortcut back to the residential buildings lining Tregunter Path for joggers returning from
the two-mile run around the top of the Peak. In fact, it was
unusual not to see some spritely local health nut. But there was
no *guay-lo* in a Hash House Harrier T-shirt, no leathery Chinese
oldster in a flapping tank top and khaki Empire-builders.

A pall has come over the Peak because of the children, she
thought. We all feel it. We want to find Leo alive and well, but
it would be unnatural not to dread finding him any other way
with each passing hour. We're all waiting for something more
to happen. You can see it in people's faces in the elevator, and
along the Path. It's nearly Christmas Day and it feels as ghoulish
as Halloween.

Something unusual struck her eye. Directly across from the
bench where she sat was a large rock, mossy and silent, piled
high on one side with dead leaves and dirt. Peeking out from
the leaves was something odd, definitely furry and small, and
bluish. In some places, it was smudged with mud. Had a small
animal been stricken while she sat there? Perhaps that was the
noise.

Caspar had fallen asleep without even tackling the other breast. Lifting herself with care so as not to wake him, Claire swung herself gently across the path and knelt slowly down against the rock. She glanced down the footpath in both directions, then started brushing the leaves away.

There lay Grover, his blue fur muddied by the pre-dawn rain. He was still smiling his silly, lovable smile, waiting for Petey, and Claire felt close to tears. At first, she thought the toy had been dragged here by a live animal, but right next to Grover, also hidden under the leaves, lay a tape cassette labelled neatly, *Peter and the Wolf*. It was Vicky's handwriting, Claire knew, from seeing her grocery lists, thank you notes, and a little roster of phone numbers pasted up next to her kitchen door.

Most days, she had barely glanced at Petey, much less his ratty, threadbare Grover. In the days before she had Caspar, it was remarkable how little she distinguished between children and their individual worlds. Now she saw each as unique, and stifling her sobs for fear of waking her own baby, she wept deeply for minutes for Petey, picturing him alone there in the forest.

Her cleansing sobs subsided. Some of the tension was gone—and it was not just to do with Petey, but the hormones flying around inside her, this silly Fabienne's visit, and questions that were coming so fast, like blows. Did Petey hide his Grover this far up the hill? If it was Petey's Grover, was Manny lying when she said Petey was playing farther down the path, closer to Tavistock, just within sight? Or did someone move these things up the hill in a hurry? Why hide his toys if there was no way to hide his death?

She heard another sound, a twig crackling somewhere in the undergrowth down the path. She was not alone. She knew it. Someone was running quickly away, but not down the jogging path where they could be seen, but straight through the dense forest. The sunlight gleaming between the trees, glinting off the water below, made it impossible to distinguish anything moving down the slope.

"Hello?" she called hoarsely, trying not to disturb the baby. Was it Ip? A jogger? Crowley on his rounds? She rose from the rock to start silently down the hill, but between the rock and the path, she immediately tripped on a long, hard root twisting over her foot. It yanked her and the harness, and Caspar jerked awake and started crying. She rocked him too wildly, wiping her eyes of tears and staring down the footpath in a futile search for the unseen observer. She stuffed Grover underneath Caspar inside the harness, pocketed the tape, and headed home, defeated and confused.

---

Despite everything, Christmas was coming like a juggernaut of mindless manufactured cheer, Claire marvelled, as she saw a truck arriving at Branksome with someone else's tree bouncing precariously off the end of the truckbed. Three toughened delivery men wearing baggy cotton shorts despite the brisk weather jumped out of the cabin, put out their cigarettes on the tarmac, and started to untie their cargo. Claire remembered she should drop off her presents for the office: a leather case for her much-appreciated secretary and researcher, Cecilia Chau, some Chanel body lotion for Cecilia's mother, and a cookbook of Asian grilling recipes for the guy filling in for her maternity leave, Hopkirk Wells. He had been borrowed from the Tokyo bureau to cover for Claire, but his was a thankless job, so she had decided she should demonstrate her gratitude.

She found Dovie and Connie finishing the vacuuming and laundry before taking their lunch.

"I'm going to leave him with you two," Claire said, slowly releasing Caspar from his hot little nest in the harness. There was a wet spot left on her shirt front where his sweaty cheek and drooling mouth had nestled for the last forty minutes.

Dovie looked at her with sympathetic efficiency in her voice. "He'll be perfectly fine with the two of us. We're double-locking both the front and back and we don't answer the door to anyone, period. Nobody. One of the Chinese policemen heard from one of the *amahs* in Century Tower that an *amah* in Tavistock said she had seen a strange young *guay-lo* hanging around Tregunter Path over the last few weeks."

Connie nodded from the corner of the kitchen. Claire sighed, but made no comment. She should trust these women with something as simple as keeping the apartment doors locked. She forced herself to hand over Caspar to Dovie, noticing Connie's look of sheer jealousy at being left to fold underwear. Grabbing the Christmas presents, Claire forced herself out the front door and waited outside while she listened to Dovie draw the chain and slide the bolt across the slot on the other side.

A few Westerners and Chinese residents in business suits were waiting for the shuttle bus to depart for Central, while Narcisa and another *amah* waited slightly apart. Of course, the Westerners all boarded first, and when Narcisa and her friend started to step into the bus, the Cantonese driver shouted, "Ten o'clock only. Five more minutes! Not now! Not now! Not ten-o'clock yet!"

The residences along the Path had a rule that only tenants had priority to use the shuttle, while the servants had to wait for the rush hours to end. This was one of the conventions that was becoming more complicated each day, as Chinese became tenants, along with their Chinese servants, while many of the white tenants hired Filipinas, Thais, and Indonesians. But, Claire reflected, it was hardly necessary for the driver to slam the doors shut right in Narcisa's face when there were empty seats.

"No sense these girls trying to bend the rules or it'll all fall apart," muttered the man on Claire's right. She turned to recognize Fiona's husband, Deputy Secretary of the Public Works Department, Barrie Reynolds.

"It's falling apart anyway, isn't it?" Claire replied. "If you mean the old caste system."

Reynolds cocked a suspicious eyebrow at her. "Trying to be amusing?"

Claire shrugged and then changed the subject, "I'm sorry to hear your wife's car was stolen."

"Nicked right out from under the carpark attendant's nose. He must be in on it," sniffed Reynolds, blowing his nose on a handkerchief noisily.

"Frankly, Fiona's such a rotten driver, the city is safer without her behind the wheel. I should have personally arranged to have it stolen months ago. She borrowed my car and driver today to do a bit of Christmas shopping at the outlets over in Hunghom. That way there won't be any more accidents, but I don't fancy riding this bloody bus. I missed the 9:07 by a hair and I'm late for a meeting with HMG."

He was the sort of man who wiped his whole face after sneezing. Claire tried to imagine him swabbing down his forehead during a long meeting with Her Majesty's Governor.

"An accident? Was she hurt?"

"Not just one. First, there was the whiplash two years ago down on Queen's Road East. Some taxi rear-ended her when she was tailgating a lorry. I don't really blame her for that one, although she could have signalled if she'd given herself more room in front. Then there was the run-in with—oh, well, why am I going on like this? Never drink and drive, myself."

The bus hurtled down Garden Road toward the U.S. Consulate.

The first stop would be the government offices near the Public Works Department. Reynolds hastened to collect himself.

"Nasty business, kidnapping the Franklin boy. Bright little chap. Got everybody jumpy. Well, got to jump off, myself, up here."

Claire was left mulling over the rather unamusing image of a tipsy Fiona Reynolds bashing into the ends of taxis driven by

Cantonese. The local taxi drivers were for the most part, volatile, rude, dishonest, and impatient. They didn't like English ladies scratching their paint jobs. It was lucky Fiona hadn't hit anybody on Tregunter Path.

# chapter eight

What a relief it gave Claire to gaze up at the old office building in Wanchai, that half-shabby, half-glitzy district of silvery new office towers overhanging faded topless bars. Suzie Wong would not have recognized her old haunts, replaced by "Chuppie" restaurants, expensive gyms, and four-star hotels overlooking the few quiet temples and sidewalk noodle shops that had survived the high-rise creep eastward from Central district.

Was it possible that in the six weeks that had passed since she hustled off to the delivery room, so little had changed here? On the ground floor of the building, the Choi family's flower shop was quiet at this time of morning, only a few funeral wreaths leaning around the lobby waiting for delivery. Claire was sadly reminded of Petey's small, quiet funeral. It would be a dignified Anglican service at St. John's Cathedral, attended by Ian's fellow pilots and their families, a few of Vicky's English school friends who had married men working in Hong Kong, and a few gray heads from Miriam and Gordon's days.

The doorman, Mr. Shuk, was sitting on the same old perch behind his reception desk in the lobby, looking as lazy and nosy as ever.

"What? No baby? What happened?" he scowled in mock disappointment.

Claire laughed, waiting for the elevator to take her to the twenty-fourth floor. "You want to babysit? Any time!"

He shook his head, laughing gruffly at the idea. "No babysitting, never, never! I too old!"

"Claire!" Hopkirk and Cecilia jumped from their seats with a huge hug for her from each as soon as she had kicked open the bureau's wooden door, warped into its frame by years of Hong Kong's relentless humidity.

"This place looks great!" she cried, dropping into her old chair and gazing around her well-worn office, and then out the window, where a sliver of harbor could still be seen between the new towers thrown up on Queen's Road East.

She didn't care that what first struck her eye was how stained the carpet looked around Cecilia's little metal desk, how the corkboard above Hopkirk's desk was broken off on one corner, and how the masking tape holding down the foam in her chair was straggling loose. Since she'd rushed out of here mid-morning, her waters broken, her step halted by painful contractions, she might have done the crawl across three oceans, she felt she'd traversed so many miles of experience in only a few weeks. Yet, the old chair fit her bottom just as well as before, even with the new pounds around her hips.

Claire had arrived at the office just as Cecilia was finishing the morning filing. Now she was photocopying and filing away stories marked by Hopkirk. Claire missed the routine with a pang, as she saw the *Bangkok Post, China Times, Wen Wei Po, Da Kung Pao, China Daily*, and her beloved transcripts of the Chinese press airmailed by the BBC's listening service. Cecilia brought in the latest pile of mail and placed it next to two other bundles, "Whenever you're ready, *Mom*."

Claire laughed, "Oh, thanks, but I'll beg off until next week and my official return. I just came in to give you my holiday goodies."

Hopkirk drooped his lanky frame around the office separator. "Tell us what's happening up there on Tregunter Path. MacDermott's back in New York from his tour of East European bureaux and I mentioned that the two boys' story is all over the front page here. He wanted to know if it ties in with any broader story. He read a *Fortune* story about kidnappings of businessmen in Guangdong province and Taiwan. They did it as a sort of travel advisory piece. You know he doesn't like playing catch-up."

MacDermott was the testy editor of the international edition of *Business World*. He was loyal to his people in the field, but impatient and painfully honest when playing corporate middleman between the forty-seventh floor overlooking half of Manhattan and the distant bureaux.

"Frankly, it never occurred to me as a story for us," Claire answered bluntly. "When you're up there, it certainly doesn't feel like a business story from any angle. There's no ransom note or demand for money, so I don't see beating up speculation just yet."

"The father of Leo Franklin is an Australian businessman. He must be fairly successful. Did you see he's offering a million Hong Kong dollars for any information leading to the discovery of the boy?"

Hopkirk pointed to two Chinese papers down on the desk in front of Claire.

Claire paused and searched mentally for her old reporter's point of view, but she still didn't see it as a story.

"If this were Taiwan, this story wouldn't even make the local papers, kidnapping is so common there. We've seen some horrific stories about kids permanently disfigured and turned into beggars on the streets of Taipei before the police could locate them in time. Really turned my stomach. I think the *New York Times* did something like it out of Delhi or Saudi Arabia."

She shivered at recalling one account of a mother stumbling over her own missing child begging legless on the street in Taipei.

"Did you remind MacDermott of the piece we did back in '94 on the Cambodians seizing and killing Western trekkers? We folded in a sidebar about 'kidnapping—a growth industry' in that," she offered.

Hopkirk nodded with thanks in Cecilia's direction. "Luckily, Miss Elephant Memory slipped it under my nose while MacDermott was on the line."

Cecilia smiled, "It was my pleasure, sir."

Hopkirk was a pro at covering the Tokyo foreign exchange market. He didn't have to hide his confusion. "I don't get it. One kid died in a seizure, then another little kid just disappeared from his apartment?"

"Like, on our floor?"

"You're kidding?"

"No, and I'm damn glad they didn't report that in the papers. We're already jumpy enough as it is." Claire struggled to find the word, waving her hands in the air. "Vanished. It's really strange. You can bet everybody is double-locking their doors. Just being down in Wanchai makes me feel like I escaped the Bermuda Triangle for a few hours."

Hopkirk had another thought. "What about that story in '95 from Singapore about the Filipina who murdered another *amah* and the kid—?"

Claire nodded, "The Contemplacion incident. She was innocent. At least that's what I think. I was convinced of it and so was everybody in the Philippines. But the Singaporean government got away with the cover-up and hung her. The Philippines recalled their ambassador to Singapore over it. Nobody's blaming the Filipina *amahs* this time without some evidence.

The *amah* working for the Franklins only got sacked with notice."

"Sacked? You've been in Hong Kong too long," Hopkirk laughed. "You're starting to talk like a Brit."

"Too right," laughed Claire, deliberately switching to a thick Australian drawl. "At any rate, the police are questioning everybody and keeping their cards close to their chests. I wonder if they have any clues, really. And my head is full of questions about things that just seem a tad weird."

"For example?"

"In the cold light of downtown Wanchai, how do these things strike you two? The policeman near the picnic site the day Petey died, who was conveniently right on the spot, has a secret life as a transvestite diva at a little no-name club off Lan Kwai Fong. His act is full of double entendres about little boys."

Claire knew her tone was insinuating, but she gave full vent to her misgivings. Although she gave John Slaughter a lot of credit for his decades of service, there were inconsistencies she wanted to pull together, and to throw her questions into the face of the veteran policeman would be insulting someone who didn't deserve her disrespect.

"Second, just a minute after Petey Sandford is discovered dead, just before the policeman conveniently rounds the corner, a car speeds away driven by the alcoholic wife of the PWD Deputy Secretary. According to her own husband, she seems to have a history of 'hit and runs.' The deceased little boy's *amah* claims she tried to flag this woman's car down before the policeman turned up, but the wife behind the wheel totally denies to my face noticing any babysitter on the curbside."

"Third, Petey's body is strangely bruised. Coincidence? Well, in case it's connected to Mrs. Reynolds' erratic driving, there's no chance of inspecting the car in question because that night it conveniently disappears from the Tavistock garage, right under the nose of the gateman."

"Finally, the autopsy confirms Petey suffered an epileptic attack, so why is some unexplained substance turning up in his little tummy?"

Cecilia and Hopkirk could only shrug.

"Fifth, only twenty-four hours later, Leo disappears."

"Where was Leo during Petey's attack? Maybe there's a connection nobody knows about? Did he see something? Know something?"

Claire looked at Hopkirk. "Good question. *Very* good question."

Cecilia piped up. She was considering what Claire had said about Crowley. "A lot of Chinese boys sell themselves to homosexual *guay-los* out in Repulse Bay. They wait on the rocks next to the beach at Repulse Bay, just in front of the hotel there, and the customers send boats to shore to pick them up for an hour or two. They might know something about your policeman, whether he is actively looking for boys or not. It's too cold to swim now, but my mother likes the buffet lunch at the hotel. I might be able to find out something this Saturday."

"Your mother doesn't mind you scrambling over the rocks accosting Cantonese in G-strings?"

Cecilia wasn't Cantonese like most of Hong Kong's Chinese, but came as a toddler to Hong Kong in the sixties, fleeing the anti-Chinese rioting in Indonesia. Her mother had worked her whole life as a seamstress in textile factories and Cecilia had worked her way to a degree in librarian skills at the local Polytechnic, earning her book and uniform money stuffing jeans and silk underwear into export packaging.

Cecilia shook her head that she didn't mind and laughed a little, a deceptively lighthearted chime for someone who had survived a nervous breakdown in 1989 over shock at the Tiananmen murders in Beijing, not to mention an unexpected incarceration in a Chinese prison in 1995 while on assignment in Guangdong for Claire.

"It's my pleasure," she said simply.

Claire rose, refreshed by the respite from Caspar and the lev-elheaded atmosphere of the office.

"Well, I meet a different kind of deadline these days, so I better get going. You know, Hopkirk, a baby boy is exactly like an editor on the international desk. He makes you feel very important for a few seconds, he won't take no for an answer to any of his untimely demands, he wakes you up at all hours of the day and night, and like any editor, he never heard of such a thing as a weekend off."

Hopkirk laughed, "I'll find it very reassuring to know that I'm so well prepared the next time I get pregnant!"

Claire nodded, "Well, enjoy your last week in our quiet corner of the empire. I liked the piece you did on Asiatech's new fig-ures for Christmas sales. It's always hard to find a new way to do the required Christmas stories."

Hopkirk bowed ceremoniously, grateful Claire had bestowed her blessing on his tenure. Sometimes bureau chiefs resented any outsider sitting in for them.

"When is your flight back to Tokyo?"

"Right after New Year's Day. After trying to keep up with events from Jakarta to Beijing, I really appreciate my simple life of yen forecasting."

Claire felt light and happy, certainly more in the Christmas spirit than any time since last Sunday morning. She missed Cas-par, but it was a novel feeling she wanted to enjoy a little longer, so she figured that before heading home, she would enjoy her freedom for another half an hour. She would stop at Xavier's office for a kiss. He worked out of a high-rise needle-shaped building on Ice House Street in Central, right next door to the Foreign Correspondents' Club.

She checked her hair in the windows of a shop and was happy to see the way it caught the sun. She reminded herself that it had been days since she'd worn lipstick, and slicked on a glossy copper salvaged from the bottom of her bag. The taxi ride to Central took mere minutes, and she hoped Xavier would be pleased to see her for once without Caspar clinging to her chest.

Opening the door to his outer office, her mood slumped. There was a woman's voice, querulous and emotional, coming from Xavier's private office. His Chinese secretary, Lornia, looked stunned to see Claire stride in without warning.

"Claire, uh, hi! How is the new baby?"

"Fine, just fine, thanks Lornia. Um, Xavier in a meeting?" The door was closed, something unusual for Xavier who prided himself on a relaxed and open atmopshere with Lornia.

Lornia hesitated, fingering the lacework holes in her handknit sweater. "Yes. He was expecting you?"

"No," Claire shrugged. Lornia looked nervous. What was wrong? Claire's hand flew nervously to an unruly red twist of kinky hair over her temple, the one that drove her crazy as a teenager by sticking out when all the other girls' hair was blonde or brunette and smooth. Lornia's anxiety was contagious.

"I'll let him know you're here," Lornia nodded, head down.

She went to Xavier's door and opened it. The sounds of a woman in tears slipped past her. Lornia said a few words about Claire waiting outside. In a second, Xavier was springing to the doorway to greet her.

"Claire, come in!" He gave her a warm kiss on the cheek and ushered her into the inner office, where Fabienne sat at the head of a small conference table, wiping her eyes with a tissue. She was wearing a black leather jacket over black suede pants and a baby blue satin shirt underneath. This was not an outfit anybody would wear if she planned on crying. She looked up to see Claire in shock and surprise. Claire had obviously interrupted an intense moment between her lover and his ex.

Claire felt betrayed by her own flushing cheeks. She rarely dropped in on Xavier during the day because she was usually so busy in her own office. With her own life, she thought. She had already been counting on the delight of a loving reception when she arrived, a warm hug and the small relish of being alone with him in fresh surroundings for a little time without the baby. These last days of maternity leave were so short, so precious, why did they have to be shared with this woman!

"Sorry, Claire, I was just catching Xavier up on some old gossip," said Fabienne.

"A friend of ours suffered a terrible motorcycle accident recently." Xavier looked solemn, and since Claire had never known him to lie, she felt her alarm subside as the pieces fell back into place.

"I'm sorry to hear that. Who was it?"

Fabienne was still collecting herself and didn't look Claire in the eye. "A girl we were both close to, the girlfriend of a member of our old commune," Xavier explained.

Claire waited for Fabienne to add something, to help Claire contribute some commiseration over someone she had never met, but the conversation seemed to have died with Claire's arrival. It seemed a fair explanation for the tension in the room, but Claire still felt uneasy.

"So!" Xavier rubbed his hands together, trying to set a more upbeat mood. "I'll get some more coffee. Claire, show Fabienne the trail we'll be taking on our hike out to Father Fresnay's village!"

This hike had been the result of Xavier's planning session over drinks with Fabienne the night Leo was kidnapped. They were going to stick to the plan, Claire insisted, because there was nothing else they could do. Privately, the thought of getting Caspar away from Tregunter Path, even for a day, was a day of escape from heavy anxiety and dread.

The two women walked awkwardly to Xavier's wall map of Hong Kong, all 400 square miles of territory, showing the islands of Cheung Chau, Lamma and Lantau, and the sprawling New Territories reaching up to the border with China's southernmost province, Guangdong.

Still unnerved by the atmosphere of ill-explained tensions, Claire pointed to the eastern coast of the New Territories and the Sai Kung Peninsula. "We'll be hiking from this part of the Sai Kung Country Park along a path to the village of Tailong and the beach of Hamtin. There's no road through these hills which means the village is preserved as it was a hundred years ago. You see, it forms part of this trail that stretches for miles, the MacLehose Trail named after one of the former governors, Sir Murray MacLehose."

Fabienne pretended to concentrate on the map, and Claire ran her finger along the coast until she found the village. They were both good actresses, but for how long?

"You must bring a camera. Did you get that broken one fixed yet?"

Fabienne bristled, "A professional never goes anywhere without his camera. Like you with your notebook, I suppose."

Claire nodded awkwardly, "Yes, same thing. Well, good. You'll get great shots of traditional village architecture, and the old church where our friend Robert gives his little Christmas Mass is very charming. Be sure and bring lots of film."

An excruciating silence followed as Claire settled herself in the chair opposite Xavier's desk, and Fabienne stood pretending to scrutinize Hong Kong's eastern coastline. Would Fabienne be excusing herself soon, or would she try to sit out Claire? Claire knew her rage was ridiculous, but she got so few chances to relax with Xavier, she was furious. At night she was too exhausted from childcare to stay up and chat with him about his day. No one who had not been a new mother could imagine that two people living together with a newborn had so little time to enjoy each other as two adults. Fabienne could never understand.

Suddenly, Claire pulled herself together. It was so ridiculous, she thought, she must forcibly remove herself from this scene. This was turning into a Henry James story, where you imagined everything was happening even though nothing was happening. Or was it? This did her no good and she wasn't vying during recess for a chance to play kickball, she was the mother of this man's child.

If there was a game going on behind her back, if there was an unspoken dialogue between Fabienne and Xavier—or worse—Claire hoped a strategic withdrawal might give her the upper hand, or at least some emotional buffer zone. If she had to share Christmas Eve with this woman, she still had Christmas morning with her man and child. She had almost thought *husband*, but caught herself.

She glanced at her watch, perhaps too theatrically. "Oh, it's late!" she exclaimed. "Time for another feeding. I'm sorry, I'm just not used to Caspar running our life yet!"

Xavier was returning with her coffee. "I screwed up," Claire laughed it off. "Nature in the form of *your* son calls! Look, I just came for a kiss. See you tomorrow, Fabienne. Wear some comfortable shoes." She could not resist this dig at Fabienne's expensive heeled boots. At five foot ten inches, Claire's own footwear tended toward flats, to her frequent regret. She gave Xavier a good, strong hug, almost a football tackle, and sipped the hot coffee standing up. Xavier looked at her, clearly startled. Perhaps he wished to detain her a few minutes longer.

Once she had escaped them and safely bid her swift adieu to the still-embarrassed Lornia, Claire pushed the button for the elevator and leaned her forehead against the cool tile of the lobby. She wondered how she would get through Christmas Day.

The taxi ride home was difficult. Claire felt waves of childish hurt, the feeling she was shrinking into nothing, diminished by each encounter with Fabienne. The importance of Caspar, his centrality in her life was one shock to her system, but to consider the idea that Caspar was *not* central to Xavier, that his own life was less than turned on its head by paternity, made her feel very wounded. There he was, in his private work domain, entertaining the latest news on his other life, his previous, carefree, single life. It was still there for him, as it would never be again for her.

She was lugging a stone of worry in her stomach. She hoped she could sneak into the apartment without alerting Connie and Dovie, and most of all Caspar. She needed time to herself. But she had forgotten the barricade of bolts and chains Dovie had erected to keep out intruders. She waited for what seemed an interminable delay for someone to answer her own front door.

Dovie's face was a deep, frightening purple flush when she finally admitted Claire. She started to speak, "Ma'am," and then stopped, shook her head, and walked toward the kitchen.

"Dovie, what is it?"

Dovie turned and spoke carefully. "I have to speak to you alone, ma'am."

"Well?" Claire tried to sound patient and warm, but in fact, she dreaded servant problems. She had seen many women lose their privacy and peace of mind over minor servant problems that blew up into domestic Cold Wars.

Dovie nearly whispered, "Please, not here."

Suddenly, a burst of angry Tagalog came out of the kitchen. Connie was standing near the sink, face turned toward the window, but she was sputtering in Filipino dialect, obviously furious over something. Fully aware that Claire was standing there dumbfounded by this unexpected confrontation, Dovie would only tersely shoot one simple Tagalog phrase back and then, appealing to Claire, "Please, ma'am."

Connie was apparently determined that Dovie would not speak privately to Claire. She walked to the doorway, her face ablaze, and shouted in Tagalog to the older woman and then started crying and shaking. Claire took Connie gently by the shoulders and sat her down at a small table in the long, sunny kitchen, as big as the living room and bigger than Caspar's nursery.

"Calm down, where's Caspar?" she said, noticing a shake in her own voice at this unexpected explosion of emotion.

"He's in his room, ma'am," Dovie said. The older woman was standing behind Claire, breathing heavily, trying to hang on to her dignity and refusing to look back at Connie.

"Please come with me, ma'am. I want to show you something."

Bewildered and alarmed, Claire raced Dovie to the nursery where Caspar was lying on a blanket in the corner, trying to pull the string on a squawking Big Bird toy but mostly wagging his fist in the air. Claire's breath rushed out of her in an explosion of relief.

"Look, ma'am." Dovie reached up to a high shelf and pulled a half-burnt candle from its perch next to some stuffed toys. "I found Connie burning this over his crib during his morning nap. She was chanting the rosary."

As a Catholic, Claire had nothing against the rosary, but the candle struck her as a bit theatrical. "Why are you fighting with her now?"

"You see," Dovie was anxious that Claire understand and she was getting excited, "she put the candle up here on this shelf on a piece of tin foil, but the tin foil got folded here, and you see!"

Claire, indeed, was horrified now to see that the candle wax had dripped onto Caspar's mattress. "Was he burned?" she turned immediately to inspect her offspring.

"No, ma'am, I found her kneeling here, like this, and the wax was dripping on this end and Caspar was sleeping over on this side, which is why she didn't see the wax, falling here, right behind his leg." Now that she had got the story out, Dovie straightened her back to collect herself and stood more calmly in front of Claire.

Claire took a deep breath. They could both hear Connie protesting and sobbing to herself, all the while scrubbing the sink, pouring out the injustice of Dovie's betrayal over the Comet.

"I'm going to speak to Connie alone. I think you can expect to be taking over a few days earlier than we discussed."

Dovie's lips tightened with private satisfaction at Claire's de-
cisiveness, but she was far from happy. "She has a lot of family
who depend on her, ma'am."

"Don't worry, she was always here temporarily, just until we
found you. She has another job waiting for her after Chinese
New Year. We'll make sure she's fully paid until the new job
starts, but I don't want her working here. She means well, but
I've lost confidence in her judgement. I appreciate your explaining this right away."

"I'm sorry, ma'am. She didn't tell me she was praying for him
every day until I found her like this. She's very frightened that
they won't catch the kidnapper. We all are."

"Dovie, do the *amahs* around here know more than they're
telling the police? About Leo's disappearance? Or about Petey's
accident?"

"They don't talk to me, because they think I'm just an old
lady and I'm new in this neighborhood. Still, I hear the gossip.
Connie got scared yesterday because of some talk on the shuttle
bus about a man hanging around Tregunter Path at night."

"Do the police know?"

"Of course we told them, but they don't pay attention to Filipina gossip. And most of the time, I would agree with them,"
Dovie shrugged.

Connie was waiting in her room when Claire knocked on her
door. "I'm sorry, Connie, but I hope you understand you put
Caspar in danger, even though you didn't mean to."

"He is already in danger, ma'am."

"What do you mean?"

"There are things going on that you don't understand."

"Like what, Connie? You must tell the police if you know
something. Are you talking about this rumor of a lurker around
the neighborhood, or do you know something else?"

"Did you talk to the policeman, ma'am? The one with the
curly black hair?"

"What about him?"

"I can't tell, ma'am. But the Filipinas, we know when something is wrong. When someone is sick in the head, we can pray, but there is nothing we can do. We have to think of our jobs and our families back home."

"And there is nothing more you can tell me?"

"No, ma'am. But don't leave Caspar alone. I will continue to pray for him, ma'am."

# chapter nine

The 24th of December started early for Claire with Caspar cradled in her arms before sunrise. Sitting tucked into the window seat in his nursery, she gazed down at the soothing stretch of harbor in the distance, still only a dark expanse of water undisturbed by ferry and speedboat crossings.

Visiting freighters dotted the waters far out to the west of the city's high-rises. It was traditional that during Christmas week, many of the sailors cruising the South China waters stopped for a rest in Hong Kong. It was only at such a crowded time of year that one could see their behemoth vessels anchored in neat rows, not randomly, as if the whole harbor were a watery parking lot outside the world's biggest shopping mall.

Christmas calm had descended on the colony, despite all the greed, hustle, and racket Cantonese merchants and Johnny-Come-Lately colonials could muster. Even the Nightclub from Hell must be dead quiet at this hour, Claire thought to herself.

She saw two police vans parked at the junction of Tregunter Path and May Road. The constables lounged inside, dozing, watching, recording, waiting day and night, for someone, somewhere, somehow, to slip up. Maybe Christmas was the time when people were weak, when sicknesses surfaced, sadnesses overwhelmed, memories too painful to endure returned. Perhaps it was a time when evil claimed its little part of the day, unable to let the birthday of Christ be an unchallenged balm to the world.

Something might break.

Let's bloody hope so, thought Claire, morbidly. The possibility that there would be no resolution to Leo's disappearance was incompatible with her sense of the world.

Caspar was now deep, deep asleep, a milky lump. He sucked so hard, a little blister puckered the center of his upper lip. Claire rose carefully, transferred him to his crib, and breathed easier. It was an echo of those first moments when the midwives at Adventist Hospital had helped her off the delivery table and she felt momentarily so light she was sure she could have defied gravity and floated away.

She moved stealthily to her books, stuffed less than methodically into shelves during their hurried move, and found her *Concise Oxford Dictionary*. Aconite was easy to find; "acme, acne, acolyte, aconite: poisonous plant of genus *aconitum*, esp. monkshood or wolfsbane; drug obtained from this."

Claire was startled by the sound of Xavier already in the bathroom, clearing his throat and humming some Christmassy tune to himself. He had a deep baritone, a wonderful voice. Claire remarked to herself, this is the first time I have heard him sing. She felt bathed in the fullness of the moment, her first Christmas present from him ever.

His family had always celebrated the birth of Christ on the eve of Christmas. Claire's parents had made the morning of Christmas a wonderland of presents opening, music and singing, and then Mass. Well, she thought, this way I'll get two Christmases every year from now on, instead of one. And just in case Fabienne ruins today's hike, I'll get a second chance tomorrow at our first Christmas morning together without her. All in all, the spirit of the holiday seemed to have pushed her enveloping melancholy to some more peaceful place.

The sun was starting to hit the silvery waters of the harbor. Where was that other book? She ran her index finger along so many beloved titles: *The History of Private Life, Volumes 1–4* so far—she'd buy the remaining volumes next time she was in New York—*The Cambridge History of China*—she had two bootlegged volumes from the old Taipei rip-off bookstore, Caves, and one genuine edition from London, all her Iris Murdoch, P. D. James, Ngaio Marsh, Robertson Davies, Robert Van Gulik, John Le Carré, that biography of Truman that had been a doorstopper in her old apartment, popular American political bestsellers, a fistful of Asian cookbooks, Chinese language dictionaries, textbooks, here we were, getting warm, her assorted guidebooks for all the capital cities she'd worked in across Asia, the dog-eared maps, art auction brochures for ceramic sales by bankrupted Chinese ship owners in the bank crash of 1983, her Carrian Trial files, warmer, warmer . . .

Caspar stirred a little, but merely pursed his lips and went on dreaming. She started along the next shelf. There it was, buried under a scrapbook of old clips, a thin little medical dictionary she'd found in one of the mainland-owned bookstores ten years before. She'd needed it for a ten-day job translating in Henan for an obnoxious BBC camera crew shooting footage of Chinese esophageal cancer patients. It had featured an appendix of chemical terms. "Aconite in Chinese: *chuan wu tou* . . . Sichuan crow's head."

"That tells me precisely nothing," she mused to herself. "But it sure sounds like strange stuff to end up in Petey." She resolved to run it past the smartest guy she knew, and that was certainly not the well-meaning Chief Inspector Slaughter busy investigating baby food and houseplants. Luckily they would be meeting him in less than an hour.

In fact, Fresnay was late by almost half an hour, but then, they were all running behind schedule. Claire and Xavier had packed up for the overnight trip as usual—frozen homemade spaghetti sauce, some bottles of good wine, bread, cheeses, salad, and eggs—and having filled all the available space in Claire's backpack, realized they still had some six diapers to accommodate, wipers for the baby's bottom, and a change of spare clothing for Caspar in case of accidents.

They were packed and just about to head out the door when they realized they had forgotten to account for one more new burden—Caspar himself, sitting innocently blowing little saliva bubbles in a carrier seat in the kitchen with Dovie.

Fabienne was waiting punctually outside her hotel, dressed in a dapper photographer's vest and jeans and well-worn shoes. Claire was almost grateful to see how slack the Frenchwoman's backpack looked; for once, this person's presence made sense. It was agreed already that Fresnay, who had the strongest pair of legs, would handle the two-hour hike with Caspar on his back. Fabienne would be able to at least carry the diapers and babywipes.

Claire had secretly packed her Christmas present for Xavier in the bottom of a sock. It was a travel clock she had ordered from New York, compact and expensive, a gold-rimmed face in a handsome lizard case and guaranteed for many years. It was the sort of thing she always wanted for herself during her many abrupt mornings in strange hotels on assignment, but she never bought expensive status goods for herself. She never bought less than top quality for presents. She was happy with her choice, and knew he would think of her whenever he was visiting one of his projects in Beijing, North Korea, Mongolia, wherever, in the coming new year.

She was disappointed to see Fresnay wasn't waiting for them

left in the care of       137

as arranged. So they had parked Claire's "rustbucket" on the side of a two-lane road winding through the brushy hills of Sai Kung Country Park, and made idle, polite conversation about the history of the New Territories, distribution of *Business World* in Asia, and Fabienne's assignment in Cambodia. She was proposing to retrace the steps of foreigners who had been seized and murdered by straggler Khmer Rouge troops at one of the ancient Angkor tourist sites. It sounded like a fairly dangerous project for a first-time visitor to Cambodia.

"You have experience avoiding land mines," said Xavier, "so I won't worry about that, but you don't have the language. I hope you have an excellent guide."

"You know I'm a survivor," said Fabienne, brushing back her dark hair and lighting a cigarette with panache. "I'm in-des-truc-ti-ble," she said, and her tone implied something more, or was it Claire's imagination?

Just then, Fresnay's motorcycle engine sounded reassuringly beyond the hills behind them and in a moment, he was unscrambling his long legs and discarding the helmet from his unruly hair.

"*Salut, salut, c'est un plaisir faire votre connaissance. Je suis Robert.*"

"Damn!" Claire thought. On top of everything else, she had forgotton that her Jesuit friend was half-Scottish, half-*French*, which, combined with Xavier's multilingual skills and Fabienne's bad English, meant that Claire was spending two days as odd-woman-out in the language department. The only other person in their party who didn't speak fluent French was Caspar.

She had forgotten how beautiful the Hong Kong countryside could be. Not heavily forested, but low-brushed and lush at this time of year with ferns and heavily fronded trees lining the water. Banana plants had to be brushed out of their way as they moved along the inlets of the South China Sea forming tiny coves around which villagers and fishermen had planted a few two-story villas or fishing shacks. At each rise, they could cast their eyes toward the eastern horizon, knowing the sea lay just beyond these hills, while below them stretched one valley after another. Sometimes they passed cows, peacefully chewing on the plastic debris left by city backpackers, or overheard the happy Cantonese racket of campers inside a neon nylon tent, their radios and CDs preventing too much urban withdrawal panic.

Still, they were out of the city and its shadows, personal and political. The fierce old battles of Sai Kung villages during the war—some pro-Communist, some pro-Kuomintang—had faded now, while the new forces still loomed, like an invisible army poised on the border to the north of them.

If the villagers who watched the hikers passing by now cared about politics, the simple fact was that there were fewer of them left for the political parties to bother about. Their sons and daughters had fled to the factories and government-designed new towns, to the urban crowds of Hong Kong and Kowloon, and along with a thousand other Hong Kongers each week for the past five years, to new lives in Canada, Australia, and the U.S., gone for good.

The incline started slowly, and Claire paced herself carefully, knowing the steepest challenge came at the end of the morning. They found a rhythm, Fresnay leading with Caspar's small head bouncing slightly up and down to his enthusiastic step, followed by Fabienne, then Claire and then Xavier. No one had said as much, but Claire knew that Xavier's slightly arthritic knees would be troubled, thanks to decades of merciless skiing and motorcycling.

She also knew that Fabienne would know that, and would understand if Claire hung back, giving Xavier "face" for lagging slightly behind. At a turn near the crest of the first hill, they paused and saw the entire peninsula stretched out before them, preserved for the teeming city as a recreation area, but also protecting, as much by accident as design, the area's few remaining authentic villages of traditional Chinese peasants.

"*Merveilleuse*," Fabienne exclaimed. "I would never have imagined such peace so close to the city."

"It is my refuge," Fresnay said. "At least once a week I have to get away from that pile of Chinese newspapers, radio transcripts, and the political database, get away from the deadlines of the newsletter, and remind myself of what I am doing here. Oh, and now, we use the Internet, and instead of less work, that just means access to more information than before. Anyway, it's my job, and not a bad way for a farmer's sixth child to end up."

"You mean spying for the Pope," Claire shouted ahead, teasingly, which only brought an annoyed glance backward from Robert. Certainly, Fresnay showed no interest in making converts, and apart from his Sunday obligations to the Filipinas, along with all the other priests in Hong Kong, he carried none of the duties of a parish priest. He and his team of Chinese analysts burrowing away under reading lamps, sifting, collating, and dissecting the news from the mainland.

Claire knew he was also secretly in touch with the Chinese religious underground on the mainland, keeping close tabs on the welfare of imprisoned priests and clandestine cells of Catholics loyal to Rome rather than to the Party. This was a subject they never touched on, and Claire had never discussed it with anyone else, even Xavier.

As for the two men, their relationship was warming slowly, even though it carried the undertones of competition between two healthy, virile men. She had introduced them more than a year ago, well before she had discovered her pregnancy. Fresnay had been cordial to Xavier, but in that challenging tone he had. You had to know that without a wife or children, all of his identity was invested in his priestly scholarship to understand him.

"Xavier is a very Jesuit name. Maybe *you* should have been a priest," Fresnay had joked.

"Eight years of monastery school with the Benedictines in Switzerland cured me of any such vocation," was Xavier's riposte.

"Benedictines! Well, of course you went astray!" Fresnay had laughed.

"We kept the Jesuits out of Switzerland for a very long time, presumably for a reason!" Xavier joked back.

"Are you so sure we weren't there anyway?" the priest insinuated.

Remembering this banter warmly as the fresh sea breezes struck her nose for the first time today, Claire smiled to herself with a shock of well-being. Part of the trick to surviving life overseas as more than a laboring drone was to create some sense of family, some belonging precisely where you didn't belong. Fresnay had accepted Xavier, and in time, Xavier would find a way of fitting in with her other friends, she felt surer every day. Was she giving Xavier the benefit of the same effort when it came to Fabienne?

They swung down the first serious slope to one of the baylets used as a dock and fishing port by a few locals. The narrow concrete path was only a short section of the MacLehose Trail. At some points, it skirted the inlet waters by only a foot or two, and Claire would have loved to have stopped there and cooled off her feet, but they had found their pace now, and had not even reached the halfway mark.

Fresnay burst into poetry, partly to show off his prodigious memory to Fabienne. He was a priest, but liked admiration from both sexes, and performing extemporaneously was the closest Claire ever saw him come to flirting with new acquaintances:

*"La langoureuse Asie et la brulante Afrique,*
*Tout un monde lointain, absent, presque défunt.*
*Vit dans tes profondeurs, fôret aromatique—"*

Fabienne joined in, "—*Comme des autres esprits voguent sur la musique, Le mien, o mon amour! Nage sur ton parfum.*"

Together they nearly sang,

"*J'irai là-bas ou l'arbre et l'homme, pleins de seve,
Se pament longuement sous l'ardeur des climats;
Fortes tresses, soyez la houle qui m'enleve!
Tu contien, mer c'ebene, un eblouissant rêve
De voiles, de rameurs, de flammes et de mats.*"

The unexpected camaraderie Fresnay and Fabienne had discovered in Baudelaire promised to dispel some of the tension, Claire hoped. Oddly, Xavier couldn't muster a smile at the sight of Fresnay pounding up the hill, Caspar's tiny legs bouncing forward and back against his torso, with Fabienne close behind, swinging her arms in time to the poetry.

"There's a possibility these two are going to get on my nerves," mumbled Xavier.

Was he jealous? Claire examined his face more carefully. And it struck her that Xavier *was* jealous, not of Fabienne's flirtation with the priest, but of Robert's proprietary ferrying of Xavier's first-born son. She realized Xavier was moving more slowly as they got into the second half hour of climbing. His face was flushed and even in the cool breeze, his forehead had broken into sweat. He was in pain, but too stubborn to admit it, and the second serious ascent was just ahead.

"You want to stop?"

"I think I had better just keep going."

"Xavier, what is it?" Fabienne had turned and was loping back toward them cheerfully.

"My knees. I'll be all right . . . just have to take it slowly. Go on, go on, don't stop because of me."

Caspar was starting to wake for his "brunch munch," as Claire called the late morning feed. She suggested they cross a small valley used by campers and grazing cows before stopping on the last and meanest hill of all. There was a cool stream where it would be good to eat some of their fruit and cheese while Caspar had his snack. They leaned against some large rocks and surveyed the neon dots of high-tech tents favored by Hong Kong teenagers on overnight adventures. Here and there a tape player broke the rural stillness with some "Canto-pop" crooning by Anita Lui or Andy Lau.

"Does that remind you of Sicily, hmnnn?" Fabienne was talking quietly to Xavier as he stretched his legs in the stream to cool down his muscles and knees. Claire overheard her, but didn't turn her head. She already felt self-conscious about breast-feeding in front of Fabienne, while Fresnay's presence didn't trouble her at all. Fresnay came from a very full house of siblings, nieces, and nephews with rambling houses in Caen and the countryside outside Edinburgh. She felt unfairly exposed to her attractive rival.

Fabienne's trilling voice carries in the soft breeze. "The tent fell down one night! Oh, it was so funny, trying to put it up again in the dark with the wind blowing and we were so drunk. *Tu te rappelle?*"

"Of course," Xavier said, putting his arm around the vivacious Fabienne for a moment for a comforting squeeze.

Claire took a deep sigh. *She's not giving up, this chick, she's just not going to give up,* and looked up from Caspar's intent little labors to find Robert's eyes firmly watching her expression from where he sat discreetly to one side. She smiled wanly. Her clerical friend was a quick study of more than poetry and Chinese politics.

"So! Madamoiselle! We take the lead and I will show you the best view in the entire territory within twenty minutes!" Fresnay was actually lifting Fabienne from the stream's side and thrusting, as much as helping, her back into her backpack.

Claire tucked herself back up as Caspar was loaded gingerly back onto Fresnay's sturdy back. She took Xavier's hand and they returned silently to the path together. He stopped for a moment and looked quietly and tenderly at her troubled face.

Words didn't come. His expression was somber, and he stroked her face as if she were a small, injured animal. Was this a sort of pity? Claire's uneasiness deepened.

Fresnay and Fabienne had already gone around a curve in the hill, and Xavier was clearly making an effort to get up to speed and maintain some dignity in the face of the priest's obvious fitness.

"I would never have suggested this if I had known you'd be so uncomfortable. Last year you didn't have so much trouble with your joints, as I recall," Claire said.

"I'm fine, I'm fine!" he protested. "It's just all those years of banging my knees around, a couple of accidents, and now I just have to live with it. You should have seen me a few years ago on my bike!"

Claire's patience and sympathy were running thin. "Well, Fabienne knew you then, as she's making clear every five minutes! I don't really need this, and it's hard to enjoy something I had really looked forward to with her around."

"Well, your pal Fresnay is here, so we're not exactly alone!"

"I thought he was becoming your friend, as well. And he's a priest, not an ex-lover! That's completely different."

"And she was always mostly a friend. Can you understand that? And now she's really only a friend, so let her be."

"Me let her be." Claire paused to collect her temper. She re-pinned some of her flying hair back away from her damp forehead. "*Me* let *her* be. Okaaaay."

Xavier had already started up the slope and sheer willpower seemed to have temporarily cured his arthritic knees.

Fresnay and Fabienne must have been waiting for some minutes when Xavier and Claire caught up with them. Fabienne looked cheerful in a forced way, and there was a wariness in her eyes.

Still, the view was breathtaking, looking beyond the little two-alley village of Hamtin's tall, skinny Chinese houses, beyond the dilapidated village wall of toppling stones, beyond the

stretch of thick low brush and paddyfields to one of the broad-
est, whitest, and most untouched beaches in Hong Kong, Hamtin. One backpacker's lonely orange tent sat defying the Pacific
winds on a bluff at the southern end of the beach, but otherwise,
the scene was unbroken and natural.

*"Incroyable, n'est-ce pas?"* Fresnay helped Fabienne unload
a camera to take some pictures, while Xavier favored the
weaker knee with a massage for a minute or two.

"Don't forget, going down can be rougher on your legs than
going up," the priest warned them, but Claire felt like a colt
returning to the stable, or in this case, one of Ah Fok's cooling
beers on the cement veranda of his little two-burner café. There
were familiar faces greeting them from the benches and tables
Ah Fok had added for the Christmas Eve festivities. A Chinese
professor and hiking aficionado had brought a new girlfriend,
and an Irish gym teacher from Kowloon had gamely dragged
his seventy-year-old mother along the same path the day before.

On the side of the veranda, a local crone in a broad circular
straw hat edged with bobbing black cotton balls laughed a
toothless greeting and waved one hand in recognition, then
grabbed Caspar without anybody's permission and stroked his
hair and shrieked, *"Ho leung jai, ah,"* sturdy little fellow, at the
top of her lungs.

Fresnay lost no time in settling them in rooms along the row
of empty houses, long abandoned now by the children of farm-
ers for a life in the crowded industrial neighborhoods of Kowloon. Claire could hear the priest showering under a hose
behind his house as he prepared to offer his tiny congregation
their Christmas Mass, so she fed Caspar in a corner of their large
cement-floored house, and washed herself off in a sunken stone
basin that had once served as the cooking wok for the former
tenants.

The little chapel behind Ah Fok's café was her favorite place
of worship in the world, and as she and Xavier took the Host
from their friend's hand, Claire prayed fervently that the con-

tentment she felt within the cool plaster walls would last. She prayed for Vicky and Ian, she prayed for Leo and his parents, and she dared to pray that her doubts about her future with Xavier would be dispelled somehow, sometime very soon.

As she prayed, the day's small and large fears subsided, draining out of her as she knelt by Xavier's side. She took his hand. She loved him and she could not afford to lose him and this new happiness for the sake of her pride. As soon as he asked her to marry him again, *if* he asked again, she was going to say yes without hesitation.

As soon as Fresnay clapped his hands together and said, "The Mass is ended, go in peace," Caspar woke up and started crying.

Laughing, they all retired to Ah Fok's veranda. Fresnay slapped some French accordion music into Ah Fok's battered cassette player and started dancing with the wailing, purply bundle. To Claire's astonishment, Fabienne grabbed *her* and started a sort of jitterbug, dancing the way French girls do together, without any of the self-consciousness engulfing Claire.

Claire's awkward torment ended within a minute or two, and they settled down to their well-earned beers, while Xavier returned from Fresnay's weekend house only a few feet from the café in a pair of knee-length shorts. One knee looked awful, visibly swollen.

"Let's open our presents now!" proclaimed Fabienne.

"Fine," said Claire. After five minutes' hustle and bustle in different directions, they reassembled at the small table and began Christmas formalities. For Caspar, Fresnay produced a tiny pair of overalls with the words, "Future Foreign Devil," embroidered on the back in Chinese and on the front in English. "Might as well be prepared for the worst," they laughed together.

"This is for you," Claire said to Xavier shyly producing the tiny box. Xavier looked very touched when he opened it and tried to set the alarm. It gave off a clear, musical chime. "Very elegant, and I can't wait to wake up in some comfortable hotel to this, instead of that little 'hiccup, hiccup' at four in the morning when that guy wants his breakfast!"

Fabienne couldn't let this rest unchallenged. "Only an American would buy a Swiss an American-made clock!" she said, trying to pass this off as a joke, and hoping the others would see how obvious Claire's miscalculation would be. Xavier chuckled, because frankly, he too, thought it was a funny thing to receive a timepiece not made in Switzerland.

"Here are my presents," Fabienne smiled, and as they were opened, Claire realized that the gloves she had coughed up for Fabienne were too large for the woman's delicate hands. Fabienne had bought a small bottle of perfume for Claire and for Xavier, an elegant sleek Swiss Army knife.

"But I have one already!" he said, producing his battered Victorinox.

"But the corkscrew is still broken, isn't it?" There was no mistaking the love and familiarity in her voice—some damn shared memory again, thought Claire with angry frustration!

Fresnay was staring fixedly at Xavier's left knee. "That needs some kind of poultice overnight, if you ever want to see Hong Kong again," urged Fresnay. "Since the eleventh century, monks have used rosemary to ease swelling. There's still lots of it in my kitchen garden. Let's give it a try." The industrious scholar was also a superb chef, growing standard herbs on a stretch of ricefield alongside Ah Fok's kitchen. Claire followed him carefully along the rows of basil, oregano, thyme, lovage, and finally, "Ahhh, here it is . . . *ros marinus*, fond of the sea. That's why it's doing so well in this sea air."

He spent some minutes in the kitchen, and Claire accompanied him inside to watch as he worked away at grinding up a huge pan of the spiky branches and then mixing the fresh needles into a paste of isoprophyl alcohol, some of Ah Fok's rice starch for thickening and wadding it all into gauze which he wrapped tightly around the mean-looking knee.

Maybe it was just the support of the bandage, but Xavier

managed one slow dance with Claire before they all sat down to heaping plates of pasta covered with freshly grated Parmesan cheese and salad, with a dessert of fruit and a tart heated up in Fresnay's little oven inside his humble but comfortable getaway.

The sun had long disappeared behind them, retracing with its fading rays the footpath to the west of them that they had struggled to conquer. Ah Fok brought out old-fashioned green mosquito coils, placing one at each corner of the little cement terrace. A brash bare bulb illuminated the terrace, but a string of colored Christmas lights along Fresnay's windows facing them told Claire that the priest, who seemed so cerebral and independent of emotional ties, had lovingly prepared for his guests with a wonderful sentiment he was shy of expressing in more obvious ways.

The wine and beer were flowing and they chatted with the other visitors sitting at nearby tables, while Ah Fok's mother, the crone who wouldn't relinquish Caspar any more than she intended to relinquish life, rocked him vigorously.

"I think this pad may be working on my knee. Can you make another for my other knee?" Xavier ventured over his third glass of wine.

"Certainly, one for every bone in your old body!" Fresnay teased him, "But don't think for a moment, man, you can ingest my magic potion. Excessive doses taken internally are fatal!"

"You're kidding," said Claire. "We eat rosemary all the time and it doesn't do me any harm."

"But not in the doses they tried in the Middle Ages. People believed that drinking infusions of rosemary water would do away with all the evils of the body, but found that too much of a good thing killed them as surely as a poison," Fresnay said, clearly in all seriousness.

Claire started, remembering her intention to tap Fresnay's encyclopedic brain. "What about monkshood? Do you know anything about that? Ever heard of it?"

Fresnay looked at her with surprise. "Of course!" He looked off into the distance. "Aconitum . . ."

"That right! Aconite!"

"Derived from *akno*, or dark in Greek," interrupted Xavier who never lost an opportunity to remind everyone he had studied Greek in a Swiss monastery school for eight years.

Fresnay nodded. "The shape of its flower resembles the cowl of the Benedictines, your friends, Xavier, which is why we Jesuits all know how sinister this stuff is," he chuckled. "According to Greek mythology, the poison of the monkshood was the foam that dripped from the mouth of the mythical three-headed dog Cerberus, when Hercules performed his twelfth labor and dragged it from Hell. Whenever the dog spit, these plants sprouted. Many educated Europeans would know it, because we learn in history that in ancient times monkshood was used to poison wells and springs in the face of the invading enemy. And it was used among common people as a sort of working class alternative to hemlock. It was a sort of classical form of euthanasia, forced on the infirm and old when people wanted to get rid of them."

There was an appreciative silence filled only by the cheerful fingering of the accordionist on the cassette player at the back of the veranda.

"It was found in Petey Sandford during the autopsy," Claire announced at last. "The forensic men told the police it might be some kind of flower Petey ate randomly while playing around the *nullah*."

Fresnay looked meaningfully straight back at her. "We must explain this to Inspector Slaughter right away, so that he doesn't spend another day wandering the hills in vain."

"What do you mean, Robert?"

"There is little likelihood that Petey just stumbled across a plant like that in the wild. Someone must have fed it to him intentionally."

Claire looked at Xavier. "But everybody has agreed that Petey had an epileptic fit. The police, his doctor, his *amah*, even his mother, who is a close friend of mine, accepts that."

Xavier wasn't so sure. "You're thinking that possibly someone fed him the poison and it was mistaken for one of his seizures, Robert?"

"If I had to guess tonight, I would say that the discovery of this substance in Petey is hardly likely to be an accident."

Claire looked at the priest straight in the eyes. "What you're saying is that—"

"That this has a bearing on Leo's disappearance beyond what the police already suspect. That you may be living, not with some random snatcher who spied on Leo and grabbed him for his charming looks when the opportunity arose, but with a very well-educated, very determined, and very, very sick murderer hiding in your midst."

# chapter
## ten

It was impossible to reach John Slaughter on Christmas Day, even though they left messages for him everywhere they could think of, and Father Fresnay, who possessed the only telephone in the village of Tailong, spent half his morning speaking Cantonese to various Chinese constables left on duty. Tomorrow was Saturday, so Claire swallowed the frustration of returning to Tregunter Path with her fears doubled, and no more answers than during those last few days of horror since Petey's death and Leo's disappearance.

Fresnay had left before nine for his solo hike back to Central. Claire was amused to see that, having warmly offered his private Mass to friends in Tailong, the next day's schedule of standing-room-only Masses and confessions with all the professional aplomb of a corporate CEO giving shareholders the annual general report.

Hong Kong's harbor was jammed full of junks, ferries, small sampans and tugs—and most dramatic to see from the hills above—military ships. Destroyers, cruisers, ships of all sizes and nationalities were still arriving for Christmas leave. Would this wonderful tradition, which always culminated with these hundreds of ships blaring their horns on midnight, New Year's Eve, end soon with the takeover by Beijing? Claire wondered sadly.

Central District was full of beautifully dressed and made-up Filipinas attending Christmas Masses, while the English-style pubs were full of sailors of all nationalities, some of them were spilling out into the streets of Wanchai, beers in one hand, girl-friends in the other, singing Christmas carols in an unseasonal midday blaze.

All of this was punctuated by the racket of construction. The resounding boom of pile drivers was a reminder that this was an Asian Christmas, and with the handover to Beijing imminent, only nominally a Western outpost any longer. While a few hundred thousand Westerners and Filipinos celebrated Christ's birthday, it was still Friday morning, a working day for millions of others in soon-to-be China, where speculation and profit would always reign unchallenged by mere concerns of the soul.

They dropped Fabienne off at her hotel. She said she would spend the rest of her day running over in a jetfoil to Macao to photograph holiday festivities. There was a children's choir of Vietnamese refugees singing on the steps of the ruins of the Church of St. Paul's and a Portuguese Christmas parade.

Meanwhile, there were thousands of Filipinas in their festive flounces, laces, and red and gold high heels streaming into and around St. Joseph's Church on Garden Road in Central. The largest corporate landlord in the city, Hong Kong Land, had installed a towering tree flown down from the northen Manchurian reaches of China in the atrium of Central's cathedral to consumerism, the Landmark Shopping Center. In the middle of this incongruous setting, splat in the middle between the Dior and Versace boutiques, a bagpipe band would be playing snippets of Handel. Middle-class Chinese who had the day off would be at sporting events or shopping malls—eyeballing goods that would be quickly marked down over the next few weeks in time for a mammoth shopping spree in time for the city's true annual holiday, the Lunar New Year break.

To her secret surprise, Claire genuinely wished Fabienne well, and as soon as she had waved the woman off as sincerely as she could without actually going, "Whoopee," she quickly forgot her. She hoped Dovie had remembered to turn on the Christmas tree lights for their homecoming. Connie had packed up her things and moved out by now. Dovie wouldn't return to work until Monday, although Claire knew that after she spent Christmas Day with her daughter, she was spending the weekend finishing her move into the servant's room at the back. Now that Connie had decamped, Dovie would be able to shove back the rolling wall and occupy the entire space.

So Claire would be with her man and child in their own home for the very first Christmas of her new life. Xavier drove in silence and she sat quietly, almost contently now, but as the festive atmosphere of the city faded from earshot below, Claire couldn't help noticing the grim aspect of Tregunter Path all over again.

For the first time, she noticed fluttering papers tacked to the railings along the sidewalk. Leo Franklin's smiling face stared out at them from reward posters attached to all the lamplights and fences along Cotton Tree Drive, along May Road, and finally, flapping in the sunny bluster of the late winter morning, from Tregunter Path itself. Giles Franklin's reward for information alone was half a million Hong Kong dollars. Obviously, no one had come forward yet.

Claire knew it would be a very difficult day for the Sandford family. And she had put off asking them if Grover belonged to Petey for fear of upsetting Vicky. Nevertheless, she intended to pay her holiday respects at a quiet drinks gathering they had planned for the 26th in lieu of a funeral reception. The day after Christmas was known to the English, and therefore most of

Hong Kong, as Boxing Day, when it was customary to throw open the doors for relatives and friends. This year, Miriam Forsythe had called to say that it was meant as a sort of memorial get-together for friends who hadn't been able to make the funeral. Claire thought she would find the moment with Vicky then to return Petey's things.

So today would be unnaturally quiet for Xavier and Claire. As they collapsed, knapsacks dumped onto the sofa, and shoes shrugged off sore feet, into their under-decorated living room, the tree stood near the large picture window, its backdrop the balcony and beyond, the glittering harbor. The tree's colored lights were twinkling, just as Claire had hoped, but there seemed to be so many of them! The ornaments she had feared were too few shone from every angle of the branches. She left Xavier standing there, drinking in this all-American spectacle with a look of amusement and affection on his face, while she laid the sleeping Caspar in his crib and came back and entwined one arm in his.

"So if you celebrate Christmas with the whole family on Christmas Eve, what's left over for the 25th?" she asked Xavier shyly.

"That's when the very private celebrations begin," he said, warmly taking her in his arms.

---

The Sandfords' party was bound to be a subdued affair. On arriving, Claire's first duty was to say hello at last to Miriam and Gordon and introduce Xavier, and then to deposit Caspar in Petey's old nursery. Claire paused in the tiny, too-neat, little room, and gazed at all the toys sorted away by Manny: the Thomas the Tank Engine slippers, the plastic dinosaurs in a row on the shelf, the foam alphabet blocks, surrounded by striped wallpaper with its trim of clowns dancing under the edge of the ceiling. It was so deathly tidy here.

She stashed her baby bag, with its supply of diapers, bottle, and Petey's Grover and cassette tape under the crib for later, if the moment came. Caspar settled comfortably into the crib for his post-brunch nap and Claire sighed, returning to the Sandfords' living room with an even heavier sense of their loss, if that was possible, than before.

She saw a brace of older people catching the fresh air on the balcony, but decided against joining them, and for the moment, seized on Gordon's offer of a gin-and-tonic and braced herself for a solacing chat with the bereaved grandfather.

"Quite a loss, our little chap," said Gordon. He added his thanks for Claire's support for Vicky, and Claire demurred, and so the formalities continued for a few minutes. Gordon was bearing up well, and soon she found herself in the middle of a political conversation between Gordon and Ian.

"I'm not entirely convinced the results had so much to do with democracy, or any understanding of political parties," Ian was saying, apparently about the last round of colonial elections before the 1997 takeover. "A couple of independents—one of them was that columnist, Margaret Ng—she got a tremendous vote just on the basis of her personality, I think."

Gordon nodded. "Well, it was their last chance to show the Communists they want these elections to continue after the handover. In England, the reporting made it seem like a clear-cut victory for the democrats, something to really stick in the craw of the Party."

Ian laughed and sipped his drink. "I think what stuck in their craw was that the Communist elements ran their own candidates in elections they condemned outright, and then were completely, utterly trounced. Beijing claimed it had to do with their lack of election experience, *of course* nothing to do with their pro-China, anti-democracy positions. So they turn around and appoint a rubber stamp Provisional Legislature on the basis of nothing but their own whims. Which just shows how much good faith they put into their guarantee of elections in the first place."

"Oh, surely back in 1984 they intended to keep their promises. I simply won't believe people who think that Thatcher would sign a document of that historical weight in bad faith. Not like the old girl," Gordon argued.

Claire agreed. "I think it's not really about elections anyway. They'll hold their elections in due course, and manage to make it look like they stuck in form to the Agreement. It's the content, not the form, that I'm worried about. The Communists are going to have their finger in every pie, whoever is elected to Legco. My friends in the local press tell me that there is already a *bo suk*, a Communist party 'uncle,' sitting in on every single editorial meeting in town, watching everyone who goes in and out of the office of the editor-in-chief from his new desk directly across the corridor—"

"—Even at the *Post* and the *Standard?*" Gordon interrupted.

"Of course," Claire shrugged. "It was a decision taken right over the head of the editor-in-chief. The owner Robert Kwok isn't about to offend Beijing. He intends to keep doing property deals with them for a long, long time. And up in Beijing, they're having meetings in the Hong Kong and Macao Affairs Office every week about how to turn Hong Kong into another ruffle-free Singapore—no free press, docile judiciary, controlled elections. Lee Kuan Yew has been personally advising them for years."

"Another Singapore? God help Hong Kong," muttered Gordon, who had seen the rancorous split between the Malays and Lee Kuan Yew in the early sixties. "What else do your friends in Beijing tell you?"

"Well, it's not just the press. A friend of mine who works in the Beijing press corps overheard an official saying with great satisfaction that since around '91 or '92, the Communist Party has had a live body sitting in all the main corporate offices of every foreign company represented in the city, if not actually on the board—"

Ian nodded, "Gordon, you must have read how they strong-armed our board into giving them a big chunk of our airlines shares at a discount to a company under direct State Council control."

Claire nodded, "And you heard that they're lining up their ducks to get control of Hong Kong Telecom? Another case of 'greenmail.' Threaten the local monopoly with mainland Communist competition and the local has no choice but to hand a piece of the action over to Beijing."

Gordon sighed and drank his gin. "Yes. Wouldn't have believed your bosses would have caved in if you told me ten years ago."

"Everybody talks about something dramatic happening on July first," Claire said, "but the Chinese are working so hard to make sure that if anything changes, it happens once all the foreign journalists and CNN go home. After all, they have all the time in the world. They're already making it clear to each journalist that we have to show our loyalty one way or another or we won't get visas into the mainland. The sinister part is that their grasp will slowly tighten, the fingers will slowly close without ever looking hamfisted. I heard out of New York that Beijing had already hired Burston and Marsteller to handle C. H. Tung's public relations six months ago, when he was only officially elected—what, two weeks ago?"

Gordon turned to Claire, "It's all good grist for you overseas reporters, eh? Won't you be sitting in the press box at the handover ceremony?"

"Of course I'll be there, but as the years have rolled closer to the date, it doesn't strike me as the Big Bang we envisioned when they signed the deal in '84," she said thoughtfully. "More of the proverbial whimper than . . . well, maybe it's just the change in my personal perspective. Before the baby, I thought about it nonstop, one of the big, big stories you could actually look forward to filing. Over 8,300 foreign reporters with their camera crews, support teams, God knows what, have applied for credentials so far with the Governor's information office. But lately, I've been off work, of course, and frankly, I've been so upset about Petey and Leo—"

It was the kind of feminine response that practically ensured the two men would turn away slightly and drift back to business. Claire felt a tug at her elbow and turned to see the white quiff of Alistair Evans-Smith on her right.

"How's Dovie working out?" he asked. "Everything all right?"

"Oh, hello! Of course, you worked with Gordon years ago, didn't you?" Claire shouldn't have been surprised to see the old colonial Asia hands stick together.

"Actually, we're going to be seeing a lot more of them in England once I join Althea. We have a cottage in England not far from their village. We've been family friends for years. I think it was Gordon who nicknamed the Evans family on the low ground below the village, the 'Evans-Below'—"

Claire laughed, "Making you the 'Evans-Above'?"

"Precisely. Anyway, Dovie making out all right?"

"Well, she had a little set-to with our temporary *amah* over saying prayers of protection at Caspar's cribside, dripping candle wax on his mattress in the process."

"Oh, Good Lord, Dovie wouldn't stand for that kind of Popery, I'm sure."

"My confidence in her doubled because she told me right away. One thing that has been hitting me all week is how these Filipinas stick together, even to the point that they won't tell us the most terrifying things going on in those back corridors. Actually, there's something else I'd like to talk to you about. Something that troubles me, but I can't really raise it with Inspector Slaughter, because it might do the person in question a lot of unnecessary harm."

Evans-Smith and she slipped out of the living room and found a quieter corner in the study around the corner. Claire was not surprised to find it was clearly Ian's sanctuary, filled with photos of him playing rugby with the airline's team and a collection of antique toy planes lined along the shelf above the television.

There Claire unburdened her tale of the night at the transvestite club with Xavier and Fabienne. Evans-Smith didn't hide his astonishment.

"You're sure it was this same Inspector Crowley?"

"Well, I think the roll of film must still be in Fabienne's possession, if there is any doubt. But yes, I'm sure it was Crowley. It just left a terrible shadow in my mind over his being there right on the scene of Petey's death. You know, I'm afraid it's some kind of unacknowledged homophobia buried inside me just leaping out and raising questions about his relationship with Petey that are just inappropriate."

Evans-Smith seemed distracted by something else. Finally, he spoke up. "I never go to Lan Kwai Fong myself, since my bailiwick tends to land me at clan festivals drenched in incense and gongs, not feather boas and beer," he chuckled. "But you're old enough to remember when buggery was a capital offense in the colony. Never took it off the books until the early '80s."

"Of course I remember."

"For years, Chinese up in Beijing gave us pretty strong signals they wouldn't let us decriminalize it—kind of a convoluted argument that it was alien to the nature of the new Chinese Socialist Man, and an English vice."

"Well, it's not as if the police and legal circles didn't have their scandals," Claire recalled. "Remember that policeman's murder or suicide, that policeman found dead in the room and shot over and over? Remember he was about to name homosexuals in the police force?"

"Yes. Those were rough days for all of us. Goodness, times have changed if coppers are prancing around in public in drag!" Evans-Smith said emphatically, slapping his thigh in surprise.

"Well, I'm not so sure it was in public, so to speak. His act is unbelievably convincing, he does it anonymously, and I only identified him through a telephoto lens. I think everybody else was too inebriated to care who he was," Claire reflected. "Anyway, would it matter if the very senior ranks knew?"

Ian suddenly popped his head in, "Refresh your drinks?" But Claire knew it was really to make sure she wasn't trying to work on family time—grilling an invited guest. Ian was the sort of corporate personality who suspected reporters of taking advantage of every waking minute to invade the privacy of others. He only respected Vicky's friendship with Claire from a slightly wary perspective.

Evans-Smith waved Ian away reassuringly and turned back to Claire. "Of course, the police force wouldn't be able to officially drum Crowley out of town, but it would look very closely at him from now on, you know, check his record for any signs of putting a foot wrong. You say he's on Tregunter Path every day? I don't like the sound of those jokes about little boys, I must say—"

Claire leaned forward and felt she had to whisper, "Exactly. But if I raise anything with John Slaughter, I might be doing an innocent man real harm to his career. He's entitled to his hobbies, I guess, and in fact, he's remarkably talented in a way. Nobody's ever accused me of being judgmental about homosexuality before, but recently I saw a report in the *Herald Tribune* about child pornography and pimping little boys to respectable men and it made me sick. Of course, now that I have a little boy of my own, I'm getting a little paranoid about the entire outside world. I feel like raising him in a social bubble just to keep him safe."

Evans-Smith patted her shoulder and rose to return to the party. "If Caspar turns out to be anything like his mother, he wouldn't sit still for life in a bubble very long. One thing I learned with Viola and Freddy, you can't save them from their own destiny." His face clouded and he said abruptly, "Leave this Crowley matter to me, my dear," and returned to the party.

Vicky found Claire sitting alone in the study a few minutes later. "Everything all right?" Vicky asked.

"Shouldn't I be asking you that?" Claire replied.

"I'm not exactly fine. But I'm putting one foot in front of the other. Really. I'll tell you an awful confession. It's almost better that Daddy and Mummy are going home tomorrow. I want to be alone with Ian, or just sit in this room and be with Petey, and take care of myself without having to put up with Mummy's constantly asking me if I'm all right."

"Sorry."

"Really."

"Vicky, may I show you something? Or rather, return something to you, not to upset you, but because it's something that belonged to Petey."

Vicky looked understandably startled and stiffened a little. "Of course."

Claire moved across the hallway quickly into the little nursery and brought back the baby bag. "I found this in the most unlikely spot. Way up the footpath above the road here, and looking as if it were hidden very deliberately." She tugged Grover out of the bag, but Vicky had gasped even before Claire had managed to deposit the well-worn toy in her lap.

"This too. I recognized your handwriting."

"My God, this tape! I chucked it into the rubbish bin almost a year ago. I had to on Doctor Trythall's orders."

"What?"

"Claire, I can't tell you how strange this is!"

"Vicky, you know I don't understand."

Vicky looked up at Claire, and took a deep sigh. "Well, I wondered about Grover last Monday or Tuesday—I can't remember when it hit me he was missing—because Petey never went anywhere without him. It was all Manny could do to get Grover out of his arms long enough to wash him every few weeks. But that's not what I can't understand. It's this tape. It makes no sense." Vicky's hands were clenched tightly around the cassette.

Claire waited and waited, feeling the edges of her patience fray as Vicky fell into a cryptic silence, lost in her own frantic search for an explanation.

"Vicky? Vicky!"

"There has to be an explanation of this. Do you remember when Inspector Crowley was here? I told him there were certain triggers, like little electrical connections, that might fire off in Petey's mind, things like noise, or stress or certain things, specific things that could set Petey off. It's one of the strangest things about his sort of epilepsy."

"Yes. So?"

"Well, the songs on this tape seemed to disturb Petey. It wasn't anything we could make out, I mean, we didn't know why or how. Dr. Trythall had monitored Petey closely and said if there was any reason to suspect the tape, just bung it down the rubbish chute at the back. And we did."

"When?"

"Well, that's it. I mean, let's see, it would have been last spring sometime."

"Did anybody else know about this tape?"

"I told Manny not to save it. Sometimes she found Petey putting things in the wastebasket that shouldn't have been there, so she tended to be careful. But I specifically told her this tape had to go."

"She didn't understand. Maybe she saved it, worried she might be doing the wrong thing."

"She's always been devoted to him, especially because her own son died, you know." Vicky looked at the Grover toy. "I'll put this up with his other things. Petey loved him so."

Claire took the Grover from Vicky, who was starting to cry, and placed him firmly on the highest shelf.

"Don't you want the tape, too?" Claire said offering it up.

"I hope I never see it again," Vicky said, brushing it away with her hand. Claire put it back into her baby bag and they left the study together, arms linked and returned to the living room.

---

Claire had already determined she would spend Sunday evening at the piano. It was, she had explained to Xavier, her Christmas present to herself. For someone who had studied the piano to an almost professional level, it was amazing she had left the keyboard untouched for so many weeks. It was a measure, she reflected, of her intense love affair with Caspar, an attachment so filled with joy and doubts from the very first hours of labor, all other pleasures had became secondary. The distractions had compounded since then and she sat down on the piano bench and rested her hands on the keyboard lovingly, as if it was a reunion with a neglected old friend.

Xavier had promised that while she played, he would take Caspar for a long walk along Queen's Pier in Central to show him the neon Christmas lights flooding both sides of the harbor and shimmering back off the waters. Claire wondered if Xavier needed some time alone and said nothing as her two men had set off on the shuttle bus bundled in warm clothes against the wet breezes coming off the water.

She pulled out her piles of music and furiously tackled the exercises in Hanon first. She had done these scales and finger puzzles in machine-gun time for thirty years now and her fingers scarcely needed coaching from the pages as she spent nearly twenty minutes on her warm-up. "Pumping ivory," her teacher had called it. Her mind relaxed into the routine, worries receded by the rhythmic rise and fall of her hands. Then she stopped and flexed her fingers. The apartment was so quiet. She realized she was completely alone.

Xavier, Caspar, Dovie—they were all of them gone. She didn't feel as comfortable as she had hoped.

She returned to her music, working through a favorite Grieg

piece and then tackled "Fast zu ernst" from Schumann's *Kin-derszenen*, a syncopated piece with five sharps that eluded her. She had to stop repeatedly as her fingers seemed to be deter-mined to tangle themselves among the black keys. With each pause in the music, the silence of the darkening living room closed in on her. She tackled the music more intently each time. She started again but it really wasn't the pleasure she had imag-ined so happily when Xavier had asked what gift he could give her.

She put her hands into her lap. A chill seemed to hang over her shoulders from the wall behind her bench. She felt so very, very unprotected and alone. Of course, it was the external wall of the building and being solid concrete, it was likely to be colder than the rest of the building.

She played ruthlessly now, forcing her fingers along, even though their stiffness disturbed her. The old adage about prac-tice—"The first day of missed practice, you notice, the second day your teacher notices, and the third day your audience no-tices,"—certainly rang true. She would get it back, she thought, but it wasn't the trade-off of Caspar for dexterity that was trou-bling her. Something in the silence of the room mocked her good intentions.

She stopped playing again. There was no sound at all, even the pile drivers and hum of construction had stopped early to-day.

She turned on the small lamp that sat on one side of the piano. She started again, but Schumann's phrases wouldn't come smoothly. She shoved him aside and tried something to keep her interest. She was so rarely alone these days, why waste the time on the gloomy thoughts that kept intruding? She tried something grand, some Paganini variations. She'd just started when a knock on the front door startled her so much she half-jumped off the piano bench and knocked the sheet music on the floor.

Standing frozen, staring at the front door, Claire was strongly tempted not to open it. There was no denying she was afraid. She wasn't expecting anyone. What was she afraid of? Thank God Caspar was with his father, safely far away in the harborside crowd. It came to her without any warning that she felt guilty. She had been meddling in the whole affair of the little boys and she had no business approaching Ip, turning Crowley's innocent music hall routine into something sinister, half-interrogating Vicky about a harmless tape.

The ringing continued and then someone started pounding on the door, again and again. She waited, bewildered at her own state of indecision. She was actually backing out of the living room when she heard a voice.

"Claire! I know you're in there, Madame! Open the door and tell Xavier to pour a man of Christ some wine!"

Fresnay! She ran to the door and let the priest in, with a wave of relief. What had she been thinking of? "Xavier isn't here. He's taken Caspar out for a walk. Please come in."

Fresnay hesitated, and Claire remembered that for all of his motorcycling, hiking, and dining-out habits, he was always mindful of his priestly profile in a godless city. He was wary of gossips and didn't like to visit a woman alone.

"I'll just stay for a moment then, but I thought it couldn't wait. I still haven't been able to reach Inspector Slaughter by telephone, but I expect I'll talk to him tomorrow about this whole affair."

Fresnay leaned in the doorway and fingered the strap of his bike helmet carefully, clearly pondering his words before he spoke. "You see, something else has come up, and I think you can help, as you live in the building. I want to talk to your *amah*."

"Well, Connie has left for another job and Dovie went to visit her daughter for the evening. Why?"

"Well, I heard confessions through Christmas Masses all yesterday—most of them Filipinas, of course. It was the usual, you know, hours and hours of impure thoughts, gossiping unnecessarily, and fiddling the grocery money. Then without breaking the seal of the confessional, I can tell you this much. A woman came into the box and her voice was shaking with fear. She confessed she wanted forgiveness for conversing with 'the Devil.' The 'Devil' that is killing children on Tregunter Path."

"No! So they know who it is! The *amahs*, I mean!"

"At least one does, indeed. I don't know the identity of this woman, and even if I did, I'm bound to keep it secret. I don't know how reliable she is. She rabbitted on and on, 'The Devil knows my sins and the Devil will get me, too.'"

"Those were her exact words?"

"Oh, I won't forget her words, lass. Exactly as follows: 'Everyone always thinks the Devil looks like a man, but he can look like a woman, too.' Then she started sobbing in the confessional box and before I could even blurt out some kind of penance for her to say, she was headed out the door."

Fresnay looked sheepishly at Claire. "I must confess something myself. I shouldn't have done it, but I stuck my head out of the door just in time to see the back of a Filipina in a heavy coat rushing to the back of the church. I've heard a lot of things in my time, but I don't mind telling you this gave me chills. Because, well, simply because it had the ring of truth."

# chapter eleven

## – Sunday –

Claire could not sleep Saturday night. She tossed back and forth, painfully aware that Caspar might awake for his breakfast feed as early as five, leaving her no hope of a deep doze in the remaining hours.

The meaning of the *amah*'s confession was crystal clear to her, if not to Fresnay. Had Fresnay been to the nightclub with the three of them on Tuesday night, he would have accused her of jumping to premature conclusions. For pretty much the same reason, she didn't mention her thoughts that morning to Xavier. Claire was sure this was no theological discussion Fresnay had heard. "Everyone always thinks the Devil looks like a man, but he can look like a woman, too," was obviously a possible description from a simple woman from the Philippine archipelago of Crowley's antics in drag.

Somehow the *amahs* knew more, but would they risk telling the police whatever it was they had seen or heard? Naturally, they would be wary of Crowley. She had seen that fear on

Manny's nervous expression from the very first, when the poor woman asked Claire to stay and witness her interview with the officer in her own quarters. If Manny's story of seeking help from Crowley wasn't true, no one knew better than Crowley how she had lied.

Now, could she prevail on Manny to tell the truth? Manny knew Crowley could have her or any of the *amahs* deported back to the Philippines in a matter of days on some trumped-up immigration charge, and was the Labour Tribunal going to take up a case against a Hong Kong policeman? Not likely.

Claire finally rose, hollow-eyed, to Xavier's offer of a welcome coffee. She wondered to herself if Fresnay had reached Chief Inspector Slaughter about the significance of the traces of aconite in Petey's stomach. Now she realized that however Petey had injested the poison, aconite might be a complete red herring, perhaps even an inaccurate identification from the lab.

Maybe the police should be thinking in a completely different direction. Following the lead of an exotic poison was unlikely to connect with finding Leo Franklin's whereabouts. Claire wondered if she should talk to Fresnay again, but realized that it was Sunday. In other words, it was an unusually busy working day for Hong Kong's priests down at the Catholic Centre, facing shift after shift of crowded Tagalog Masses, great distaff assemblies of prematurely aging virgins and lonely wives and mothers. But that thought led to another; today was a day off for most of the *amahs*, and possibly Manny and her friends would be returning to the picnic site for their usual mix of prayer and partying.

Around eleven, she left Caspar sleeping in Xavier's lap in the study, and set off for the picnic site. She wasn't sure how to approach the group, how many there would be, or even whether Manny would be willing to talk to her in private. At least her hunch was right; she heard women's voices singing to guitar strumming coming from the clearing on the hill above her and she quickened her pace along the Path, over the bridge just wide enough for a single car that spanned the drainage *nullah*, and to the entrance of the familiar footpath ascending to the Peak.

She paused. The music had stopped and she heard a low chant of prayers, very light, like Tagalog ripples along the recital of rosary beads. She didn't intend to interrupt their prayers, so she started up the footpath and aimed to pass their gathering and settle a little bit above them to wait for their lunch to begin.

Sure enough, she could see four women, kneeling on garish beach towels in the dirt of the construction site reciting Hail Marys, the gaudy clear plastic pink and blue beads of their rosaries catching the sun. It was a startling tableau to see these women removed from their hours of servitude. In a way they had become entirely different females.

With their hair dressed, their faces made-up, their plain blue and white uniforms discarded for the day in favor of tight denim jeans, bright shirts, hair ornaments and incongruous high heels, they seemed to have morphed into fully-fledged female citizens. Having painted their faces, they seemed to Claire to have reclaimed their personalities from the anonymity of domestic service.

Manny, being the oldest, was the least flashy; she wore a black dress with a white collar and black flats. Claire noticed Regina, one of the girls who had prayed with Narcisa in the carpark, but Narcisa wasn't there. The other two girls looked familiar from the neighborhood.

Claire resigned herself to a long wait. In fact, she was losing interest, her idle thoughts drifting dangerously back to Xavier and Fabienne and wondering if they had arranged any other meetings behind her back, besides the office encounter the previous Wednesday, when suddenly Manny took up the guitar and started strumming a loud song. The other three women joined her in song, and for a few seconds, it sounded like nothing more than a modern religious tune—trite, and certainly an insult to the ears of any god who had once enjoyed the services of Handel and Mozart.

The strumming grew more insistent, and without warning, Regina began to switch from singing to a kind of moaning babble. Claire strained her ears for clues of Tagalog dialect, but nothing she could make out from where she sat sounded like language. The utterances were more animal in nature.

Taking her cue from Regina, the third woman, whom Claire now recognized as an employee at the Tavistock building, and the fourth woman joined in with their own uncoordinated mumblings and groans, their bodies starting to shake and hands waving rhythmically up and down according to some otherworldly dictate.

The sight frightened Claire, who felt she had intruded on something too private, it smacked so much of sexual hysteria. Only Manny remained cogent, strumming the guitar undisturbed by the wildness emerging around her, with an unemotional expression Claire found stranger than the antics of the three younger women. It was almost as if Manny had incited them into these fits intentionally, and the longer it went on, the more Claire realized that this was a ritual of some sort. She had heard of the Charismatic movement, an evangelical offshoot of the Catholic Church that priests like Fresnay frowned upon, but could do little to stem in a relatively uneducated community of Filipinas. It was so unrelated to the cerebral theology Claire had been raised with, it was unrecognizable as the same religion.

In fact, Claire found it amost unbearably embarrassing to watch, and just when she started to think of abandoning her mission, the unearthly performance started to wind down. Slowly, the three twitching, howling women drew themselves together, and at Manny's behest joined hands and began to sing another simpering song, this time in English about being all one together that made Claire think of home Masses of the sixties back in Berkeley with her parents working hard to seize on the results of Vatican II.

When the song ended, the party began and finally Claire felt free to show herself by walking back down the Path and waving hello to Manny. Manny nodded and smiled, apparently assuming Claire was striding down the footpath like just another jogger. She looked startled when Claire turned toward them and entered the circle of construction piles.

"Manny, could I talk to you for a few minutes?"

"I'm busy now, ma'am, could it wait until tomorrow?"

Manny clearly knew her rights to ignore all employers other than her own during her sacrosanct hours off.

"I would appreciate very much if we could talk privately," Claire pleaded, leaving Manny the privilege of showing her companions how generous she could be with her time.

Manny joined her near a flat rock wide enough for them to sit on side by side, but the Filipina pointedly refused the place Claire offered. She wanted this to be a short interview.

"Manny, I can't help but notice that a lot of the Filipinas look up to you as their big sister, and I thought perhaps you could help me, or rather, Father Fresnay."

Manny's eyes widened at the mention of the priest, perhaps because it was an honor to be singled out by a priest, one of the most important men to the Filipinas in all of Hong Kong.

"Yes, ma'am."

"Father Fresnay heard a confession that, well, alarmed him and although he doesn't know the identity of the woman who confessed and would never divulge her identify even if he did know, he was worried about something she said, something to the effect that there is a Devil killing the children of Tregunter Path."

"Really, ma'am? A Devil?" Manny's eyes widened with curiosity.

"Yes, a Devil who can be 'like a man or a woman.'" Claire

stressed the exact words. "Can you imagine what it means for a Filipina when she says that? I mean, do you think this woman was trying to tell us something useful in helping answer questions about Petey and Leo?"

"I don't know anything, ma'am." Manny looked confused. She was starting to redden and look as if she would cry any minute. "This upsets me, very much, to talk about Petey. I miss him very much, every day."

"I know, I know. It just occurred to me, just between ourselves, that the person confessing might have been Narcisa."

"Narcisa? Why Narcisa?"

"Because on the night Leo disappeared, she was screaming something about the Devil taking Leo, as if she really knew who it was. When I asked her about it, she said she really believed in the Devil."

"I don't know, ma'am. Why don't you ask her?"

"Where is she today? Doesn't she usually come here with you?"

"She spends the whole day crying in her room, ma'am." Manny's face had hardened, Claire thought, and it became clear why with Manny's next words. "Mrs. Franklin went to her mother's house—"

"Yes, I know."

"And her mother has a lawyer asking for Narcisa to be charged with neglecting Leo. She wants to break the contract with Narcisa and send her home right away. Mr. Franklin doesn't want the lawyers. He is fighting all the time with Mrs. Franklin on the telephone. Mr. Franklin told Narcisa to stop working and just stay in her room in case the police want to talk to her. Anyway, Narcisa doesn't want to see anybody now. She is feeling ashamed. I think you should leave her alone."

Claire thought Manny might be right in other circumstances, but saw no reason to give in that easily when Narcisa might know something.

"Don't you know Narcisa well? Couldn't you help us out a little?"

Manny seemed to consider this for a moment, but instead turned unexpectedly talkative.

"I feel very sorry for Narcisa and also for Mrs. Sandford. I cannot tell you how sorry. You know I lost my own little boy because he got pneumonia in the Philippines. I asked Mr. Sandford for airplane money to go home and take care of him, but he said it wasn't necessary, that all we had to do was send the money for antibiotics back to my village and that pneumonia was an easy sickness to cure.

"So he gave me a lot of money to make sure we could buy the best, the kind that come from a famous company and not one of the phony imitation medicines the poor people in Bontoc use to save money, and fortunately, another *amah* was going home on her vacation to a village near my village, so I gave the money to her." Manny paused for breath.

Claire waited, unwilling to stop Manny from talking, even if it had nothing to do with Petey and Leo. Manny had tried to tell her once before about Ramon's death, during the interview with Crowley, and it was obviously a story that Manny needed to retell. Somehow the death of Petey and Ramon were tied up emotionally inside her, and why not? She had lost two little boys she loved, not one.

"How much money?" Claire asked out loud, politely prompting Manny.

"Two hundred U.S. dollars for the medicine, plus another fifty dollars for her to travel to my village and buy food for Ramon and my family. I was very grateful to him then."

"He could have let you go home," Claire said against her better judgement.

Manny was graceful enough to overlook this disloyalty on Claire's part to her friend's husband.

"This *amah* was so stupid, ma'am. She spent most of the

money on makeup and clothes to make a good impression on one of her boyfriends, thinking Ramon could be cured by traditional herbal medicine instead. When my mother got a letter from me telling her the money was on its way, they caught her and she told the truth, and then this Filipina tried to raise more money from her own family and I did everything I could to get more cash, too. I didn't dare ask Mr. Sandford for any more, so I worked Sundays cleaning other apartments."

"And did you get the money together?"

"We almost got it from friends and everybody, but not fast enough, and Ramon died." Manny's expression of composure threatened to disintegrate as her grief surfaced with the telling of the tragedy and Claire took her hand.

"I'm very sorry, Manny."

Manny nodded needlessly, "I know, ma'am." She withdrew her hand.

"What happened to the other Filipina?"

"The priests said I should forgive her foolishness, that God wanted Ramon in heaven, and that my boy was happy at God's side. They told me that forgiveness and friendship would bring grace to my soul for eternity." At that, Manny collapsed into sobs and there seemed to be nothing for Claire to do as the woman shook off Claire's gestures of sympathy.

Claire waited for what must have been two or three minutes before she spoke again. She thought it might help to change the subject back to Tregunter Path.

"Manny, excuse me, but let me ask you the most direct question I can, because I know you want to get back to your friends. Do you know something about Inspector Crowley that we need to know in connection with Petey and Leo?"

Manny wiped her eyes with the back of her hand and looked up surprised at Claire.

"No, ma'am. Did anybody say anything about him to you?"

"No, nobody. But Connie, who worked for us between regular jobs, was scared by talk of a man hanging around the Path. Nobody said he was a policeman, but I wondered if without the uniform, maybe someone would mistake Inspector Crowley for a loiterer, you know, someone with no business hanging around watching the kids. That's really what I wanted to talk to you about. And just another thought. Petey's body had strange bruises on his chest and it occurred to me that perhaps he was hit by a car and you didn't want to say so for fear of getting into trouble, or getting someone else into trouble, because he shouldn't have wandered down to the road."

Manny wasn't stupid and her eyes flashed briefly with recognition of Claire's drift. "You mean Mrs. Reynolds, the Crazy Lady."

"Is that what you call her, the Crazy Lady?" Claire had to suppress a smile.

"She drinks a lot of wine all day, and she keeps a bottle of it in her dressing table drawer. Her previous *amah*, Concepcion, told me."

"Yes, she's very lonely, Manny."

"She misses her boy a lot, but she could bring him back to Hong Kong any time she wants. Nobody wants to work for her, ma'am, she is always changing her mood and firing and hiring the Filipinas who are sent to her by the agency. Nobody wants to recommend her to their friends anymore."

"Did she hit Petey with her car that day? Is that what really happened?"

Manny seemed shocked at the suggestion. "No, ma'am, although everybody is very careful walking around the curve to the vegetable truck because maybe she is driving out of Tavistock at the same time."

"Really."

Manny saw no humor in Mrs. Reynolds' driving skills.

"She is a drunk driver, ma'am." And Manny drew herself up, apparently impatient to rejoin her friends.

"Thank you, Manny. I appreciate the time you spent with me. Oh! I nearly forgot to ask you something."

Manny was already turning away to return to her friends, who were unsuccessfully trying to hide their curiosity, casting glances at them from lowered faces.

Claire reached into her backpack and pulled out the tape cassette of *Peter and the Wolf.*

Manny gasped.

"You recognize this?"

"Yes, of course, ma'am. It is an old tape of Petey's."

"You seem surprised to see it. So was Mrs. Sandford. She said she threw it out, or rather that you threw it out, but I found it up in the forest, way up there by the gazebo, with Petey's Grover."

"Where, ma'am?"

Claire pointed up the path.

"Petey was never higher than the place over by the *nullah* where I could see him."

"So you said. But what I can't figure out is why something tossed into the garbage would turn up again."

"I don't know, really, ma'am. I threw it out a long time ago." Manny did look bewildered. Claire detected something behind Manny's eyes—were new questions occuring to her, some realizations that hadn't hit the woman before?

"Please try and help us figure all this out, and think over what we talked about, I mean about the Devil stuff."

"I will, ma'am," Manny nodded slowly and walked away.

---

Claire wanted to talk all this over with Xavier when she got back to the apartment, but the phone interrupted her return. Fabienne was back from Macau. Claire knew this because Xavier took the phone call in his study and closed the door before continuing the conversation in a voice well below his usual Swiss mountain-man volume. Claire was too proud to ask what her rival's plans for the day were, or whether she had booked herself a flight out of Hong Kong soon.

She felt as if she were literally choking on her own pride and she found it hard to admit to herself that even on that lovely return to their bed on Christmas afternoon, the first time they had made love since Caspar's birth, she had hoped he would propose again. He hadn't.

His silence had grown very heavy since she had decided to seize this chance at happiness without any of the guarantees she had foolishly thought were necessary. Just watching Fabienne swinging back and forth on an emotional tightrope without a net was enough to embolden Claire. Life didn't come in fairy tales with happy endings. Fabienne had arrived armed and ready to battle charmingly to stay in Xavier's life on any terms. The gloves were off—and suddenly Claire's ring finger looked awfully bare.

About midday, the phone rang again. Claire raised her eyebrows meaningfully at Xavier, unable to hide her annoyance at the possibility that Fabienne was pushing for yet another adventure. Instead, it was Alistair Evans-Smith.

"Whether your curiosity was fed by homophobia or not, some quiet inquiries with some retired friends at the London end have turned up something quite distressing about our young Inspector Crowley," he said.

"Did you ask Slaughter?"

"No, no, no. Not at first. I was afraid John might see it as unwarranted meddling and it might have just created ill will. However, as it turns out, he is now very aware of Crowley's history."

"He has a record. As a criminal?" Claire sank down slowly into her well-worn rattan desk chair.

"Not quite, but there was a troubling reason he left England and joined the Hong Kong police."

Claire felt the journalist's selfish satisfaction of her instincts being on target.

Evans-Smith was obviously being careful in his choice of words. "Crowley was once questioned, then totally exonerated, *totally*, on suspicion of child molestation. There was a case involving a young boy in his district in south London. Crowley had taken a friendly interest in the boy, to the annoyance of the boy's mother, and then the boy reported some hanky-panky with a friend of Crowley's, not a police officer, as it turns out. Crowley was questioned and another police colleague reported seeing some, well," Evans-Smith cleared his throat as he reached for an appropriate phrase, "well, so-called, 'man-boy' love magazines in Crowley's locker."

"My God!" Claire exclaimed. "How did he manage to get into the police force here?"

"Times are hard for recruitment here as far as Europeans are concerned. There's absolutely no opportunity for promotion to the upper ranks, as you know, but we still need a few Europeans on the beat. To be fair, I warn you, Claire, before you speak to anyone about this, it turned out there was no connection between the case and Crowley's private life. None whatsoever."

"He wasn't involved at all with the little boy?"

"Beyond friendship, apparently not at all. The little boy's mother was away at work a lot and she'd given the father the boot long before. But Crowley's career in England was over. The other men in the ranks put the hard word on him to get out."

"So, what happens now?"

"In the end, I had to ring Slaughter because he should be aware of it, which he wasn't. However, I think that should be the end of it, my dear. It doesn't answer the question of where that poor little chap, Leo Franklin, has spent his Christmas. By the way, the investigation had turned up one strange new fact— Leo's passport is missing."

Claire started at the implication, "Isn't that good news? That means he's been taken somewhere else? Maybe across the border or to Macao?"

"That's what we hoped, but there's no record of him departing the territory at any of the border controls," said Evans-Smith.

"Anyway, it leaves a little hope that whoever took him might have some plan. Each day I pick up the paper expecting to see they've found his body somewhere in the harbor or up on the Peak." It was the first time Claire had admitted out loud that she feared Leo was dead.

"I promise you that at least out here in the New Territories, the Field Patrol Detachment teams are on alert for anything like a dead body, and believe me, what with the sharks and the gangs coming across the border every day in vegetable trucks, it wouldn't be their first, by any means."

---

That evening, after a long bath, she fully faced herself naked in the mirror for the first time. What she saw was frightening and strange. She had someone else's body. At least the breasts had slipped at least an inch lower and their shape was even more conical, less wide and high. Her stomach was pulling in nicely, and there were no stretch marks, thank God, but around her navel was a halo of little, tiny puckers. It wasn't exactly as bad as a painting by Lucien Freud, and it wasn't Rubenesque anymore. Well, it was, at any rate, Claire's body, and they would just have to go on together.

She reached into the back of her closet where she had stuffed all her kimonos of yore, a proud collection of antique silks and newly tailored satins she had routinely wore after meeting a big deadline to New York and returned from a particularly gruelling assignment outside Hong Kong.

All that was before she had moved with Xavier to Tregunter Path. It was a sort of secret costume party for the soul, a departure for a few hours from the stress of sustaining long-distance working relationships and making cold calls to people who generally didn't want to talk to the press. A retreat to a world of Chinese poetry, tea, her books and music, had often helped her through a lonely week.

Where had her sybaritic side gone? In the diaper wash? Why was she being such a ninny over this Fabienne? Claire brushed her red hair high up onto her head and clasped a long tortoise-shell comb into the depths of the wave at the back. She found her L'Air du Temps bottle still behind the hair conditioners and nursing pads, exactly where she had put it when they first moved, for God's sake. What had she been wearing each morning? Baby oil mousse? It was time to rise like a phoenix from the ashes of self-pity, self-examination, and self-mourning. She wanted this man, and for Caspar's sake, she had to have this man. He would never have another father and her child deserved more than a half-way, half-uttered, half-defined life.

Claire had just pushed her arms through the long sleeves of a long-favored dark green damask robe and tied the cider-colored sash when she heard the doorbell ring. Xavier was working in the study, and she called, "I'll get it." She pulled the robe more tightly across her for modesty's sake and ran to the door, opening it without hesitation.

She instantly regretted it. Anthony Crowley stood within a few inches of her and lurched halfway through the doorway, yelling, "For my own good! For my own good, he said! A voluntary request for temporary transfer, oh yeah, right! Bloody right! Voluntary! You bloody, meddling cunt! You think I've got a chance with me asking for temporary transfer *voluntarily*," Crowley crowed bitterly at the top of his lungs, "and everybody asking why? You're going to regret this. I'm innocent of everything, I was trying to help, you stupid, stupid, cow."

Claire stood back, but as she gave ground, he moved right into the living room, trying to grab her arm with his right hand

and hold her rigid in front of him. He missed once, and grabbed at her gown instead, catching hold of the belt.

"You'll regret this, you bitch! You can't do this to me without paying for it." He leaned into her ear, "Just a little word in the ear of some ponsy colonial twit, just a little harmless inquiry, eh? I finally figured it out. You were in the club that night, weren't you? You were with that 'nice gel' with the camera?" he wheedled in a frighteningly good imitation of an upper-crust English accent.

Inches away, Claire saw his eyes flicker strangely. She felt the blood draining from her face and her feet rooted to the floor. She saw him pulling back from her and knew in the next minute he was going to slap her or worse. She knew it and yet she couldn't move. She heard a roar from Xavier coming down the hallway, but even before she could turn, Dovie was pushing her aside, wielding a huge Chinese cleaver threateningly in Crowley's face and shoving him back into the corridor.

As Claire pulled back, she saw the two men struggle, the violence coming out of nowhere and filling the room, while Dovie stood like a rock. There was a split second when the men parted slightly and Dovie seized the moment when she could slam the front door on Crowley's startled, raging face. As the three of them stood there, stunned into silence, they heard Caspar in the nursery, starting to whimper.

# chapter twelve

" 'I am afraid, I am afraid,' that's all she cries all day," Dovie sighed. She was leaning her matronly torso over the railing of Caspar's crib to whip the little bedsheets under the mattress corners with an efficiency that belied her age. Her strong brown hands worked expertly, fixing one corner of the sheet tautly over the other. The thin pad sprang to attention.

Caspar was replaced firmly but gently in the center of the bed where he stared obediently up at a mobile of dangling ducks. Claire admitted to herself that Dovie's confidence translated itself through touch to her baby, who seemed more settled than before. He was squalling less and less and practically gurgled with happiness as Dovie swung him unceremoniously from nursery to kitchen. He was just as composed when she bounced him up and down in the balcony doorway in a kind of swing on a mini-bungee cord suspended from an old ceiling hook installed years before by someone keen on hanging plants.

Claire was jealous of Dovie's experience, but wasn't ungrateful. There would be a time any day now, she knew, when it would make all the difference between giving her job full concentration or feeling nagging doubts. If she had harbored any doubts about Dovie's physical agility or quick-wittedness, she had seen ample proof in the way Dovie had wielded her cleaver in Crowley's face until Xavier had managed to grapple one arm, and then the other to twist the younger man around and out the doorway.

The two women had fallen into a conversation about Crowley and Narcisa as Dovie started her morning rounds of the bedrooms. "Having seen that police officer throw a wobbly last night, I don't wonder the *amahs* around here are scared witless. What a display! That's not the kind of young man they sent over in the old days." Dovie threw her shoulders back and surveyed the crib. "I'll change over to the Paddington Bear sheets on Wednesday."

"What made you visit her?"

"Narcisa? I was worried about her, ma'am. She missed Mass. That's a mortal sin. She's been hiding in her room the entire week. You would think she'd want a day away. She told me there were a lot of things I didn't understand . . ." Dovie paused, as if to wonder what kind of things *she*, another, older *amah*, couldn't understand, then shrugged. "Of course, we all know what Mr. Franklin had done to her and why he can't just dismiss her. She might tell on him, how he abused her body. Then his wife would know and Narcisa says she would never get another job."

"It seems so incredibly unfair. All the *amahs* know?"

"Of course, ma'am. They all try to avoid Mr. Franklin. They say they cannot look that kind of master in the eye."

"And Narcisa? Is she hiding information? Not just about Giles Franklin or Jun? About Leo's disappearance? She's got to go to the police. She can't go on forever if Leo's in danger."

"She knows about the passport missing—she told Inspector

Slaughter it was gone from Leo's baby book where his birth certificate and and medical records were kept."

"Isn't it odd she was looking for his papers in the first place? Did you ask her why?"

"Yes, I did. When I asked her why she would have thought to check such a thing, she said she was dusting and said I didn't trust her because I am from Manila and not from the north, and then she shut up and just cried and cried. She's on her knees, the poor child."

"What about the boyfriend, Jun? Does she talk about him?"

"Probably up to no good, that one, ma'am. She hasn't seen him since the police questioned him the very morning after Leo disappeared. Narcisa says he's gone away because the Chinese police beat him up, but I think that's a Filipina exaggeration. I don't think the Hong Kong police would ever do such a thing."

Claire wasn't so sure, since the number of complaints about police brutality had risen sharply in the last year, but she had to smile to herself to hear Dovie talking as if she were an English village dowager rather than a Filipina herself.

Dovie's conversation was a welcome distraction, but Claire felt uncomfortable getting too chummy with the older woman. Already Dovie had the edge of simple age, not to mention experience with children, over Claire. Claire had heard of women losing their authority over domestic servants who did everything from selling their shoes secondhand out the back door to borrowing cosmetics and perfumes on the sly.

Yet she liked Dovie more and more.

As if the wet winds of the South China Sea had lurked stealthily off the coast of Lamma Island to carry off what little Christmas cheer the colony had mustered, Monday had given birth to an ugly, watery haze. Claire faced her last hour of maternity leave in her study, ruefully reliving Crowley's attack. Only someone driven by impulsive fury would have caused a scene that could only backfire by causing more negative attention to himself. She had considered reporting him to the police last night, but thought better of it. Why not give him more leash and keep an eye out for him? Let his frustration grow. Let him betray himself once and for all, if he had any real reason to be fearful. If not, let it go.

Her hair at this time of year seemed to suck up half the humidity in the harbor, ballooning it into a coppery cloud. She brushed it back into a long, unyielding plait for work. She was due in the office at 9:30. Everything was supposed to be back in place now—child, *amah*, career, sanity. Instead, she was terrified of stepping outside her own door because even though Crowley was suspended, he was free to make trouble for her wherever and whenever he liked. Moreover, he was a police officer and in Hong Kong, police officers were the only people allowed to carry guns.

She stared out at the windswept roads crisscrossing the slope below Branksome and shivered, "Well, who you gonna call?"

She felt little cheered by her feeble joke. Everyone knew the police force was in a shambles. People like Slaughter had already booked the moving men for next June. In a matter of months, Major General Liu Zhenwu and his People's Liberation Army troops, some 8,000 of them, would be taking over the military garrison of Hong Kong. The nervous breakdown of a Johnny-Come-Lately Brit cop would be of no interest to the new regime. Her eye travelled along May Road as a green pickup turned down Garden Road and headed toward Central. The back of the truck held a delivery of carefully wedged-in potted trees, swaying side to side. Mr. Ip was off to see a customer, she mused.

Claire jumped up, knowing that staying hidden in her study was the silliest possible response to Crowley's threat. She dressed quickly for work, squeezing into a khaki pantsuit. She threw on an ankle-length rain slicker and rainhat and tucked her well-worn leather carry-all that doubled as purse and briefcase under her arm. Reminding Dovie once again to double-lock the door behind her, she headed out to the parking lot.

Crowley was nowhere to be seen. Her nerves settled a bit and she knew what she had to do. A dense fog closed in behind her, obscuring Branksome's lower stories as she moved across the one-lane bridge and branched off the jogging path over to the lowest of Ip's green terraces cut evenly into the slope.

Now was as good a time as any to get Ip off her list of niggling doubts and to answer a question that had lingered in her mind since that dinner with Fresnay in Tailong. Crowley was their man, she was sure of that, but Ip could well have played a role. Somehow, somehow . . . She had half an hour before she had to head to the office. And Ip needed half an hour at least to do any kind of business in town.

The undecided drizzle had drenched the beds of low brush plants, ferns, and bougainvillea pots set in neat rows, cross-hatching the gardener's property. Ip's finely dug irrigation gutters were already overflowing with last night's rainfall. Claire noticed for the first time that behind the ramshackle shed that doubled as Ip's residence there was an herb garden. She saw at least fifty bunches of sweet basil in the distance, but closer to the shed lay dozens of little plants, some with tiny flowers, some with spiky branches of no aesthetic appeal whatsoever. She wondered who the customers for those could be.

The door wasn't locked as she had guessed, since Ip wouldn't be the kind to keep valuables in a structure that could be carried off by tomorrow's typhoon. Nonetheless, the shed's interior was a shock.

The tiny building was completely whitewashed inside from top to bottom. Claire would have expected a dirt or wooden floor, but instead she was walking, treading muddy footprints in fact, on spotless white-painted cement smoothed and varnished right to the edge of the wall. A chart of a naked young man was pinned on the wall, and Claire saw quickly that its

main feature was a grid of meridians running from the head to
the feet and hands. The rest of the shed's little wall space was
jammed with bookshelves, some loaded with reference volumes and others lined with jars of roots, seeds, and unidentifi-
able compounds of earthy colors and unworldly textures. She
stepped back for a moment as the glistening eyes of snakes met
hers from their resting place next to animal penises and horns
floating in large glass vats.

The desk's wood surface looked freshly dusted. There was
only a cheap large radio and a small cellular phone recharging
next to a simple lamp. Apart from the desk and a simple chair,
there was a narrow wooden cot doubled up on itself and
propped against the wall for the day. An antique model of a
dehumidifier sucked and ratttled noisily next to the cot, laboring
to empty the mist into a plastic bucket of water slotted into its
back. The smell of a musk incense stick penetrated the moist
air. Ip had put an orange and an apple with the still-smoking
joss stick in front of a small red shrine to the Chinese kitchen
god. The kitchen itself consisted only of a wok sitting next to a
tea kettle on a two-burner gas stove in the remaining corner.

"He's not a gardener," Claire said to herself with finality, feeling the bone-heavy chill of the cement penetrate her leather
soles. Pungent chemical smells coming from the fleshy jars
around the room mixed with the incense. Fresnay had feared a
murderer who was "very well-educated, very determined, and
very, very sick." Ip did not strike Claire as very sick at all, and
she saw the room as belonging to someone with an orderly
mind, albeit an orderly mind in an ornery, stubborn old body.
But then, Crowley had not struck Claire as a very well-educated
man, certainly not one to make an obscure poison his criminal
signature. It was all coming together in her mind—but something about the picture felt wrong, at the same time.

She heard an engine along the road close to the shed and
quickly dodged to the door to see if Ip was returning, but it was

only the diesel grinding of a taxi moving slowly in the fog along Tregunter Path like a heavy bottom fisher cruising along the seabed for wayward passengers to gobble down. Claire realized she had been holding her breath and moved back into the shed. This expedition was rash, she realized, and resolved to spend only five more minutes in Ip's home.

So who was Ip? Claire took a tiny tour of the room but couldn't risk the leisure of scrutinizing the heavy volumes lining the shelves. She ran her eyes along the jars' labels, feeling each minute tick off as she struggled to translate the traditional characters of complicated botanicals she had never studied. Many, even most of them, were beyond her training in standard newspaper-level Mandarin and taxi-driver Cantonese. She took a small notebook out of her bag and worked her way along the shelves, noting what she could.

"*Ban xia*," she wrote, "Middle summer." It was clearly a root, and Ip's faint handwriting in scratchy fountain pen underneath had recorded, *Pinellia ternata.* The next jar carried an identical label, but appeared to contain processed powder and smelled of sulphur. She continued down the row, searching for any others she could make out. She found a jar of dried white flowers that looked to her untrained eye like common clematis, but Ip had labelled them with the characters, *wei ling xian*, meaning "holy root of the temple," and underneath, *Morus alba, spath-olobus suberectus.*

She lost more valuable minutes before she found an easy one, skipping the Chinese and translating, "ox gallstones," from Ip's Latin, *bos taurus domesticus.* The gallstones sat next to *cou teng*, "hooky branches," called *uncaria rhynchopylla*, according to Ip's precise labelling. Claire moved the jar of creepy-looking twigs to see another glass jar of strange tubers, and read *chuan wu tou.*

"Crow's head," she murmured to herself. "*Aconitum carmi-chaeoli bex, radix aconiti.*" It was the herb from Petey's stomach, found during the autopsy. She had known she would find it. She had feared she would find it, and at the same time, hoped she wouldn't find it.

She stood still for what must have been more minutes she shouldn't have spared, wondering what to do. The dehumidifier churned away accusingly next to her. She should alert Slaughter, let him go through the right procedures, get a search warrant. She wasn't supposed to be here. Ip might come home at any minute. But he would know what to hide, and where, in an instant's notification of a search. She put the jar in her bag and glancing around the shed to make sure her exit hadn't been observed, darted toward the road. She was negotiating the final, expectedly dangerous leap across the *nullah* which had filled with water when she heard another engine coming toward her.

Standing still on the hillock at the foot of his terraces, Claire and Ip's eyes locked. His truck veered away from her path, but she had registered the shock of surprise on his face at seeing her descending from his slope. There was no old man's confusion in his glance. Could he guess from her guilty expression where she had been and what she had discovered? She would call Slaughter as soon as she got to the office.

---

Reaching the Inspector wasn't as easy as she had expected. Cecilia put in a call right away, while Claire called Father Fresnay with the news.

"Tread very carefully now," Robert said. "I will pull out some of my reference books here on Chinese pharmacology."

Slaughter was on the telephone immediately, just as livid as he was impressed that Claire had discovered the source of the aconite in Petey's stomach. "Illegally obtained evidence is useless in court," he shouted at her. "I appreciate your interest in solving our problems, but with Crowley suspended and Ip's poison in your pocket, you've made my life bloody complicated, Claire. Bring the stuff round to the lab by lunch-time."

Claire put the phone down, shaken by Slaughter's entirely justified tirade. She was going to be glad to unload the evidence into official hands. She was sure that Slaughter would find a way to handle Ip. Cecilia would personally take a taxi with the herb to Police Headquarters. Before she could reach for her raincoat, however, the phone rang and Cecilia passed it to Claire, "It's your *amah*."

"Ma'am, the Immigration Department has telephoned this morning. They say that the transfer of my papers to your name is ready and I have to go to Kowloon Immigration to collect them."

Claire sighed. "Don't they usually give us more notice?"

"Yes, ma'am, but as a favor to you, Mr. Evans-Smith asked them to waive the usual six weeks' delay because he is leaving for England before that, so they are urging me to come right now."

Claire hadn't ever imagined there could be a downside to Evans-Smith's old boy network. Now Connie had been dismissed and she had too much work piled up on her desk to return straight home the first day. She knew there would be conflicts in the life of a working mother—but not in the first ten minutes. She called Xavier.

"I'm sorry, but Dovie can't take the baby with her today when she goes to collect her immigration papers. Could you work from home today? I can't be seen my very first day back at work spending five minutes in the office and then going right back to Caspar."

There was a long pause. Xavier would try to do his best, she felt sure.

"I'm sorry, but it's impossible. I'm sitting in a planning session right now with Chinese provincial officials from Hunan. After this, we're supposed to go straight into another session with the financial people and the engineers."

I don't believe this is happening to me, thought Claire. She tried to focus. She looked at Cecilia, but Cecilia had to leave now for Slaughter's office. It saved Claire from herself, in a way. She knew within an instant that asking her secretary to babysit was a major breach of Cecilia's employment terms.

"Xavier, I have a job too, and this is my first day back! Maybe you don't realize what Immigration is like—second only to the Transportation Department's Vehicles Licensing Bureau, it can be the Great Sucking Hole of Hong Kong. There'll be a black mark on her file if she isn't there. Filipinas don't win trying to negotiate with this bureaucracy. She has to go today."

Xavier's tone make it clear he was drawing the line. He had offered a lot, but never had he been willing to play the house-husband or second fiddle to Claire's career. She had run up against a brick wall of Swiss chauvinism.

"I know who would be happy to babysit!" he crowed with male pleasure at solving a domestic problem. "Fabienne! She has nothing to do! It'll give her a sense of belonging and being useful. She'll be happy to do it."

Claire felt her face flush. Hating the other woman already made her feel guilty, but now on top of her jealousy and suspicion, she had to be grateful to her for small favors. Every fiber in her body wanted to say no.

She looked at the mountain of newspapers, BBC broadcast transcriptions, correspondence, and E-mail messages, printed out and neatly readied on her desk by Cecilia. If only she had cleared this off last week during her little Christmas visit. How blithely she had assumed there would be time and tranquility on her first official day back!

"It's unnatural," she said to Xavier in a sullen voice. "Anybody but her."

"Why, Claire? She'll probably be thrilled. Call her right now. She's probably at the hotel just counting the hours until her departure."

That's right. Fabienne was actually leaving, having filled the last day or so with sightseeing and camera maintenance. Why begrudge her this final gesture of acceptance? Why be so mean-spirited? The woman was leaving. Claire had survived her. Sheer time, and the extraordinary exercise of keeping her lips pressed together one day at a time, had won her an important psychological victory.

"You call her. She can't say no to you. And I don't have a spirit generous enough to beg. Caspar is your child, too."

Xavier's male ego was pleased by this solution. Two of his women tending his tribe. Ancient Man's polygamous perogatives were actually proving useful. "I'd be happy to. Any instructions?"

The emotional crisis seemed to have passed. Claire tried to sound practical, even matter of fact. "I'll call Dovie back and tell her to give Fabienne all the instructions she needs, the back-up bottles of my milk are there in the fridge. It won't be complicated."

"Fine," Xavier's tone sounded loving and managerial at the same time. "Everything will be fine, so don't worry. When shall I tell Fabienne that Dovie will get back?"

"Probably not later than four. It'll take an hour for Dovie to get there, pull a number, and wait for her file to be delivered to the right officer. As I recall, they stop calling new cases to the window around four or four-thirty every afternoon."

The only way to cope with this development was to file it in the back of her mind as fast as possible. She called Dovie and told her that their friend would be babysitting, to relax about the Immigration appointment, and to give Fabienne all the instructions on care and feeding she needed and then to attend to her affairs as completely as possible so that there would be no call-backs. Dovie sounded as competent as any mother could have wished.

Meanwhile, Cecilia was eager to brief Claire quickly on what she had found out in Repulse Bay the previous Saturday.

"They know Crowley very well, the boys I asked. It wasn't

so hard. It was so cold that instead of sitting on the rocks to be picked up by the *guay-lo* launches, they were all sitting in a *daipaidong* eating noodles. My mother went to the hotel for her buffet lunch with a friend and the friend's daughter came with me. We said we were looking for my little brother who might have gone with a policeman with dark hair, good-looking. It was a family emergency. But they said the policeman hadn't been around lately. They had a dirty nickname for him." Cecilia blushed before she uttered the Cantonese equivalent of "Big Badge."

"So they knew him. Any details on him?"

Cecilia nodded. "He likes young Chinese boys, that's certain. But so do a lot of them, Claire, that's why they go there. Some of these boys were maybe thirteen, fourteen, hard to say. There was an older one there who didn't like my questions."

"Did they know anything else about him?"

"They knew he sang at an expensive club they couldn't afford. They said he liked to teach them naughty songs in English and they would teach him some in Cantonese. He told them he was trying to get together a new act and maybe one of them could be in the show with him. He seemed to be very popular, but none of them had seen his performance. Said it was too expensive unless you got a *guay-lo* to pay for you."

"Then they knew it was Crowley for sure."

"Oh, yes. They even knew he organized day trips across the border into Shenzhen. Looking for virgin boys like a lot of the foreigners who are afraid of AIDS. Sometimes they said he took one of them along as translator."

"More like purveyor," Claire mused. She had heard about the hunt for HIV-free conquests, and not just in the Hong Kong area. Burmese virgins, peasant girls from the Chinese interior, and Vietnamese orphans were all valuable commodities on the international sex market.

Cecilia looked intently at Claire. "You Europeans are so inscrutable," she joked. "Do you think now that Inspector Crowley intentionally hurt Petey and Leo behind the *amahs'* backs?"

"I'm not sure. Considering the way he lunged at me last night, he certainly seems to be acting guilty. But since I found the poison on Ip's shelves, I've been confused. I'm not sorry now that I reported him to Evans-Smith. He shouldn't be a police officer. He should leave the buggery to its traditional home, the Legal Department."

They both laughed, knowing well that Hong Kong's most famous queen was not pictured on the colonial currency, but had enjoyed two decades as a Queen's Counsel in the territory's courtrooms.

To keep her mind off Fabienne's invasion of her private domain, (turnabout and fair play from the gods for her own trespassing on Ip's property?) Claire buckled down to work. It was going to be a nightmare of cramming to catch up with six weeks of past news, but Hopkirk had done a magnificent job of not letting too much of the drudgery pile up on her desk.

For today, though, the most important thing was to edit down a stringer's file from Bangkok and to work through the story ideas tentatively suggested by Hopkirk and propped next to a welcome bouquet of flowers on the rickety metal typing table that had outlived its usefulness, but never seemed to get thrown out.

The day passed in a trance of concentration achieved only by blocking out all thoughts of Tregunter Path. The fog had burned off and the sky across the harbor was clear. By four she was exhausted, her eyes red-rimmed from staring at the computer screen and her wrists throbbed with strain. She had known she could skip one feeding, but she had pushed her luck. It seemed like a very, very long time since she had held Caspar, as if he were a stranger from another life, a brief dream between yesterday's working agenda, and this morning's labors. This desk, this chair, were more familiar to her than her own child.

She leaned into the cracked plastic backseat of a spacious old taxi with appreciation for its surviving the newer fleets of low-slung Japanese interlopers. The driver happily chatted to himself in broken English about his own children, his family in Guangdong, and God knew what else. Claire felt she had been away from Branksome for a week, and she wondered if Caspar would greet her with recognition after a whole day away.

She was paying the taxi driver the fare and heaving herself out of the car when she heard herself hailed, "Claire, back so soon! How was your first day?"

Claire stared at Fabienne in bewilderment. She was dressed in jeans and a lithe cotton knit cardigan that clung to her petite figure, leaving a sliver of tiny, flat belly visible above the waistline. She was, inexplicably, carrying one of Xavier's squash rackets. It was all too obvious that babysitting had begun to pall on Fabienne and she had run downstairs to practice her forehand.

Claire felt sick to her stomach and then remembered that she hadn't eaten lunch in an effort to get her work done and get home early. She should have something to drink and eat before she wakened the baby for his feed.

"Is Dovie back already?"

"No, no, she called and said she'd be back by five. So, how was your day? I can guess," Fabienne cocked an eye confidentially at Claire like an indulgent older sister. "Maybe it was a relief to be back on the horse?"

"Back in the saddle," Claire muttered. She could not lose her temper, not yet. But she wanted to buck and run up the eleven flights to her apartment, the elevator seemed so slow.

"Oh, oh, don't worry about the little one. He is taking a deep nap. He was actually snoring just like his father! We played and played and played. He kept trying to flip over and he learned to clap his hands!" Fabienne made a reassuring face and said firmly, "He is really a very intelligent little man."

Claire unlocked the front door, slightly consoled, and Fabienne followed, tossing the racket on the rattan sofa and heading to the kitchen. A second later, Claire heard her run water from the tap into a glass.

She slung her leather case off her shoulder and her immediate thought was to open the nursery door to check on Caspar, but first she wanted to get cleaned up into something fresher than the sticky shirt she'd been wearing all day. There was crusted mud on her pants' hem from Ip's gardens that morning. All that seemed like an adventure belonging to another life.

She struggled out of her jacket and shirt and checked the mail left by Dovie on her dressing table that morning. She saw with pleasure that even though Dovie had left midway through the day for her appointment, the bathroom was spotlessly clean, the bedroom dusted and swept, the drycleaning organized ready for the pickup the next morning.

She ran a quick shower and stepped under it for a moment. She chose a clean cotton kimono instead of one of her silk ones, laying it out on the bed. She brushed out her hair and retied it in a more forgiving knot at the back of her head, jamming a couple of geisha needles through it.

In a couple of minutes, she felt transformed and capable of continuing with what had already been an extremely full day. Her thoughts glanced back to the morning and Ip's shed. The story was coming to an end and approaching an explanation, she thought to herself. There will be someone held responsible, at least for Petey. It would lead somehow to Leo, or at least to some truth about Leo. There had to be more. Branksome Building and its unhappy tenants could not live in a limbo of fear forever.

She returned to the living room to perform the minimum of courtesies.

"Can I get you a drink or something? Some wine or something more interesting than water? I have to feed Caspar now, so you'll have to excuse me just for a few minutes." Claire was determined to be alone for this important reunion.

Fabienne's uncertainty flickered in her light glance. She seemed unwilling to impose herself any further on Claire's privacy, but Claire had tried hard to sound sincere and conciliatory. Her gratitude toward Fabienne was more genuine than it had been this morning. With Dovie on the job within a few hours, the poison found and delivered to the police, Crowley suspended, and Fabienne leaving Hong Kong for good in little more than a day or two, all the tectonic plates of Claire's life seemed to be shifting slowly, if still unclearly, into a stable position once again.

"No, thanks, but I'll stay a bit, if I may. I'll be fine with my water here. You go ahead. I understand."

Claire was actually humming to herself a snatch of music learned as a child, "In the Evening," by Frederick Low, a duet she had played with her Viennese teacher in the low, orange dusks of a Berkeley autumn. She looked forward to the day she and Caspar would play at the piano side by side, his little pale face intent on the simple melody and his small white hands playing the parallel octaves as her freckled fingers supported him with the interweaving harmonies on the lower octaves. Oh, the pleasures they had in store!

She returned to the corridor and gingerly entered Caspar's little nursery. There, in an instant of immeasurable scorching hurt, she felt herself hit like a soldier on a battlefield pushed off the ground by a shell and hurtled emotionally through the air like a legless doll.

Caspar's crib was empty.

# chapter thirteen

– Monday evening –

Claire's eyes were swollen shut, but even with them closed, she sensed an unusual cool around her reclining body. What had happened to her? She reached through the fog of her thoughts, wondering why she felt so dull. No, not even dull, she felt nothing but a shifting blanket of sleep. Nothing at all.

She turned in her bed and started to fall alseep again, but a small thought pierced her sedated mind. Caspar was missing. She knew this was a terrible thing, but her emotions didn't protest. Her mind crawled back in time. She saw herself walking into the nursery and holding back shock, walking quickly back to ask Fabienne where the baby was. She had been insisting to herself, the way rational adults do, "There's an explanation, there's an explanation."

Lying quietly, she heard a lot of pacing and conversation outside her bedroom door. A lot of short exchanges between Cantonese men. She breathed out, waiting for the feeling of horror to flood back over her. She turned over. Pulling the curtain aside, she glanced out the window and saw the lights of the territory spread out below her, broken by the dark stretch of harbor. Night had fallen.

Claire tried to rouse herself, but her body felt weighed down. So heavy, so very tired, she thought. I've been so drained lately, literally by breast-feeding, of course, and then this woman showed up. This woman who left my child alone. This woman who lost my child.

She wanted to call Xavier who must be home by now. He had to find Caspar. He had to call the police.

Oh, yes. Fabienne had called the police while Claire had been trying to hold back her tears of panic. That's right, Xavier had come home just as Fabienne had been asking for Dovie to help her find Dr. Sui's telephone number. Xavier had called Inspector Slaughter. Dovie had started screaming, but then she had stopped and controlled herself and Xavier had taken Claire to the bedroom.

Claire felt a lump underneath her damp midriff. It was Caspar's little blankie, still fresh from the morning laundry. Her emotions rallied from somewhere deep below the sedatives holding her under the danger zone. She knew there was a hole inside of her. The drugs filled the hole with numbness, but for how long?

She had to talk to Xavier. Where was he? Where was Fabienne? He would know what to do. He would talk to Fabienne. He would find out what she had done with Caspar. What had happened?

Her foot knocked over something resting on the end of the bed. An electronic toy fell off the end of the bed and started playing a nursery ditty. The four little lines of the song were just ending when Dr. Sui leaned her head into the room.

She sat on the edge of the bed and took Claire's hand. "How are you feeling?" Her doctor was a Chinese woman of northern stock and over six feet tall, with a hint of a moustache and a penchant for girlish blouses and heavy shoes. She would have made a perfect senior officer in the women's ranks of the People's Liberation Army. Trained at MacGill University, Dr. Sui had delivered Caspar decked out in a yellow slicker and matching shower cap that made her look like a mad Chinese pirate in a sou'wester steering through a storm between Claire's knees. Her only concession to Claire's discomfort was handing her a face mask connected to a tank of laughing gas, childbirth old Hong Kong-style.

"Where is Caspar? Do they know anything yet?"

"Xavier is doing everything he can. The police will need to come in here pretty soon, they're doing the fingerprinting and examining the whole house for fibers and hairs."

"What did you give me?"

"I knocked you out. And I'm going to give you another sedative to see you through the night."

"I thought you didn't believe in painkillers. At least not when I needed them." Claire feebly joked. Why did she always feel obliged to perform for doctors?

"You didn't need them then. You need them now. And these aren't painkillers, they're tranquilizers."

"I want to see Xavier."

"He'll be back in a few minutes. He went outside with the Chief Inspector. Your friend Fabienne is outside. Do you want her to come in and keep you company?"

"No, thanks."

"I didn't think so, but she offered."

Claire glanced up. It was dark outside where Xavier and Fabienne had gone. It would be hard to find Caspar on such a black night. Claire realized her thoughts weren't making much sense. She thought she heard new voices.

"Can you get Xavier for me?" she asked Dr. Sui.

"That's the police crew finishing outside. Try to be patient. It's a critical time right now, when any clues might still be fresh. They have to talk to everyone on the street, the jitney drivers, the *amahs*, the man at the vegetable truck. They radioed all the bus and taxi drivers on shift asking if anyone had carried a red-headed baby away. I heard it."

Claire started to cry, slow waves of fear for Caspar engulfing her in terror. Wasn't he hungry? How many feeds had he missed? Dr. Sui's tablets started to work, and she fell into a dreamless, cold, and sour sleep.

---

She awoke to angry voices outside her door, Xavier's low, threatening rumble and Fabienne's now-familiar chirp. Only now, the light Gallic tone sounded more like a broken flute, the air caught in wrenching sobs.

"They haven't found him yet," thought Claire, her breath shortening as the fear returned, a claw on her breast. Determined that she would get up before anyone had the chance to sedate her again, Claire heaved her feet to the floor and bracing herself against the wall, started down the corridor.

They were speaking French and English, back and forth, as if English was the language in which Xavier could think clearly and Fabienne could only bare her heart in her own tongue. Claire struggled against the drugs, and was almost halfway toward the living room, moving hand by hand, before she realized the conversation wasn't about Caspar at all.

"*Tu as dit, non, non, je ne veux pas des enfants.* No children, that's what you said. *Il n'y avait pas de discussion avec toi, pas de question!*"

"It was a different relationship, a different time in my life!" Xavier argued in a voice somewhere between a shout and a hiss of fury. "When I said I didn't want to have children, I was speaking as a man of thirty-five, not forty-five, or forty-eight!"

"I know the little boy is everything to you, but she, this American woman, can't mean that much. She's not your type, Xavier. Whatever happened, *tu es revenu a moi, j'etais sur, il ne m'inquietait pas, mais maintenant . . .*"

"Well, I'm not coming back this time. It is totally different now. You have to see that." It sounded as if Xavier had struck a piece of furniture with his fist.

"It's more complicated, that's all," Fabienne sniffed and seemed to be finding her composure. "*On peut parler, faire des arrangements. Je peux accepter le petit—*"

"You can accept him? I don't recall putting him on offer to you or anybody. Thank you, thank you. You know, you are talking like my wife, which you are not. Try to remember that. It was never like that between us."

"*C'etait possible, c'etait simplement tu ne voulais pas, mais pour moi, c'est toujours possible.*"

There was a long pause. Claire held her breath and leaned, sodden and sleepy against the inner wall of the corridor.

"How many times?"

"What?"

"How many abortions did you have?"

"Two. And they disgusted me, so then I had it done. *C'est fait.*" Now Fabienne's voice took on a taunting air. "Oh, but you could change your mind, after all, you didn't really know, did you, what you wanted and what you didn't want. You just said something for convenience at the time, now I realize that! And when I realized, it was too late. The operation was done."

Xavier didn't reply. Claire felt an entire minute tick past in the pained silence in the next room. Then Fabienne seemed to have refueled her fury and burst out again, this time from a different part of the room.

"Whatever happened, *tu es revenu a moi, après le project en Malawi, et après l'autre fille à Beirut?*"

"That was diff—"

"Let me ask you something," Fabienne spit out at him. She had moved across the room, closing in on Xavier in a fury so intent on punishing him with her bitterness that she didn't notice Claire, now visible to her from the hall. Claire pressed herself back against the wall. She felt unable to enter the room and unwilling to retreat, stuck to the corridor wall by her frayed nerve endings.

"Will you still want to marry her, would you want to marry her at all, if there were no child? You told me you didn't want children! And I agreed because I loved you! What did she ever do to earn your love? Would you have wanted her without him?"

"Of course, I would. That is why there is a child. Because I wanted to be with her in the first place. And I will stand by her because I want to be with her. Do you have to hear every single word of it, word by word by word?" There was another long pause as Claire heard Xavier seat himself heavily in one of her old rattan chairs. He sighed, "I can't stand this kind of fighting. You love it. You always loved it. You lived for it, fighting and making up. I think it makes you feel more real somehow. Anyway, why didn't you tell me this before? When you were pregnant? You should have told me."

"I didn't think you needed to know."

"But now you do." He laughed derisively.

"It just came out."

"No, it didn't just come out. You picked the worst day of my life to get back at me. I can imagine what you thought when you saw Caspar."

"*Non, j'avais peur jusqu'au moment quand je l'ai vu. Il n'etait pas comme toi, pas de tout.*"

He roared, "Don't you dare say that he wasn't like me, he *wasn't*, as if he is gone. He is alive!"

"Xavier, Xavier, where are you going?"

"I'm going back out there with the police to find my son before Claire wakes up. I swear it. You can stay here or go to hell. If you'd stayed in the apartment, this wouldn't have happened."

"It wasn't my fault. Obviously, someone was watching, was waiting for the chance. I've upset you, I'm sorry, it was the wrong time."

"What a bitch! What do I care about your sterilization? Your self-mutilation is none of my business! How could I trust you with my son? Was I crazy? All that garbage in my office about how you could accept my new family, how you liked Claire, how you needed my help to get used to the idea, the tears, I felt sorry for you! I even felt guilty! Why? I never made any promises to you. *Jamais, jamais!*"

Claire had noiselessly slumped to the floor as she sat and listened to what Fabienne had been feeling all this time. Her arms clenched around her midriff, she could only imagine the emptiness, the defiance, and the finality of Fabienne's decision to have her tubes cut. Not only had Fabienne not borne Xavier's children, she had not even *kept* Xavier's children.

All week she had looked at the child of the man she had loved for so long, knowing that she would never have anyone's children. Though Claire had never given the matter much thought before, there was a horror in the timbre of Fabienne's voice, the fury of someone who had seen herself making a practical birth control decision only to find out she had undergone a virtual amputation of her deeply repressed hopes. What if things had been different between Claire and Xavier? What if he had been cooler at the news of Caspar's conception, what if she had panicked and taken the easy way out? Suddenly Claire felt too close to Fabienne, pretending over and over she didn't want what she might have allowed herself to want by challenging the course of events.

"I want you out of here before Claire wakes up. I have to think of my family now," Xavier said in the other room.

"What family? You have no family, you are no husband, you have no rights over anyone, nor they over you."

"That's enough!" Xavier roared at her.

"It is a truth of life, a fact, and no child gives her permission to own someone!"

"I want you out!" Xavier demanded as if all the force in his body were behind it.

"Let me stay and see Claire. I want to say I'm sorry. I should stay until Caspar is found," Fabienne said weakly.

"Get out and wait at the hotel. No, go to Cambodia. Better yet, go to hell."

Fabienne was moving now across the room and gathering up her bag and cigarettes. "I'll be in my room if there's any news," she said in a small voice.

For a few moments, Fabienne didn't move. Claire knew, as any woman would know, that Fabienne was waiting for more, for some good-by that would reassure her of a place in Xavier's life. That was what she had waited for all week, and Claire realized with a wave of relief, it was what she had not received. Finally the front door slammed shut.

She had had enough. The only thing that mattered was their son.

"Claire!"

He held her so tightly, he was pushing the fear right out of her pores, fear of losing him and not finding Caspar. The fuzziness in her mind was expelled like a foul cloud. She felt even weaker than before his embrace and he led her over to the sofa. They sat down as she fought back more tears and asked him, "Where is John?"

"He's with his officers right now running checks on the taxi and bus drivers by radio. They're interrogating the watchmen of all the buildings along Tregunter Path, doing all the routine things they have to do as quickly as possible."

"Routine, routine! Routine hasn't found Leo Franklin, now presumed dead. Xavier, there must be something we can do besides sit here."

He wrapped her in his arms, "Give them a chance, Claire, give them a chance."

"Where's Robert, does he know?"

"I called him. He's on his way and should get here any minute. He's going to stay with you while I work with the police."

"Where is Dovie?" Claire mumbled.

"She's in her room, or maybe in the kitchen, I think. I excused her to get a rest. She's deeply upset, too. No one had any time to spend with her when she got back from the Immigration Office. John talked to her for a few minutes. I asked her to make you some soup."

"I'm not hungry."

Xavier sat quietly with Claire stroking her hair back from her damp forehead. Claire spoke quietly. "The front door was locked, I unlocked it myself. Did they check whether the back door was locked?"

"Yes. It had been locked and there was no sign of breaking in."

"Xavier, that means that whoever took Caspar had a key. Dovie was in Kowloon. I have my key and you have yours." Claire couldn't think beyond that.

"No, no, Claire, you're still a bit confused by the drugs," Xavier said. "Fabienne had Dovie's key. We had to let Dovie in."

She thought of Crowley. "Do the police have keys? Like skeleton keys?"

"No. If they need access to an apartment, the gatehouse man uses his and comes with them. We've gone over that already with John Slaughter. He was asking me how many keys we had."

Fresnay arrived just then and the sight of him was so comforting that for a moment, Claire could almost believe he might have stashed Caspar in his backpack and the whole nightmare was over. After comforting Xavier with a bracing hug, he sat down and gently took Claire's hand.

"I can't just sit here like a drugged zombie, Robert. What can I do? I will not just sit here!" Claire pounded her free fist on her knee. "You've seen what the Franklins have done for over a week now and how much good it did!" she glared at Xavier. "We can't just let the police put up their posters, play their stupid announcements on that weekly police show and even if we had a million dollars to offer as a reward, you see how much good it did Giles Franklin."

"Calm down, Claire," Robert said, but he looked at Xavier and nodded. "She's right. What's happening downstairs?"

"Exactly what we've seen twice already," Xavier told him. "They're interviewing everybody in the building, door by door. They're stopping cars leaving the buildings and coming into Tregunter Path at the junction of May Road. They're radioing to all the taxi drivers and bus drivers."

The drugs were wearing off Claire. She was crying, despite all intentions to stay composed.

"Crying is not going to help Caspar," Robert said to her, brutally withdrawing his hand. "Think, Claire. Stop crying."

She took a deep breath and wiped the back of her hand across her exhausted face.

"I have one idea," the priest said, finally putting his motorcycle helmet at the foot of the sofa and leaning back to catch his breath. "I was already trying to work on it when Xavier called me. As soon as I heard that Petey Sandford had aconite in his stomach, I had one of my friends in the doctoral program over at Hong Kong University fax me some research on it. You remember when we were treating Xavier's knee with rosemary, I said something can be both good or bad depending on the dose."

Claire nodded. "Ip has aconite on his shelves. We handed it over to Slaughter this morning—Cecilia did. I thought it proved Ip was Petey's murderer. Ip knows I found it. He saw me coming down his slope this morning."

Xavier interrupted. "They released Ip after questioning. The police told me this afternoon. Ip was in police custody the whole afternoon, literally with them, when Caspar was kidnapped. It was a perfect alibi. Ip told them someone must have taken the aconite without him knowing it and replaced it. He doesn't lock the shed. He's been completely cleared and back home. They're running fingerprint tests on the container."

Fresnay shook his head. "He may be telling the truth or he may be lying, but why? We have to confront Ip ourselves. I think he gave Petey the dose and I think I know why. Read this." Fresnay shoved into her hands a couple pages of fax paper.

Claire read out loud. "Sconitum Chinese paxton and *Aconitum carmichaeoli bex*, or *radix aconiti*, is a tuberous root, pungent in flavor, toxic in crude form, used to relieve spasms of arms and legs, paralysis of limbs, twitching and numbness, to remove 'wind.'" She looked up at Fresnay. "Wind?"

Fresnay nodded. "When people with certain kinds of epilepsy suffer a seizure, they sometimes give a shrill cry and fall unconscious. The Chinese ancients called this the 'goat wind,' referring to an imbalance in the system of 'winds' and because in traditional lore, Chinese herbalists reported that the cry of an epileptic in seizure was similar to that of a goat."

"Robert, are you saying that they used aconite as a medicine?"

Fresnay nodded. "In combination with other natural herbs. Read on, Claire."

Claire's eyes skipped across the lines, as she scanned. "Used in combination with the dried bodies of centipede, *scolopendra subspinipes multilans*, for tetanus and convulsions, decoct with *uncaria rhynchopylla*, in Chinese *gouteng*—"

"Hook-like branches," Fresnay translated.

"—Common name gambir, from the *rubiaceae* family, the branches have a sweet flavor, their energy is slightly 'cold,' um, let's see, to reduce anxiety, stop involuntary movements, calm down convulsions, stop dizziness, stop convulsions in children and twitching, counteract epilepsy and convulsions; *gouteng* is an ideal herb for light cases of convulsions at the beginning stage."

Fresnay spoke rapidly, almost as if talking fast would help them find Caspar all the faster. "Aconite is a powerful poison and wouldn't be very hard to obtain. It has such a classical history in the East and West, it implies a murderer with education, a doctor, a botanist. It didn't fit with the profile of an ordinary gardener, but I couldn't discount it. My guess is that Ip—"

"He was trying to stop an epileptic attack when Petey died," Claire said.

Xavier shook his head. "But why would he just happen to have a dose of epileptic tonic around the house, even if he was some kind of herbal hobbyist? It's too much of a coincidence."

"We have to ask him, now, tonight. Are you ready, Xavier?" Robert turned as if he expected Xavier to follow him immediately right out the door.

"No, you're not leaving me here," Claire pleaded.

"You want us to leave it to the police?" Xavier moved toward her, his arm reaching for her understandingly.

"God damn it! Xavier, don't you know me at all? Leave it to the police? I have no intention of leaving this to the police and sitting in a heap of secluded sedation like Lily Franklin, hiding in her mother's apartment all week."

"Well, someone has to stay here in case the police call." Xavier was trying hard to be practical. He was looking at Fresnay and Claire as if they had lost their minds. But Claire was already headed back to their bedroom. She reached for a T-shirt and sweater and realized that her breasts were overflowing with milk. She would have to release the milk and it would take valuable time. She ran to the kitchen to get the breast pump and a small spare bottle. They were kept cold in the refrigerator after Dovie sterilized them.

"Xavier?"

"Yes, Claire?"

"Where are all my bottles of milk?"

The two men rushed to join her in the kitchen. Dovie was standing behind her. The two women were staring into the refrigerator at the shelf along the inside of the door where bottles of her own milk ready for Caspar were stored. There was not a single bottle left.

"I don't understand." Claire looked at the two men.

"Someone has taken the milk along with the boy," Xavier muttered in explanation to the priest.

Fresnay murmured, "Maybe we can allow ourselves a little hope, Claire. Whoever took Caspar is feeding him."

"Why? What could anybody gain from taking him, especially if they are taking care of him? That means they intend to hand him back safely? Do you think he's being held for a ransom?"

Fresnay took his pipe out of his pocket and rubbed it thoughtfully. "Finish changing, Claire."

She ran back to the bedroom and finished changing her shirt and shoes. She put on a jacket.

The two men were staring at her almost accusingly. Xavier was the first to speak, as if by right.

"Claire, do you have anything, anything of value, or that someone would want in exchange for Caspar?"

She glanced at Fresnay. Xavier knew about her discovery of the tape recording of *Peter and the Wolf.* She hadn't fully explained to Xavier yet everything about her discovery in Ip's shed, but she had telephoned Fresnay within hours. She felt that the accusation was prompted by the priest, who dared not directly imply she was responsible for the danger Caspar was in now.

The priest didn't wait for her answer. "We're going now." Fresnay took her arm and said to Xavier, "You know where we are, just up the slope. If the police have anything to tell us, come right up and get us. Otherwise, this won't take long. This time, Ip is going to talk."

# chapter fourteen

Claire first went through the back of the kitchen and knocked on Dovie's door. She heard the faint rattle of a rosary as Dovie rose and answered, still clutching the beads in one hand. Her expression was calm and grave. Her hair was awry, as if she had been running her hands through it, or holding her head between her fists.

"I'm going with Father Fresnay to ask the gardener some questions about Caspar. My husband is staying here with you in case the police come with anything new to report."

Dovie nodded gravely and went into the kitchen, leaving her bedroom door open. Claire saw a brand-new little photo of Caspar on the *amah's* nightstand, next to the one of Freddy Evans-Smith standing on the English lawn, and another of a Filipina bride, presumably Dovie's daughter on her wedding day.

Seeing Caspar's happy toothless smile in her mind caught her by surprise. She felt overwhelmed by cold, nauseous fear. For

the next minute or so, she found herself in Dovie's small bathroom off the back door, her empty stomach drawing up drugs
colored by bright yellowish-orange bile. Robert waited patiently
in the corridor.

Finally, she took a deep breath, and feeling the surge of new
anger fill her lungs, followed Fresnay out to the servants' lift. It
was much larger than the residents' posher elevators, since it
was designed to accommodate furniture and machinery as well
as people. Fresnay seemed very far away as he leaned against
the wall facing her.

"You looked almost guilty when we asked you what evidence you have that might frighten someone into taking Caspar."

Claire nodded. "The aconite wasn't the first thing that came
to mind. I thought of Crowley and how angry he is, angry
enough to attack me the other night. I wondered if he realized
Fabienne still has that photo of him in full drag at the nightclub.
He figured out it was us that took the photo, but maybe he
thought because I took the photo that the camera and film were
mine. I don't know. It just seemed to me that if he's denying
anything to his superiors, then he might want to get the photo
out of our hands. Do you think he could be holding Caspar
ransom for that photo or something crazy like that? He sure
seemed crazy when he attacked me."

Fresnay held his tongue. They left the building for the night
air cooled by the heavy stucco of the building on one side, and
a few feet away, a cement wall about ten feet high damming
up the hillside. The cicadas' relentless chant filled the air now
that most of the traffic had died down for the night. What remained was a muffled, undifferentiated urban rumbling from
the tightly packed, overflowing city spread out below, hundreds
of feet down the slope and stretched away, a blanket of garish
Chinese neon lights broken by the dark blue stretch of harbor
and the strange hulking shadows of the distant Kowloon moun-
tains.

In the darkness, she thought, anyone could enter this building, climb the steps slowly and quietly to avoid people riding the elevator, and then, very gently, very sweetly, descend the steps again, holding her child. Since Leo had disappeared, every car on Tregunter Path was checked out, discreetly but effectively, as it went through the gatehouse by policemen on duty with Mr. Lui. The shuttle bus drivers were on alert. The taxi drivers were reminded each day on their radios to watch passengers travelling with small children carefully.

How many red-headed babies were in Hong Kong? Who could enter her apartment without a key? How would they get away without being seen?

They rounded the back corner of Branksome and exited the gate of the carpark. On the other side of the road stood a police van with two policemen quietly passing the time making notes and quietly talking into radios to colleagues taking stock somewhere nearby.

Her lanky companion led the way to the left. They drew no comment from the police who had identified him on the way in. They made their way swiftly along the twenty or so feet to the bend in Tregunter Path where the *nullah* came closest to the Peak side of the road. They leapt it easily. It was the same spot Claire had chosen to return to the Path when Ip's lorry had nearly collided with her.

Ip's single desk light was lit, and in the glow of the lamp coming through the window, Claire could make out the silhouettes of potted plants readied for delivery near his door, moist and glistening in the bulb's glare. Everything around the hut lay in darkness and it was hard to find her footing, she realized, as she leaned on her friend's arm.

A young Chinese police officer stepped out of the shadow to block their path to Ip's door. "Would you mind to inform me what you are doing here?"

"This is Ms. Raymond, the mother of the child who was snatched this afternoon."

"Excuse me. I'm very sorry, ma'am."

"I'm Father Fresnay, attached as a pastor to the Catholic Cathedral on Caine Road. *Ip Sin Saang. Hai m hai do-ah?* We'd like a word with him."

The officer wasn't moving out of their path. He regarded Claire cautiously and then turned back to Fresnay. "Inspector Slaughter was talking with you today, I think."

"Yes, I'm the same priest. I'm a family friend of Ms. Raymond and also spiritual advisor to many of the *amahs* who work along Tregunter Path and attend Mass at the Catholic Centre."

The officer's silver identification numbers pinned to his epaulets reflected the light streaming from Ip's window. It was hard to see his face beneath his hat and it was easy to see why they hadn't noticed him on surveillance duty on a dark night in his blue-black uniform.

The officer was a careful man. "You want to speak to Ip? We've already examined him. He was just released from questioning this afternoon. I'm not sure—"

"We won't be long, officer," Fresnay said.

Claire turned to the priest. "Robert, I need a minute to think about what we're doing. I only want to save Caspar. We know Caspar isn't inside here. I want to avoid doing anything that might harm my baby. Are you sure we're doing the right thing?"

"Think clearly, even though I know it's hard. The doctor was trying to keep you numb so you wouldn't feel the shock, but think, this man was in custody when someone took Caspar. Someone who had a key to your flat. We've never been able to completely trust the stories we heard from Narcisa about Leo— the timing, her attentiveness, the door left open for the boyfriend. This time we know. Your flat was locked. Someone took Caspar, took his milk, and maybe will ask for something back in exchange. The thing you must remember, you must cling to, is the assumption that your baby is alive. He is alive. Maybe this man can help."

"I'm confused, Robert." She was leaning on his shoulder, diz-
zied by the quick sprint up the slope.

"Don't you understand? I'm convinced that nobody poisoned
Petey at all. But as of today, I realize this story is very compli-
cated. Ip has an alibi, he had the aconite that was found in
Petey's stomach, whatever the story is, he hasn't told it so far.
But maybe he'll tell it to us. Think of him as your only link to
your son. Stay calm."

The officer had turned away from them to radio into headquarters. Claire heard the rumble of the Peak tram cars passing
by on the nearby steep slope, their brakes creaking to stop at
the May Road station and then rolling on toward Robinson
Road.

A thought suddenly struck Claire, not a thought actually, but
an image of the tram in her mind, but it was instantly interrupted
by an unfamiliar voice. "*Chin lai*," said the wraith-like silhouette
standing in the light of the hut's doorway. It was Ip, inviting
them to enter. He gestured to the officer to move aside. The
officer hesitated, wondering whose authority came first. Claire
guessed he was supposed to watch the old gardener, but had
no orders to hinder him.

The priest led Claire past the officer with a nod of thanks and
they followed the old man inside. Claire felt Fresnay's hand still
holding her upper arm steady. She was shaking now with cold
fear, hunger, and fatigue. She sat on the edge of the cot next to
Fresnay as Ip slowly lowered himself back into his chair at the
little desk. There was a long silence. Claire saw again there was
a tiny radio on the desk, now barely audible, broadcasting in
Mandarin. Ip had been listening to the news from the mainland,
removing himself from the day's events in the grief-stricken
neighborhood.

As she glanced at the radio, Ip's slender hand reached out
and gracefully turned the plastic dial. There was a long silence.
Finally Ip extended a pack of cigarettes, but both Fresnay and
Claire declined. Ip himself did not smoke.

Fresnay took the cue and removed his pipe from his pocket, tamping it down as he began to speak to Ip in Mandarin, his Scottish burr unable to completely obscure the northern Chinese "rrrrring" accent that betrayed the long secret years spent disguised as a mere foreign student, a lay wanderer, in Beijing. "We've come in the hope you will help us, not frustrate us. Three women in that building have lost their sons. This mother and the father are my friends. I am a priest."

"You are from the Catholic faith?"

"Yes."

Ip sniffed audibly with disdain. "I've seen your worshippers every Sunday down there," he pointed to the *amahs'* picnic site. "Throwing themselves around on the ground, screaming and singing like crazy women. I thought the Catholics were very good people. We knew Catholic missionaries in my families for many generations in Jiangsu province, but I don't understand that way of worship."

"It's a kind of movement called the Charismatics. I am not a follower of the Charismatic movement myself, but it is a powerful community in the Philippines."

"I see," Ip answered quietly. His fingers played with the corners of pages in a large volume opened in front of him. Otherwise, his entire posture, expression, and especially his silence, frightened Claire. She realized she was still not breathing very well.

Ip spoke suddenly. "But I didn't know until this afternoon that two more little boys were dead."

"Not dead, so far just missing," Fresnay corrected him.

Claire examined Ip's face for any clues to his emotions. There were none she could fathom. She needed this man's help. She had to rely on Fresnay.

Ip continued suddenly, "I didn't know anything about these two missing little boys. This the police told me. Today." He pointed with a slender finger at the desk to mark his point. "Just today. I understood before. I understood the questioning. I know you came into my home without my permission." He glared at Claire, "And I saw today what you gave the police. I have been thinking about this all evening."

There was a seemingly endless pause. Ip was considering something carefully. Claire and Fresnay waited long seconds while the elderly man gathered his thoughts. Claire started to speak, but the slight pressure on her arm from Fresnay silenced her into patience.

Ip drew himself up. He seemed to have made a decision. He walked to the door and opened it. He returned quietly and Claire realized he wanted to make sure the officer outside was beyond earshot.

He switched into English. "You will have to understand why I have said nothing. When you came to me demanding help before," he turned to Claire, "you will think I was protecting myself, me, the killer, the poisoner. Now you are confused because I was with the police when someone took your son. But you still think I had something to do with poisoning the little *Pei-tei.*"

Ip cleared his throat and looked up at the rows of books and medicinals along the narrow homemade shelves.

He sighed with resignation. "You will be wrong. I was protecting myself. I am not the killer of that little boy, but I have killed, accidentally killed. I was protecting myself, yes, and someone I felt very sorry for, no, not really sorry. I want to say, I understood this person. Someone who has killed without understanding."

Ip's face was drawn. His tones, his diction, were clear and slow, enunciated enough for Claire, whose comprehension would have been dulled by drugs and panic, to focus on as a drowning woman clings to a floating shard of wreckage.

Ip turned to her directly, his face shadowed sharply by the harsh light of his single lamp. "That Sunday, what you said about it was right. I could see what the *amahs* were doing, as I could on every Sunday. They would pray like crazy people, speaking in strange sounds like animals, looking for signs from their God. Waving their bodies and hands. Curling up on the floor like dogs in pain." Ip shook his head in disgust.

"*Pei-tei* made fun of them when he was with them. He was the only one who wasn't scared of his *amah*. The foolish little boy loved her. But the other women, they are afraid of her. They called her the 'Witch of Tregunter Path.' "

"Why?" Claire burst out. Again, Fresnay restrained her, but too late this time.

"Because she charged them money for prayers to their dead, for casting spells to keep their husbands living faraway in the Philippines faithful to them, to get better jobs. I saw them take the money out of their pockets. I saw her take the money, every Sunday. I saw a lot. I said nothing, but I saw a lot. I saw the money given and taken. I heard the silly women with their thanks to this *amah*."

"What happened that Sunday?" Fresnay demanded.

"I will tell you. You must understand everything, or you will understand nothing at all. It is very simple. One Sunday last September, I think, I saw *Pei-tei* in the middle of their group, playing I thought, but I didn't understand more.

"A few weeks later, they were holding one of their meetings, and *Pei-tei* was with them again, right there, in the middle of their group. This time, I saw from here, he had an attack of the sickness. They came running to me for help, probably because I was right there, they saw me watching them, but also because they were afraid of their *guay-lo* bosses. They were afraid, and I saw, very frightened, very guilty. I told them I could give *Pei-tei* a concoction for this type of sickness, 'the wind' in his system was very bad. I ran back here right away and took some ginseng tea I was drinking and mixed crow's head and—"

"We know, we've already guessed." Fresnay nodded.

"You are a knowledgeable man, then. You have my respect." Ip cleared his throat and sighed. "This is what you don't know. The medicine worked. When *Pei-tei*'s attack had subsided, he was very quiet and needed to rest. I asked this *amah*, this Man-uela, how the attack began. She went wild with anger and told me to go back to my hut. But later, many days later, another one of the *amahs*, came to me."

"Which one?"

"I don't know their names. They all look alike to me. One of the younger ones."

"Would you, or could you, identify her if we asked you to?"

Again, Ip had to silently acknowledge to himself what he had given in to. Finally, he conceded, "Yes. Yes, of course. She came to me and explained what had really happened."

"Was it something to do with the policeman Crowley?" Claire could not wait for this old man to tell his story. She wanted her son back now.

"No, no. I think he is a troubled man. I see him walking up and down the Path, up and down, sometimes in his car, but often walking, just walking. But he is not part of my story. The *amah*, the *amah* Manuela, had used a tape recording to start *Pei-tei* talking nonsense, *hu shuo ba dao*, bullshit talk, blind talk. She believed she had reached her dead son. She believed this dead son would talk to her through *Pei-tei*."

"Ramon!" Claire exclaimed in English, turning to Fresnay in astonishment. "Why then she told us the truth herself, from the very beginning. When Crowley interviewed her, she asked me to stay and listen. She seemed to be afraid of him. She started crying, telling us 'if only I could talk to him once again, but *now* I will never talk to him again.' Crowley made her shut up, cut her off. Neither one of us saw the connection. So she must have thought Petey's seizures were some link to the afterlife."

Ip nodded sadly. "She used the little tape cassette to make him shake and babble. I warned this girl Narcisa that she must stop this woman from playing witch."

"She did it again?"

Ip nodded to Fresnay's question. "*Duey-le*. Of course. She

was sad and sick and happy to be powerful over the other women."

Claire turned to Fresnay, "So that was why Manny looked so startled and defensive when I asked her about the *Peter and the Wolf* cassette. Vicky had thrown it away months ago because something on it aggravated Petey's attacks."

Claire thought back to her conversation at Vicky's small drinks party, when she had returned Grover and the cassette to her saddened friend.

"We never guessed at the importance of it. The idea that someone would use it to *make* Petey sick never crossed our minds."

Fresnay added, "That's also why that Englishwoman, Mrs. Reynolds, didn't see Manny on the road trying to flag down help for Petey. She wasn't so drunk as you thought—"

"Manny never went down to the road when she said she did. It never occurred to us that Manny was lying and the soused Mrs. Reynolds was telling the truth."

As the implication sunk in, anger flooded Claire in waves. "Why didn't you tell anyone? You could have saved Petey's life!" Claire screamed at Ip. Fresnay pulled her back down on the cot, she was so close to assaulting the frail Chinese.

Ip raised and lowered his thin shoulders as if to admit the weight of guilt they carried.

"And now we come to my responsibility. You see, if you have not yet guessed, that I am not a gardener, not a hobbyist. I was a traditional doctor of Chinese practice in Kowloon. I studied in Shanghai with the best teachers and for a few years, I practiced very successfully in Beijing, even treating many famous members of the old government. I came here with all the others, running away from the Communists in 1951. I set up a clinic on the streetside in North Point in the Shanghai refugee section, then I got more patients and moved to Nathan Road. It was easy to get new patients and soon I had too many. One too many."

"Who was that, Mr. Ip?" Fresnay leaned toward the man gently. Ip was no longer looking at his visitors. He was staring back in time at a face only he could see.

"She was a lovely young girl, a *guay-po*, but locally born. She could speak fluent Cantonese, like many of the local European children. English parents, the father was a *dai lo* in the government. She came to me one day, no appointment, just off the street, and told me she was pregnant—by a Chinese boy. She knew her father would accept it, but she was afraid it would kill her mother's love for her, her hopes for the girl's future in England.

"It's an old story. I gave her the herbs she needed, but they didn't work. That can happen. Under my care, she could have tried again, but with careful supervision. But instead of coming back to me, she did not trust me anymore. She went to another doctor, a *Chiu Chow* in Mongkok. Then she took all the drugs we gave her, all the medicine I gave her, all the medicine this Chiu Chow gave her, all the herbs in a single tonic."

Ip shook his head and carefully folded his hands in his lap. "And finally, that was the drink that killed her baby."

There was an awful silence.

"It killed her, too." Fresnay had to finish the story for him.

Outside, the cicadas droned their reverberating humming, and Claire felt the ghost of the girl; it was as if she knew the terrible, awful detail yet to come. Outside, she heard the tram rumble by again, and suddenly, the image that she had lost sprang back before her. The kidnapper had escaped with her baby down the Peak on the tram. That's why none of the drivers had reported seeing Caspar. The tram driver's back was to the passengers behind a partition. There was usually a ticket-taker too, but somehow the kidnapper had managed to slip the baby past him.

But Ip was speaking again.

"This girl's father, a big government man, found the herb packets with the name and address of my clinic in her room. He knows Chinese very well and he came himself to my office to hunt me down. He didn't want a scandal, he too didn't want to upset the mother more by making everybody in the whole city talk about their family. The mother told the newspaper a story about an accidental drowning.

"I thought about running across the border, but I figured they would be more likely to find me there with the cooperation of the mainland police than if I disappeared right here in Hong Kong."

Ip sighed to himself and shook his head. "It wasn't even that difficult. You know Hong Kong—very small place, very big city. I never went back to the office. Not once. I tried never to cross the harbor again in case somebody from the old neighborhood recognized me. I hid in North Point around the old Shanghai neighborhood for a while, then came up here and bought this shack from a distant cousin. I became a simple gardener with a simple hobby."

Without warning, Ip's face turned to them, indignant and proud. "Now you think I am going to go to the police and admit I was practicing illegally on an epileptic boy, and that some-times my tonic works and sometimes it is too late because of some idiotic witch! I will go to jail for the rest of my life because of some ignorant Filipina *amah*!"

"We understand." Fresnay gently put his hand on the gar-dener's bony knee. Ip looked up in a sort of shock at the kindly touch of the Jesuit.

Claire spoke in her clear, workmanlike Mandarin. "We still don't know where my baby is. Where is Leo Franklin? What has happened to them?"

Ip looked intently at Claire and spoke carefully in English, not sure how much of his Chinese she could follow. "I told you already. I didn't know anything about the two little boys missing until the police took me to their headquarters today. You must be prepared to learn that perhaps there is no connection."

Claire felt her courage crumbling away.

"No, don't tell me that." She started weeping and felt the

priest's arm comforting her, holding her up as they left the gardener's hut.

"He explained so much, about the tape, the poison, even about Viola Evans-Smith. Now we know why we knew so little about her death. That was the way Alistair wanted it. Now to think that there is no link between Petey and Caspar. I assumed, I hoped, I—"

Now all she could do was cry her guts out, dreading the return to the apartment to relate everything to Xavier and seeing the disappointment and frustration in his eyes when he realized there was no good news. She passed the police van at the entrance to the building in a daze. She felt the energy draining out of her legs. She knew she would not sleep and saw no end to the horror. She was afraid of seeing Caspar's face in her imagination, so she pushed out all happy memories of his touch and smell and so the harder she pushed them away, the faster they flooded her with a longing more intense than any sexual or other physical sensation she had ever had.

Fresnay explained most of their story to Xavier in the living room, while Claire gave way to all restraint and went into Caspar's nursery and sobbed. The building was a deathly silent sleeping tomb. She felt exhausted and scarcely heard Fresnay when he explained he would talk to the night officer on duty and request that Slaughter come to talk to them as soon as possible in the morning. He would spend the night in the apartment and wait for that dawn meeting.

"But why? We know Ip couldn't tell us any more than he did."

"Maybe there is a connection, one that Ip didn't see. Because Ip doesn't know the whole story. It's in our hands and now we must put it together until it makes sense. We thought the key to this story was Crowley, then we thought it was Ip, and now we find out the central figure was a little boy who died years ago, a little boy named Ramon. You said yourself, Claire, Manny told you the meaning of the mystery herself the first day—you just didn't understand the importance of her words. You get some rest, if you can. Tomorrow we're going to follow any trail we've got, and God willing, Claire, it is going to lead us to Caspar."

Claire looked at Xavier. He held her tightly, and helping her to lean on him, he took her to their bed to wait for the next dreadful day to dawn.

# chapter fifteen

"Claire, here, take these. Doctor Sui left something to help keep you calm," Xavier said gently when he had closed their bedroom door. He held out four small blue pills. Claire turned away shaking her head. No one had drawn the curtains, and looking down the slope toward Central, she could see the street-lights of Tregunter Path shining their futile vigil. She looked back up at Xavier through swollen eyes that felt like two stone weights. The energy and determination of the previous few hours had drained away.

"It's not going to help. It only makes me useless to everyone. Especially to you."

He took both her hands in his. "Don't give up now. Tonight you learned the truth about Petey's death. We might be only hours away from finding out the rest of the story. You might have Caspar in your arms in a matter of hours."

"Don't, Xavier. Don't raise my hopes. I've read stories like this, stories about kids who disappeared with no explanation, and their parents live in some kind of limbo ever after, always wondering whether they're alive or dead, filling their lives with good works and campaigns to protect other kids because their own kids will never come back! Those are the kids whose faces stare up at you from posters and milk cartons for years, and they just never, never come back. I just never imagined it would happen here in Hong Kong, or happen to me."

Xavier sighed, put his arms around her, but it couldn't stop the rage pouring out of her.

"You get this false feeling of security here, nothing happens to you because you're not Chinese, you're not a local, you're living this privileged life on a street paid for with overseas housing allowances, guarded twenty-four hours a day by goddamned royal policemen like Anthony Crowley!"

Xavier's expression was grim. "They stopped being 'royal' last year, remember? Take these, Claire. We're going to make it through tonight and tomorrow, and whatever happens after that together, but I need you to be as calm as possible. Please."

He went into the bathroom to get her a glass of water.

Claire was adamant, almost yelling at his retreating, unyielding back. "I would take the pills if I thought they would bring Caspar back faster, but they only make me stupid and numb. What I realize now is that the police were wrong, totally wrong. Fresnay is wrong. Ip is right. There is no connection between Petey's death because of Manny's stupid seance games and the disappearance of Leo and Caspar. That's the first thing that hit me when we were talking to Ip. I know Fresnay wants to find some kind of connection—that's his logical, goddamn Jesuitical mind at work. He can't accept the possibility of coincidence. But there is no connection at all. Some sick wierdo has got our baby, and the misery we feel is nothing to what has happened to our little guy."

Xavier grasped her by both arms, his fists digging into her muscles almost painfully rousing her from despair. "That's the point. We don't know yet what has happened to him. We can't give up, or think the worst, until he's found."

She rolled over to him and let herself collapse in his arms, her voice no longer her own, but a new voice, like the dead's— waxen, emotionless. "But they never found Leo, did they? He's been gone exactly seven days now, there are no clues at all, no fingerprints, and no one in this whole city has reported seeing him. You know what that means, don't you? You know that as well as I do. He's rotting in some rice paddy in the New Territories."

Even as she was muttering this, muffled by his firm embrace, she wondered at how selfishly she was allowed by everyone to fear and grieve, while he was expected to stay on his two feet fighting for information and alert to signs of hope. They both knew, but hadn't dared to say to the other until now, that every hour that passed without Caspar made it more likely their baby was dead.

---

It must have been a few hours later that Claire awoke. She realized that in her exhaustion, she had dozed off. Xavier was gone, but she found him sitting on the balcony outside with Fresnay. The lights from the living room reflected the grave concentration of Fresnay, smoking his pipe, leaning his elbows on his knees in the semi-darkness.

Strain lines gripped Xavier's mouth, and his normally ruddy skin looked putty-colored. Even so, Claire suddenly saw a startling likeness between Xavier and Caspar, a likeness that had never hit her so hard. What must this loss mean to him? How many chances did a man in his late forties have to start a family? What must he be thinking? Everyone had made such a fuss about the red hair Claire had passed to their baby. Hadn't anyone noticed that the chin, the mouth, and probably one day, the nose, were all the father's?

One day? She wouldn't give up hope, she would push herself through one full day of hope before she surrendered to the nightmarish possibility that Caspar was dead. Fresnay discreetly excused himself and said he wanted to lie down on the sofa for a while.

"I heard you and Fabienne," she said to Xavier, not daring to look him in the face. He didn't reply at first, but pulled away from her a bit, not ready for this conversation.

"It's an old story. It's over. I told you that from the start. Okay, I realize I didn't know all the details of her side of it until last night. I didn't realize what she'd done."

"But now you do know. For her, the relationship wasn't completely over until she had told you. She wanted you to feel some pity, or regret, or responsibility, or something."

"It's more than that. After all, she could have stayed in Geneva and written it all down in a letter. Yesterday I saw something in her face that she had hidden before. Now that she has seen you and the baby, she hates me as much as she ever loved me. Maybe because I denied her the kind of love she wanted, she wasn't really a friend. She was addicted to the challenge of changing me while pretending to be my perfect partner, to being more me than I was myself."

Xavier's expression changed, almost cruelly. "And she conveniently forgot that, at least in the old days, she also said she didn't want any children, that she had to be a free agent, ready to go or do anything. She was afraid of being tied down, or so she said. Now she blames me for everything, but I certainly don't remember it the way she does."

He rubbed the exhaustion lines across his forehead, as if trying to erase the years themselves. "I can't help her bitterness."

"I wasn't sure about children either," said Claire. "You know Caspar just landed in our laps. But you didn't suggest an abortion to me, or was I so bewildered and thrilled and," she fought for the words to describe those heady, frightening weeks, "so overwhelmed that I missed your hints?"

"You missed nothing, nothing," Xavier said vehemently. He reached over and took her firmly by the shoulders and held her close. "I could see the change in your face, in your body, the sheer joy of it all. I wanted you that way, I admit, much more than I had wanted you before. Suddenly there was more of you there to love, and I don't mean the baby inside you. I saw all the love that was promised to me and to us together by that sudden change in you."

His voice dropped even deeper than usual. "And I never saw that in Fabienne, even when she got pregnant, so how could I have known she wanted children? She won't admit it now, but she didn't change with that joy because she didn't feel it. She didn't want to allow something she couldn't control into her life, into her own body. It's not that I want to marry you now because of the baby. It's not the baby that I'm marrying—it's you, because of who you are becoming, and how it came out from under that lonely reporter's shell you were hiding in."

For Claire, words had always flowed rapidly and fluently out of her fingertips, into the keyboard and onto the page. But the word she said next, that simple word "yes," came out as if its only syllable contained a book of meaning to them both.

Coffee was brewing in the kitchen, and Fresnay returned to the balcony with three mugs. The priest offered them the drinks with a stalwart smile.

"I tried to rest, but my mind won't relax. Now I realize what that confession on Christmas Day was all about. One of the *amahs* who attended Manny's seances knew how Manny had caused Petey's attack and death. Remember? 'Everyone thinks that the Devil looks like a man, but he can look like a woman, too,' she said. She confessed her dealings with the Devil that is killing children on Tregunter Path."

"I thought she meant Crowley, who dresses up as a woman," admitted Claire.

Fresnay shook his head. "I don't think our mysterious confessor meant him at all. She knew we were looking for a man

after Leo was snatched. She might even have been making an
unconscious allusion to Manny's name. You see, I'm convinced
that the confessor thought she herself had more to really fear
from Manny. She wanted Manny stopped."

Claire sighed. "Robert, it's just as likely now that Manny and
Petey had nothing to do with Leo and Caspar's disappearance."

"I don't agree. This Filipina who spoke anonymously to me
in the protection of the confessional connected the death of
Petey with the disappearance of Leo. Who was she? What did
she fear from Manny? Was she trying to lead us to Manny in
order to prevent something worse?"

Fresnay rubbed his stubbly chin. There were dark circles beneath his eyes and Claire realized his frame stretched well beyond the dimensions of the cheap rattan sofa he had tried to
rest on.

He went on, "Quek told me there were no unusual fingerprints. How do you avoid leaving fingerprints? Wearing gloves.
Who wears gloves in a semi-tropical climate without raising an
eyebrow? People cleaning, digging, working with their hands
like gardeners, pool men, delivery men, *amahs.*"

"Police," said Claire.

"All right, also the police. Then, how do you get into the
servants' entrance of an apartment without arousing suspicion?
You see, I think," he leaned forward with excitement, "the latch-
key is our only real starting point. Who had a key?" he insisted.

"Only the *amah* and us, just like Xavier told John Slaughter's
men earlier tonight," Claire shrugged.

Xavier added, "Fabienne had Dovie's key. I saw it last night
on the cookbook shelf where Fabienne told me she returned
it."

"But you have two *amahs,*" Fresnay said, puzzled.

"No, just one."

"But when I stopped by Christmas evening to tell you that I
had heard that strange confession and wanted to talk to your
*amahs,* didn't you mention two Filipina names?"

"Connie!" exclaimed Claire. "What happened to Connie's key when we dismissed her? Dovie!" She raced to the kitchen where Dovie had fallen asleep, her head on the table. They woke her as gently as they could. She was still dressed in her Sunday church dress, worn for the Immigration Department.

"Dovie, when Connie left here Thursday morning, what happened to her keys?"

"She gave me the front door key, ma'am."

"And the servants' entrance keys?"

Dovie paused, taking in the implication of Claire's frantic questions. "I don't know, ma'am. I assumed you asked for her to return her set of keys."

"No, Dovie," Claire replied, turning to the two men. "She didn't give them to me. When I saw Dovie using the same keychain, I thought Connie gave *all* her keys to Dovie."

"No, ma'am," Dovie protested. "I duplicated the servants' key to the elevator entrance and our back door from Connie's keys. She gave me the front door key, so one of us would have it, but for a few days while we overlapped, we both needed to come and go through the back door at different times."

"Xavier, we must find Connie and ask her what she did with those spare keys."

Claire now regretted the haste with which she had dismissed Connie.

Xavier asked, "Dovie, do you know Connie's new phone number?"

"No, sir. We weren't on good terms when she left so suddenly. She was still angry at me for telling you about the candle wax."

"I'm going to call the Sandfords for Connie's number," Xavier said.

Fresnay turned to Claire. "In the meantime, Claire, try to recall the story of Ramon once again, exactly as Manny told it to you that day at the picnic site," Fresnay reached into his back pocket and started to tamp down his battered pipe.

"It's so hard to think straight, Robert. I just want Caspar back."

"I know, my dear, just humor me. Try to remember what Manny said about Ramon."

Claire took a deep breath, thinking back to the sun-bleached scene of the Sunday meeting of the Charismatic group—the primitive strumming of the same three guitar chords, the writhing, babbling, and swaying figures of the *amahs* in the clearing. She told Fresnay how she had watched them from a distance and waited for a chance to talk to Manny about Petey, not expecting the subject of Ramon would come up again, just as it had with Crowley's interview.

"She said he died of pneumonia. When she asked the Sandfords for permission to go home to the Philippines, Ian assured her it wasn't necessary, that all Ramon needed was a dose of good antibiotics and medical supervision. So he didn't let her go, but he promised that he'd give her a lot of money to send to her mother for Ramon's treatment. She was afraid of getting some cheap generic drug, and he promised he'd give her enough for brand name antibiotics. She gave the money to another *amah* to carry back to their village."

"What was that friend's name, the other *amah*?"

"I didn't ask," Claire realized, as much to herself as to the priest.

"That could be important."

Claire nodded. "Especially because of what happened. That *amah* spent the hundreds of dollars she was carrying on clothes and makeup, and left only a little for herbal medicines for the sick boy."

"And by then it was too late."

"Manny's mother caught up with the ruse, and Manny hustled more money together, but then you know the ending."

"Not necessarily. What happened then?"

"Her story kind of petered out. Your colleagues in collars down at the Catholic Centre told her to pray, forgive, and forget," Claire couldn't hide her growing frustration with the conversation and at the impotence of her own situation.

Fresnay sighed and leaned back in his chair, perversely exuding an air of satisfaction. "I'm beginning to understand, I think. In her grief, Manny resorted to spiritualism instead of faith. She twisted religion around on its head. Used Petey to 'talk' to Ramon, she thought. She didn't find peace. And the *amah* who betrayed her, now I really wish I knew who it was, because I think that was the *amah* who came to me in the confessional. Who feared Manny's revenge."

Suddenly Fresnay blurted, "Claire, where does Manny's family live?"

"Bantac? Bantoc, I think she said."

"Bontoc. That's in the north of the Luzon," Fresnay pondered. "Who were the other *amahs* with her that day?"

"Regina was another one. Vicky knows her as a good friend of Manny's. I knew the face of the third one, but I'd never seen the fourth one before. Anyway, you've got to remember we haven't lived in this neighborhood more than a few months."

"I know, I know."

Xavier was dialling again, explaining carefully to the "master" Bridgeway why he was telephoning in the middle of the night to speak to his new servant. As he waited for Connie to come to the phone, he asked Fresnay, "Do we want her to come here?"

"That depends on her answer, I suppose, and the police," the priest said.

In a few seconds Xavier turned to them again. "She gave them to Narcisa."

"It's what I suspected. Hang on just a bit longer, Claire," Fresnay murmured.

"She's just next door," Claire said, trying to take in the speed of events.

"Come on," Fresnay said, and he led Xavier through the

kitchen, followed closely by the two women. They crossed the back landing and facing the back of the Franklins' apartment, pounded on the servant's door, shouting in Tagalog for Narcisa to answer. There was no one home.

"She might have snuck out to be with her boyfriend," Claire said. "Especially since Lily Franklin is living downtown these days."

"Giles must be there," said Xavier. He led them quickly back through the apartment and across the carpeted front landing to the Franklins' front door.

Giles Franklin answered the bell wearing only a sarong, his beer belly folding over the knot he was gathering at the front with meaty hands, already in a foul temper at being wakened. His expression changed when he saw Xavier.

"Hullo. I wanted to come over this morning and offer my help as soon as it was a decent hour," he said simply. "Although I'm sure the last thing you want is what I've been through for the last week with Lily."

"Could we have a word with Narcisa?" Fresnay pressed him. "We think she has the keys to their back entrance or passed them to someone."

"Go right ahead," Giles said sourly. "Don't think you'll get anything out of that one. She went to bed straight after serving dinner last night. A few more days and we'll be well rid of her. Maybe then Lily will come home. I swear we'll never hire another maid again, and I don't care what Lily says."

He was already trailing them through his apartment at doublespeed, bewildered and pathetic, and Claire could see why Lily Franklin packed up her grief and confusion for the sanity of her mother's apartment across the harbor. The Franklin apartment was overlaid with the dust of a week's trauma, and as she passed hurriedly through the dining room, Claire almost knocked over a porcelain dish on a sandalwood stand.

Fresnay had already pushed open the reinforced doors separating the dining room from the kitchen, and the kitchen from the servants' corridor. He was knocking on Narcisa's door just as Xavier pointed downwards and said in a strangely careful version of his usually fluent English, "Please look down at your feet."

From underneath Narcisa's door, on which they saw pinned a postcard from Bontoc, Luzon, spread a sticky pool of thickening dark blood.

# chapter sixteen

– Tuesday dawn –

They sat in the Franklins' living room while the police guarded the entrance and the Scene of Crimes team worked around Narcisa's body in the back of the apartment. Photographs were being taken of each wall, each angle. A constable named Lim had asked them to wait quietly in the living room until he had a chance to talk to them, but no one could put Fresnay on hold. He spoke to Claire, Xavier, and Giles Franklin quietly and deliberately.

"One wonders every Sunday, staring out at all those women, those patient, tireless, devoted women, what they might have been, what they could have done, with more luck in their lives," he sighed.

"Well," he continued, looking up at Claire, "that was her drama—her conscience, her intelligence, her deep, deep grief. Petey's death was a sort of accident, but Manny was a well-educated Catholic woman by Philippine standards. She hadn't intended to kill Petey with her seances, but morally, she knew her experiments made her responsible for his death. Even when there was no hint she would be found out, she was laying her plans to get out of the territory. All she needed to escape from Hong Kong was to distract the investigation and buy herself a little more time."

Claire listened to Fresnay's narrative, but as she sat quietly, her eyes were looking inward, distracted only when an officer walked through the room carefully carrying an open cardboard box containing the drying cleaver. The rosary had been left in a clear plastic bag. Each object ceremoniously brought past her stunned mind took her back to a snapshot, a fleeting glimpse of Narcisa's face and body. Manny, who had every evening so matter-of-factly sliced meat into inch-wide strips of stir-fry for the Sandfords' dinner, had slashed Narcisa's beauty into strips of pain, again and again, using a wide Chinese cleaver.

The broad steel blade had lain grinning up at them, grotesquely caked with flesh and blackening blood in the light of the corridor's bare bulb. One hand, nearly severed, clutched at the lethal cutting edge, while the other hand held a black-beaded rosary. In Claire's dulled ears, Fresnay's voice sounded both familiar and strangely distant at the same time.

"Petey died a week ago Sunday, and I can only imagine that for the last eight days, Manny has lived in suspended terror, first from Inspector Crowley who might have seen something odd, something incongruous, at the scene of Petey's death, and then from Narcisa. Although Manny was a calculating woman, she was probably in a state of cumulative shock. She hadn't recovered from the loss of Ramon, she had lost Petey in the process of trying to stay close to Ramon, and all she knew every waking day was that she wanted her son back."

Xavier looked at him. "Or perhaps anybody's son?"

Fresnay admitted, "I can't fully understand the psychology of such a profound loss, or a kidnapping. But in the case of Leo, it was a practical, vengeful precaution, as well as easy. She knew about the back door left unlocked, as well as the appointment with the gardener, because the silly twit Narcisa had told all her friends. We can imagine Manny did her duties at the Sandfords'—minimal because she was so discreet in the face of Mrs. Sandford's grief, and she watched, she waited, and she took Leo from Narcisa the very next night to shut her old friend up. Leo was her hostage until she could get out of Hong Kong. She took his passport too, just in case. Keep in mind that it was easier for her to smuggle Leo out of the neighborhood and hide him somewhere downtown—probably in one of the apartments unemployed *amahs* share by the dozens when they hide from the Labor Bureau after their visa runs out—easy, because Leo was Eurasian. We have to hope, because otherwise, the question is what *did* she do with him?"

Giles interrupted, "You're saying our *amah*, Narcisa, knew it was Manny all along. Narcisa was the *amah* who spent the money for the antibiotics on makeup to impress her boyfriend and didn't take it up north to Manny's mother."

"Exactly." Fresnay drew his finger in a line along the dusty coffeetable starting from the ashtray. "This is Manila, and," he traced his forefinger toward Xavier opposite him, "northward, this is Narcisa's hometown, Banaue, that she mentioned to Claire in passing the very morning after Leo disappeared. This, almost half a day's bus ride farther northward, is Manny's home in Bontoc."

"You see, the Ramon story might have told us everything we needed to know the same day Petey died, but Crowley, and you Claire, Vicky, the other priests, and I—we just didn't listen. She was talking about staying close to her son through Petey's seizures when she said to you she couldn't talk to him anymore, but she was also going to tell us more if Crowley hadn't been so impatient—a tale of anger and jealousy for the beautiful, young Narcisa that she could not bury, no matter how much she led the prayers for herself and for others."

Claire looked at Fresnay, trying to concentrate her thoughts away from the bloodshed behind the kitchen.

"Manny has known all week that Narcisa was the one that would have the guts, or enough fear, to betray her to the Sandfords or the Franklins or the police, because, after all, Narcisa had already betrayed her once," she said.

Fresnay nodded. "Narcisa had to protect her family back home in the Philippines from Manny and her relatives who, I assure you, have not forgotten their loss. If she came straight out, there might be hell to pay back home for generations to come. She tried to clue me in with her Christmas confession last Friday. She was, no doubt, the girl who went to talk to Ip about the seances. He'll be able to confirm that. But Ip did nothing about it. I'll bet it was Narcisa who planted the tape and the Grover toy for you to find on your walk that day."

"I had the impression I was followed, that's right!"

"Yes, I think Narcisa was watching to make sure you picked it up. If you had missed it, she probably would have tried again and again to place it in someone's path until it was brought back to Mrs. Sandford."

Claire counted back the days. "I found it last Wednesday and I'm sure Connie saw me come home with it," Claire said, "and it was that very same afternoon while I was at the office that Connie started burning candles and praying over Caspar to protect him."

Fresnay thought for a moment. "I'm not defending the candle wax ceremony over your son's extremities, but Connie knew what Dovie couldn't have known because Dovie was too new in the neighborhood to have joined the Charismatics group. When Connie saw the tape and the Grover toy, she must have incorrectly jumped to the conclusion that you knew the implication of the music and the seizures already. That put Caspar in danger, she thought."

"I didn't understand until Saturday when I gave the toys back to Vicky. Even then we didn't really understand."

Fresnay continued, "All the *amahs* along Tregunter Path feared Manny as a self-appointed religious leader. You remember my sermon a week ago about witches? None of them would tell us priests who the witches were, but Narcisa was different. She feared Manny in a very specific and perfectly rational way. She knew Manny had taken Leo. Maybe Narcisa even felt she deserved Manny's revenge, had murdered Ramon, in a way. She wouldn't really feel free until Manny was removed from Hong Kong."

"Bloody hell, and I thought she was hiding from me all these days in her room," Franklin muttered.

"But all that talk about a *guay-lo* lurking around Tregunter Path?" Claire interrupted him.

"It might have been just any *amah* mistaking a plainclothes officer on duty, or maybe the rumor was intentionally started by Manny herself after watching too many serial killer movies on television."

"Crowley," sighed Claire. "I was sure it was Crowley, especially after Cecilia talked to the boy-toys down at Repulse Bay, but then I was confused about the poison and Ip. But Ip was only trying to help Petey."

Fresnay nodded, "I was wrong earlier this evening on that point. Ip didn't know anything about Ramon or the hatred festering between Narcisa and Manny. He could only take us part of the way."

Giles Franklin pulled himself together and demanded their attention. "Then what happened yesterday? Where is Leo? Where is your child?"

"I should have known it was a woman who took Caspar. Only a woman would remember to take the breast milk from the refrigerator," Claire murmured.

She felt Xavier's arm tightening around her. She saw him look soberly at Fresnay, warning him with his eyes to slow down. Giles Franklin was sitting behind them, and as they turned, he put his head in his hands and they realized suddenly that he was quietly crying. Fresnay went to comfort him and at the priest's touch, the huge Australian started to openly sob, his sweating chest heaving with the strain of the nightmarish week, saying over and over again, "I need Lily, I need Lily. I don't care what time it is. Call Lily, please. Tell her I need her now, here at home."

Constable Lim came into the room, bringing with him the small but now-familiar sounds of authority; the brisk walk, the static of his walkie-talkie, the murmured Cantonese asides to his assistants.

"Father, could you bring your group with you to our cars now?"

Xavier looked up, "At least, couldn't my wife rest before she has to make a statement?"

My wife, he said my wife . . .

"I'm sorry, sir. We're not going to Arsenal Street. We're going to join Chief Inspector Slaughter at Kai Tak. The *amah*," he checked his notes, "Manuela Gacad, has just tried to board the first flight to Manila by Cathay. Would you mind to come right away? Please."

"Has she got Caspar with her?" Claire blurted at Lim. Xavier held Claire's hand tightly, as if to hold her back.

"No, ma'am, but she has the Franklin boy with her. She's trying to pass him off as her illegitimate son."

"Oh, thank God," Giles Franklin was sinking under the relief, and Fresnay caught his bulk and helped him toward the corridor. "I'll be fine now, I'll be fine now, just let me get dressed," Franklin blurted, stumbling back toward the bedroom.

Xavier's arm stayed tightly around Claire as she waited for Lim to say something more. She stared. She took a deep breath. She tried to speak, but Lim was already walking away from her and had disappeared back through the kitchen to give instructions to his team. She could not breathe. He had said nothing, nothing more, nothing about Caspar.

It would not take long to reach Kai Tak before the early morning commuters started crisscrossing the harbor by ferry, by car, by high-speed underground rail, to Mongkok, to Hunghom, to

Kowloon City, to Kwun Tong, to Central, to Wanchai, Kennedy Town, North Point, and beyond the border to the north, to Shenzhen, Panyu, Foshan, Zhuhai and all the destinations of cement blocks, old and new, that made up southern China's success story. Now, from the van, Claire saw only the still-quiet streets at dawn, soon to be given back, relinquished to the tune of a band and the change of a banner.

She kept her slender hand with its long freckled fingers and short musician's nails in Xavier's wide, strong, fist as they rode behind Lim and his driver. "My wife," he had said to Lim. They were going to hold on to each other and come out the other end. They were indissolubly joined, now, she realized, not by joy, but by tragedy, but married they were, even if it was in a sense she had never desired.

Where was Caspar? Where was her baby? He was gone. She had the sensation that someone had gripped her throat, his fingers digging deep into her clavicle. She could not look Xavier in the eyes, she was so awed by his strength, and she wondered at herself, dazedly asking deeply within why she had feared he was too frivolous, too unsteady, to partner her? How cruelly she had typed him as unreliable, underestimating the depth of his reserves. She had worried so much about past relationships, her fears had eclipsed from her his true character, masked his potential and hidden his needs.

Lim was talking to Xavier now. "An escort is going to pick us up as we turn past the offices of Hong Kong Aircraft Engineering and run us to some side gate."

Something was wrong. Claire saw it in Xavier's eyes and the recognition of alarm in Fresnay's expression. Something had been said between the two men.

"Xavier, has Manny said anything to the police about Caspar? What did she do with him? Did Lim tell you something?"

Xavier looked at her as if to judge her state of mind. "Manny isn't talking to the police. They don't have her in custody. She's holding Leo as a hostage until she gets on the plane. They don't want to tell Giles if they don't have to. They just want to get us all there."

"How?"

Her question was answered within a few minutes.

As they drove through the security entrance at the side of the airport, Claire remembered an occasion in the 1980s when she had stood along with the rest of the press corps, presenting passes, to be allowed into the VIP waiting room. Who had she been waiting to interview? She couldn't remember. Some politician from the U.S. in transit, no doubt. She had done so many stories in Hong Kong, her memories of the individual assignments, the years, even the editors they were written for, were beginning to merge in her mind. She had loved this city so much. It held her youth, her energy, and her freedom. And all around her, she saw the end in a pool of darkening blood.

The airport tarmac stretched beyond the parked police van and the runway lay directly in front of them, its end dropping abruptly off in the brown-gray waters off Hunghom, one of the most notoriously tricky landing strips to navigate in the world.

A flight was taking off, speeding in the direction of Taiwan. Half a dozen police cars and airport security vans stood in front of them, and beyond, Claire saw as she jumped out of the van behind Xavier, stood a huge Cathay Pacific 747, its engines running.

A passenger bus stood thirty feet away, emptied out of its hordes of travellers who had innocently stepped onto the tarmac, and heedlessly shoved around the clumsy *amah* dragging a confused and unwashed toddler with one hand. With the other hand, she was lugging behind her the kind of cheap red-and-blue striped plastic carrier bag used by half of Asia as a temporary suitcase for gifts and goods needed by relatives back home. The *amah* hadn't made it into the plane yet and for a reason that was horribly clear, their flight was being delayed.

Manny had reached the boarding steps. She had clearly been

denied entry to the plane. She was shouting at the police who stood at attention, waiting for a command. Nothing could be heard above the engine's roar. Claire started to feel she was going to throw up. The *amah* held a short knife in her right hand, her arm tightly wrapped around Leo's neck, her left arm holding Leo around the stomach. Every few feet she reached back to drag the carrier, filled to bulging with all her worldly goods, never taking her eyes off the row of security men moving forward.

For a moment, Claire realized, Giles Franklin stood beside her, taking in the extraordinary predicament of his son. Leo's dirty curls were flying in all directions with the wind of the engines, but he had seen his father. As he made a move, Manny pressed the knifepoint into his throat. He began screaming. Franklin was moving so fast, Claire realized that Manny's shouting out her warning to him was futile.

She saw Giles' bulk move with unbelievable speed, but he was not as fast as Manny who had already cut into Leo's neck, but was turning to press the child into a better position for a final, lethal stroke of the knife in a desperate attempt to halt the onslaught of Chinese security dashing behind the Australian. Whether the uniformed men wanted to stop Giles or to assist him in attacking Manny was impossible for Claire to guess.

Claire leaned back as she saw in a second what was about to happen. Xavier was behind her, half supporting her. For a second, it seemed Giles would reach his son in time, then behind him, Claire saw Manny's arm lift again to strike. The enormous Australian grabbed at the knife, kicking Manny to the ground. She scrambled up and insanely yanking her belongings into her arms, scrambled and stumbled back up the boarding stairway. People inside the windows were silently screaming and pointing, Claire realized, some gesturing wildly inside to the crew.

A stewardess looked down the stairs and saw Manny wildly struggling with the overpacked carrier, lugging it up a few steps at a time. The stewardess started to jerk at the door of the plane, which on the commands from the police, relayed through the tower, had moved slightly away from the steps. Seeing the plane inching away from the top step, Manny finally tossed the carrier bag over the banister of the stairway down to the tarmac, and dashed up the final steps, pursued by Slaughter and his men.

For a second, Claire saw with disbelief the *amah* leap and fly toward the ever-narrowing opening and desperately grab at the door which moved slightly forward and then to the side in the direction of her right arm. When Manny snatched back her arm, she stumbled forward, and the door closed completely on her head. The door was pushed back open by the terrified stewardess within a second, but too late, knocking Manny brutally off the side of the plane and directly down onto the tarmac. The confused pilot and his co-pilot, their mouths moving frantically but silently within the cockpit to the tower, was backing up the plane now, to return it to its original position.

In the next moment, the plane's front wheels were moving toward Manny's broken and unconscious body. Claire screamed out her own private hell of disbelief in a cacophony of confused Cantonese shouts.

The shouting stopped as the engines finally died. As Slaughter and the airport team rushed underneath the plane, the sounds of construction, of ferry horns, of any morning in Hong Kong, went on all around them. Another plane took off, this one in the direction of Guangdong Province.

Minutes must have passed as Xavier held Claire, her eyes welling up with tears, because then another plane smoothly lifted off in an indifferent roar. Would no one come to them? Would no one explain, "Here is your boy. He was here all along? He is safe. It was all a mistake, ma'am."

Fresnay came up to them. He spoke to himself, more than to his two friends. "Like the *magtatangals* who appeared headless by night. Or the *asuang* who could fly. But she couldn't fly fast enough."

The three of them stood together for many, many minutes.

Everyone seemed to have so much to do. Everywhere there were so many trucks, cars, police and airport officials. Claire watched as an ambulance for Leo and his father arrived and then left for Queen Elizabeth Hospital. No one spoke to them, and Claire realized there was no time for the three *guay-los* standing at the edge of the tarmac, staring at the crowd around the transit bus.

Finally, Fresnay moved to Manny's body, and kneeling in the bloody pool, recited prayers for her soul in a fierce act of concentration. When he indicated that he had finished, her corpse was carried away.

Claire and Xavier could not look each other in the face. While they stood watching dumbly, the plane for Manila had been washed, the pilot and stewardess involved had been exchanged with as little delay as possible for another team, and the flight was now being cleared for takeoff.

Down underneath the plane, a small airport service truck was signalling to Lim and in response, a police officer was directed by Lim to collect Manny's bulky carrier bag out of the path of the truck. He gestured to stuff the thing into the back of one of the police vans headed back to headquarters.

It was all over.

From the bag, Claire heard a baby's sudden desperate squalling.

# epilogue

– Two weeks later –

"So, in the end," Robert looked down at Xavier and Claire standing in front of him, "we can rejoice that God has included the possibility of marriage and family, among all the different kinds of relationships, or paths of spiritual growth, offered to us. For every one of us, married and unmarried, beloved or lonely, benefits from the promises made before us today. We hope for a stable partnership between two people in love, but more than that. Let us as witnesses, not just friends, pray together for a partnership that says love is not an accident, it is not a hit and run vehicle! It is not infatuation—what a great word for that!—no, let us pray for a partnership that says love, real love, best grows out of the active decision, the aggressive commitment, the opening up of the will to feed that devotion and support it to the best of our human ability.

"A partnership that carries these overwhelming vows, *until death*," Fresnay widened his eyes dramatically, "—this promise before friends and families transcends the fact of love that exists in us today, and says it will be nurtured, it will be protected, and it will be recognized not only by this couple, but by all around us.

"Merely a social contract? Yes, yes! It is a public declaration that says, 'We will make love!'" Fresnay raised his arms and threw up the long sleeves of his plain vestments in a happy gesture of abandonment, getting a good laugh from his small congregation. He dropped his voice and said slowly again, "But it is also a gift to all of us here today, one in which we all share. It is a declaration from this couple, who are saying, we will not just enjoy our love, we will *make*, we will create, love!"

Soon it was Caspar's turn. Fresnay baptized him with all the pomp one could give a restless baby whose head had been shaved clean of all red fuzz for his journey to Manila, and whose left shoulder was still sore from bruising. Manny's desperate attempt to smuggle him home to Bontoc had included removing his telltale hair with a dull razor.

Without a passport for Caspar, Manny had drugged the baby and laid him on top of her clothing in the huge striped carrier with newspaper crumpled lightly over his face before she stood in line at the ticketing counter. Then she had held him in her arms while the carrier bag was X-rayed, but smuggled back into the bag again through check-in at the gate and into the commuter bus headed to the plane.

The Band-Aids dotting his skull were covered by a sun cap until Robert lifted it off to pour holy water on his forehead. Predictably, this triggered a miserable wail and the rest of the ceremony turned into a high-speed wrap-up and race to the luncheon banquet next door on Ah Fok's terrace.

Ah Fok's two grown sons had grumbled on foot all the way into Tailong Bay with crates of champagne and red wine strapped to their sturdy backs, and Dovie had enlisted her daughter to help her with the forced march, carrying the ingredients for a cake, which was beyond Ah Fok's repertoire. Berkeley still lingered in Claire's core and she had asked Dovie for banana bread filled with walnuts and large enough to feed a crowd. It had been cooked in three sections in Father Fresnay's little Sanyo oven and then assembled and frosted on the terrace an hour before the party began in the chapel.

Claire had been brought close to tears of appreciation to see the arrivals straggling down that final slope toward Fresnay's house in their hiking clothes. Alistair Evans-Smith hiked in with the Forsythes, chatting the entire time with Miriam and Gordon about developments in the New Territories, the choice of the Chief Executive to replace the Governor, the likely lineup of his future cabinet—and making it clear as they marched gaily down the path and into the shade of the cement terrace, that all the three old colonial civil servants needed was an impromptu branch as a walking stick and they could make light work of a two-hour hike in the sun.

Vicky had bowed out at the last minute, on the excuse of her pregnancy, but Ian, said Gordon, "was toddling along" behind, and sure enough, Vicky's husband arrived a full ten minutes after his in-laws. He was breathless, red, sweaty, and clearly unfit from a life of long hours in the cockpit.

Though many of the other guests had lived in Hong Kong all their working lives, some had never visited Tailong, particularly Claire's fellow foreign correspondents who had used the city more as a regional hub than a home. But Lornia was quite at home, and was her bright self again, joking with Claire that "Every girl in the office is sorry to see the boss get married."

Cecilia had hiked the Sai Kung hills all her life. She came with her brother Winston Chau whose backpack was armed with congratulatory E-mails from all the editors in New York and correspondents around the region. They were filled with rude jokes about the order of events, like, "We hear this story carried an interesting side-bar in diapers," or "Are you sure you didn't get your deadlines mixed up?" which drew predictable chuckles and toasts.

There were Chinese friends Claire and Xavier had made during their weekends with Fresnay in the village, sitting together
along a wooden bench on one side of the terrace eating already
and telling Cantonese marriage jokes. There was a businessman
Claire had worked closely with on a story a few years back, and
curiously, Barrie and Fiona Reynolds. Claire hardly knew them,
but they had heard of the wedding from the Sandfords and
invited themselves without debate. Fiona formally wished Claire
well, and helped herself to a drink or two. They had ploughed
up to Sai Kung from Queen's Pier on a speedboat and had their
"boat boy" ferry them through the rough surf in a dinghy.
Fiona's gold-laced boat sneakers were drenched with saltwater
and dry dirt from the clamber up from the beach, but she
seemed in good spirits.

"Sorry about your car," Claire said to Barrie, more as conver-
sational filler than anything else.

"Turned up in Canton in a round-up of stolen vehicles,
dragged out of the harbor in an airtight cover, and then driven
north," chuckled Barrie, his mouth full of Ah Fok's shrimp dim
sum.

"You mean another Benz-in-a-Bag scam?" asked Claire.

He nodded, "Right. Bloody clever. The cars don't surface 'til
they're out of Hong Kong waters, and frankly, I won't be in a
hurry to get it driven back down here. I think we all had a lot
more peace of mind after it was nicked and Fiona had to be
driven everywhere." He looked at her, eyebrows raised, "Rather
like the feeling of relief you got at the end of *Jaws* when they
killed the shark." He was chuckling to himself strangely.

"You sound like you personally arranged to have it stolen!"
Claire joked and was startled when Barrie slowly turned full face
to her, winked slowly, and then dodged off to talk government
with Gordon.

Claire got the feeling that she should spend time with Alistair,
but didn't know whether or how to tell him she had discovered
the tragedy of Viola's death. When she sat down to eat her cake

with him, he surprised her. "You know, your favorite police officer announced a major life change."

"Not a sex-change operation!"

"No!" he laughed. "God, woman! You're a bloody Victorian with all your little sexual nightmares! No!" he caught his breath again and stopped laughing finally, "He's seen his main chance, and it's clearly not in police work. So, he's quit the force to start a Balinese restaurant with an Indonesian partner. He's in love, happily with someone his own age. Or at least that's what he told his immediate superior last week."

"So I wronged an innocent man."

"With a closet full of child pornography," said Evans-Smith dryly. "Yes."

"Well, good luck to him. I trust he'll be performing something on his own stage."

"Apparently he sings straight songs quite well. His mother was, as it turns out, a pretty popular cabaret artist from Leicester in her day. Worked the cruise lines to Marbella, that sort of thing."

"So that's what she did to support him. He certainly admired her for raising him on her own."

Evans-Smith drew himself up proudly and announced, "And more news! After ten weeks with the Evans-Below, Althea already loathes England, can't get good help, finds her friends have all withered up into boring old sticks and she has decided to come back here, effective as of yesterday. If I know her, she'll be completely unpacked and back to barking orders at the Kwun Tong Women's Health Advisory Coalition by, um, let's say, next Thursday."

"Then, you're not leaving!"

He turned and the sunlight caught the top of his white hair, "I'm not leaving!" he mocked her. "Not only that, I'm going to work for the enemy!"

"You're going to stay on in government? I thought Beijing wouldn't allow it. Everyone they fingered for the future elected legislature is going to be some toadie or well, you know, no offense, but certainly not you!"

"No, not in the government itself, of course. Beijing wouldn't stand for that. Some of my old Chinese friends out in the Territories here have hired me as a consultant, to act as a sort of liaison of information and support system to London as things here along the border undergo what you Americans call 'meltdown.' "

"I hope you know what you're doing. You know, the old 'staying on' syndrome. Didn't Paul Scott write a sad short story about it, some old couple laying down to die in India, laughed at by all the locals?"

Alistair rolled his eyes. "Do I act like the Raj type, molting underneath some mosquito net? I want to be useful, keep my hand in, *watch the deluge*, if you insist."

There was an extraordinary youthful glow on his face and he danced up to refresh his drink. He was not renouncing home, she realized as she heard him correct Ah Fok's elder boy on the proper drinks proportion in Cantonese dialect. He was already home. Claire envied him, knowing that protecting Hong Kong in his own way against Beijing's detailed planning and vast manpower would be his greatest, if ultimately futile, challenge yet.

Fabienne had not been invited to the wedding, nor did she send a gift. Claire realized as Xavier's silence about Fabienne stretched for hours into days and weeks that this was Xavier's choice. Fabienne would always be to Claire like a parallel line running within Xavier's reach, but not crossing, as the three of them moved into the future. Claire digested the understanding that she would never know what their last words had been, on the phone or by letter, or if they had resolved their anger at all.

She had decided to risk more, to risk all, with him.

He stood with Fresnay directly across the terrace from her, the two men intently discussing something. She enjoyed watching Xavier from a distance, so clearly comfortable now with her friends, new and old, confident as never before in his place in her life. Now he was laughing at something. Now he was listening intently and nodding. She had never seen him look so youthful, and she was pleased when without warning, he looked up for her and found her eyes across the crowded space.

She wondered briefly what point it was that Robert was trying to make to Xavier, what subject so amused and concerned both her lover and her friend. Although her better sense told her otherwise, in her vanity, she hoped they were gossiping about her. After all, she had already become the wife and mother, but it was her one and only day as the bride.

# acknowledgements

*The Christianization of the Philippines: Problems and Perspectives*, Miguel A. Bernad, S. J., The Filipiniana Book Guild, 1972

Martina Burns Bertoni of Grosse Pointe, Michigan, for accounts of epilepsy triggers and symptons as well as for passing on:

*Seizures and Epilepsy in Childhood: A Guide for Parents*, John M. Freeman, M.D., Eileen P. G. Vining, M.D., and Diana J. Pillas, Johns Hopkins Medical Institutions

Another book that was quite useful was:
*Seizures, Epilepsy, and Your Child*, Jorge C. Lagos, M.D., 1974

"I Wonder Where My Easy Rider's Gone," Mae West, from the film, *She Done Him Wrong*

The poem by Charles Baudelaire, one of Father Fresnay's favorite poets, is translated by William Rees in the *Penguin Book of French Poetry, 1820–1950*, (Penguin Group, 1992 edition) as follows:

*"Languorous Asia and burning Africa, an entire distant world, absent, almost extinct, lives in your depths, aromatic forest! As other spirits sail on music, mine, O my love, swims on your perfume.*

*"I will go there, where trees and men, full of sap, swoon in a long slow trance in the burning heat of the climate; strong tresses, be the sea swell that carries me away! You enfold, ebony ocean, a dazzling dream of sails, of rowers, of pennants and of masts. . . ."*

Information on herbal poisons and medicines were gathered primarily from the following sources:

*Herbal Pharmacology in the People's Republic of China*, from the National Academy of Sciences, 1974

*Legendary Chinese Healing Herbs*, Henry C. Lu, Sterling Publishing Co., Inc. New York, 1991

*Illustrated Dictionary of Chinese Medicinal Herbs*, Wee Yeow Chin and Hsuan Keng, CRCS Publications, 1992 (originally from Times Editions, 1990, Singapore)

And last, but not least, thanks to the Mystery Writers of America Mentor Program—in particular, author Justin Scott who volunteered to serve as an MWA mentor